LUDLOW'S DAUGHTER

DR. HENRY LYDO

D1712365

LUDLOW'S DAUGHTER

DR. HENRY LYDO

Reverend Crown

Table of Contents

CHAPTER ONE

DRUNKEN RUN, NC

1793

The late October air was already crispy as a chest-length brown and gray bearded farmer dressed in cotton tartan homespun coveralls milled around inside the horse stable. The sun slightly lighted the wooded horizon with a bewitching pink, and the horses nodded their heads in approval as the tall, large-boned, slightly arthritic man slowly hobbled passed back and forth, dragging two large new bales of dry golden hay. Long ago, he learned to function perfectly in the moonlit morning or evening darkness without using a lantern, being a genuine security and fire risk. He paused suddenly before the horses.

"I know you-uns 're happy to see me this morning," the man spoke as he stroked the three's fur gently along their necks and backs with his crusty, calloused right hand. "It's hard in these fields on ya, I know. You-uns er the best I've got around here. You kin do what no man by himself can."

The late middle-aged man smiled as he spoke in a low rumbling tone echoing in the early morning air. The horses grunted in approval as they sharply nodded their heads again.

The man reached behind himself, grabbing a tight bale of fresh hay with his left hand. He retrieved a twist of molasses soaked tobacco from his coverall bib pocket with his right, ripping a chunk from the curled leaf strand with his teeth, chewing thoughtfully as he broke the bale and began stringing it out

1

inside the trough before the impatient horses.

"We got a job to do, all of you 'n me. With the field hands sick, it'll be us doing this thing all by ourselves. That dirt must have a break. Takes three a year. Thankfully the collards, turnips 'n beets are on the ground already. The plantation general store, The Dream Wagon, next door, 'll pay top dollar to us for 'em soon coming. We'll cut, split, 'n haul wood from here all the way back to Ramah Plantation, a mite near twenty miles away. That'll free old man, Craig Burney, up so he can keep on contracting out his carpentry services, rather than messing around with that truck himself. We'll be busy as all get-out boys, but that is what it'll take to build a productive, fine looking money making, big house estate here on Drunken Run.," the farmer rumbled low as he labored dutifully in the chilly morning air.

He turned and spat black juice upon the dry straw laying all around in the manure of the horse stable. Outside the stable door, he heard the crunching footsteps of someone cautiously approaching. The thin, nearly muscular, springy figure of his middle-aged wife soon strode her plain tartan patched cotton laborer's skirt and labor worn boots across the stable threshold, pausing before the farmer with her tightly curled fists perched upon both hips.

"Have you heard anything from Jarlan?" she asked firmly to the point of nearly being a screech.

"Who?" the farmer asked as he abruptly commenced shoveling manure, tossing it into a pile in the corner of the stable.

"Don't act dumb like that first thing in the morning here, Reuben. You know who I'm speaking of. Jarlan Clark!" fired his wife in a quick flush of anger.

"He came by here 'bot three days ago," the farmer replied as he labored, chewing thoughtfully.

"And?" his wife fired again impatiently.

"Said he paid his share on our new tenement. He cut me our share of the rents."

"How much was it, I shudder to ask?" inquired his red-haired wife, with harsh cutting firmness in her voice, and a questioning appearance in her general demeanor.

"Three Spanish doubloons," snapped the farmer as he turned, tossing another shovel full of manure.

"My word, Reuben, is that all, for sanity's sake? I don't think the hot shaft is sinking in as smoothly as it was supposed to, here in this love-dove business we have with him myself," fired his wife in a flash of temper, as her ice-blue eyes widened. "My wild eyed Scottish blood simply won't let me rest when I feel some son of a bitch is intentionally stepping on me! I have far too much rattle snake in me, Reuben, to simply lay right down and take it straight up the ice like that."

"It's a good beginning, Ruth," returned the farmer with a soothing calmness in his voice.

"I mean, Reuben, we went in half with him for eight tenements, plus the dining area, way over in town yonder. It takes people this far out two days to travel these wagon rut roads in. Most do it during the harvest season, when they sell their cured meat, animals, and crops at the Market House there in the middle of town square. Spring planting time is big too, you know, with the numerous festivals and all, but it'll be awhile now before that. We could rent by the day and the week during the fall until New Year. We could net in three doubloons every other day with a place in town at this time of the year. I mean, Reuben, we could fetch three doubloons from the new general store at the plantation next door, selling turnips, beets, and collard greens in small batches, saving us a day trip into town and the hassle of renting out property, if such a frivolous amount was all we ever designed to take in."

"I know, dear Ruth," sighed the farmer as he continued to labor dutifully at the shovel. He turned his head to spit tobacco juice again.

"I mean, buddy, you just wait!" fired his wife in another flush of anger, "our collards 'n turnips'll be ready soon, maybe by tomorrow should it frost tonight. I'm in the process of smoking and salting that pig you killed a day ago. We'll load the wagon up with these dresses I've sown and the food items I've made, then we'll ride into town and check on our property. Honestly, Jarlan should have already been back here to Drunken Run, Reuben. He owes us work too, you know."

"I know," replied the laboring farmer, as the two suddenly paused in their conversation, glaring hard at one another. After a minute or so, the conversation resumed. "I tend to give him the benefit of the doubt since his parents were such good, God-fearing people and all, Ruth. His grandparents, going as far back as one can, were fine folks, to say the least."

Ruth paused as she glared at the farmer hard, clenching her teeth slightly as she did. She almost spoke the words, dirty rotten dog, as she thought them out loud. She spat a wad of snuff juice she held tightly underneath her lower lip instead. She fought with herself while knowing well about Reuben's anticipated reaction to her slur, where he would apply it to Clan Clark at large, rather than the individual person, Jarlan, as she meant it to be.

"I'm a gathering in the dried beef and salt-pork now. I'll be finished soon. I know the cow needs milking and the eggs taken in, but the wagon needs inspecting as well. Since the weather is clear and sunny, I want to make sure everything is in ship-shape. We could also check the collards and turnips since it may have frosted last night. If everything checks out, we could load the wagon by nightfall, Reuben, and be ready to pull out by break of day tomorrow. It's quite a ride out to Mount Horeb Village, but we'll make it to the ole Tory landing there by evening. We'll book a room for the night, unless there is one available in our new place."

"Sounds good," replied the farmer as he labored. "How are the girls doing?

"Savannah is asleep in the loft. April and June are out in the garden working the crops. June is the eldest and fully comprehends her responsibilities, Reuben."

The farmer paused, gazing backward toward the manor house, taking a deep breath as he slowly resumed chewing.

"She's making a fine woman, Ruth."

He turned to spit.

"I can't believe how much she's already filling out. That gal looks mite near five years passed by fourteen, Ruth. We need to consider marriage arrangements for her soon, I think."

Ruth sighed, then glared again with a hot flush of anger.

"I can believe it, Reuben, and that is the whole problem I have with you. You simply don't have the ability to foresee potential problems."

"Potential problems?" the farmer sighed as he turned to commence shoveling again.

"That's right, Reuben. With a doe's body filling out right, there's a horn-wearing buck out there a lurking in the woods somewhere just a licking his slobbering joules, like a drunken dog gone mad. These things don't take a genius to figure out, and are natural as sunshine and rain."

The farmer paused in deep thought for a moment.

"You think she'll be o.k. tomorrow and the day after though, don't you, Ruth?" asked the farmer with a look and sound of sudden concern.

"The odds are with her, but the devil always saunters in from the darkness when people have their backs turned, Reuben. Two days is a spell, and a fine chance for anything."

"Ruth, I know, honey," sighed the farmer with no expression on his face, "but in reality, we must go. I reluctantly accept. Our time frame for netting an income is short until those tenements are rolling. The wagon'll be full, and there's only enough room for our wares and us two."

"I know, but knowing it doesn't ease my gut feeling about us being absent overnight," Ruth replied.

"We have to watch her ice until we can arrange to tie her up with a good buck. The puny short horns and dirty dogs, I have to say, 'll come in from miles away, and neither of us nor Clan Ludlow, dear God save our souls, simply can't have it. Only God in Heaven above knows what kind of earthy scum 'll work its way in here just to slice her tender, luscious cake with his filthy, good-for-nothing knife, Reuben."

A serious expression assumed Reuben's face.

"She needs to be matched up soon, I agree. Ruth I was thinking about one of Jake McPherson's boys, James, the surveyor. He's a fine fellow and has a great job with a decent income. Jake has an immaculate plantation estate he inherited. The McPherson family comes from noble blood, you know."

His wife, Ruth, made no reply, but only stood erect, gazing hard at her husband through narrowing eyes while she listened.

"What about the plowing though, Ruth? That break has to go," replied the farmer. "On second thought, maybe we could put this trip off for another day or four."

"It'll be right here a waiting for you when we make it back," fired Ruth, as she turned and walked back out across the stable threshold. "Meet myself and the girls out in the garden when you have the wagon and everything ready,"she fired as she walked away in a series of snappy jerks.

When Ruth made it back out to the house and the garden, all three girls were busy gathering in the cut collards and large armloads of freshly cut turnip tops. Every now and again a turnip root was pulled, but they appeared not yet completely ready for harvest, since the purple top hadn't formed in all of them. These armloads were dropped at the edge of the plow line, where the wagon would usually pause.

Rather than immediately step out into the open, Ruth cautiously paused by the corner of the house, observing. Curiously, after pulling three arm loads of turnips, June would pause in her work, then walk rather nervously across the garden to the wood-line on the opposite side. Ruth strained her eyes to catch sight of specifically what this young woman was doing.

She appeared to be whittling on a maple stick, maybe an inch and a half in diameter. June seemed rather meticulous in producing a special shape, although this shape was not immediately discernible to Ruth in the distance. Whatever she was crafting was obviously twice the width of her right hand. Ruth could easily discern that much. Every now and again June would glance upward to gaze about rather nervously, then hastily commence her delicate carving.

Ruth strained her mind to figure it all out, as she strained her eyes. Finally, June turned her back, seemingly burying her object underneath the leaves, then arose to stride back out into the collar patch, and commence cutting and pulling arm-loads of these and some of the purple topped turnips. Ruth stepped from around the house corner suddenly.

"All of you women are doing mighty fine work, I must say. We'll have these turnips clipped or pulled, and collards cut in virtually no time flat. I must fetch my own articles from inside the house that I have to sell, along with the crops."

The youngest girl, Savanna, was clothed in a plain, ankle length of white cotton dress, of the type field workers wear. She wore a cotton sunbonnet on her head. The bonnet was stained a perfect wood green by boiling it in unripe black walnut hulls. She liked the color since somehow it allowed her to sneak up close to squirrels before they ever noticed. She tilted her head to one side as her eyes sparkled suddenly.

"Where are the field hands, Mamma?"

"They're all sick, child," Ruth explained.

"Why doesn't Papa buy more?," asked Savannah.

"Field hands are expensive, and even more so if they are conditioned to plantation life, and experienced," explained Ruth.

The middle daughter, April, was nearby. Her dress was colored in bright red and black squares. Her dark brown hair was pulled into a tight bun behind her head. Her complexion was pallid, yet her emerald eyes sparkled with a cat-like glint of gifted intelligence.

"Why doesn't Papa just rent some field hands, mother? Several plantations around here would rent them out for the asking."

"News of this disease has gotten out. No farmer wants it to infect his household. We, ourselves, could come down with this scourge, for heaven's sake!" Ruth gasped to her daughters.

"So it's us who must keep Ludlow Estate here going, right?" asked April.

"That's right," Ruth replied, "it's us who must keep Ludlow's family and estate up, since we are the Ludlow family," she laughed slightly with a smile. "So let's keep on working."

"Where's the doctor?," Savannah asked, as she squatted and labored.

"He's on his way. He had to come in all the way from Ramah Plantation. He'll be here tomorrow some time, I think."

"You and Papa are pulling out tomorrow, right?" asked April.

"Yes, but who told you?" Ruth asked, with a puzzled expression on her face.

"I can sense these things," April replied. "My sixth sense is always right.

"Oh please, doll!," Ruth snapped, "we haven't time today for foolishness."

"No, seriously, you and Papa are going to Mount Horeb Village tomorrow. You are going to sell these wares inside the Market House there in the center of town. You are also going to check out a piece of property you went in with Jarlan Clark and purchased. You are thinking he might be there, but he won't be. You and Papa are not going to like what you find out tomorrow, mother," April spoke in a serious tone of voice.

"Oh please, daughter, enough of this talk. We all have more crops to pull, chickens and rabbits to feed, horses to look after, and so much more. Tomorrow 'll be a busy day, so let's keep to it."

The sun was virtually directly overhead. Even though it was fall, still when high noon arrived, the rays could cut some if one was outside directly in it all day long. It could also warm to a point it felt hot when one was busy moving around. By the time a sizable portion of the vegetables was pulled, Papa had the wagon inspected, repaired, and loaded up for the long trip the following morning.

When the sun was four O'clock high, everything commenced to slow down for the day. June made her way back outside and across the garden, to the edge of the wood-line. She dug carefully underneath the leaves, retrieving her newly crafted wooden keep-sake. She carried it carefully, tucked away underneath her dress until she could make it into the barn. A foot tub filled with water sat on a wooden stool inside the work-room. She removed her secret treasure from underneath her dress, dipping her right hand into the water, then coating the wooden object with sand. She scrubbed the object hard with a well-used cloth until the sand abrasive rubbed every place on this precious keep-sake's wooden surface perfectly smooth. She glanced around the wood working area until she discovered a castaway wooden disk discarded from a cheese container. It was strange that Papa would toss such a treasured reusable object down on the ground so carelessly. He must have dropped it by accident, she figured.

On a wooden shelf filled with one by one foot wooden spaces used by Papa for storing various tools and items, she discovered a cake of lard underneath the space for a stone hone. Carefully she cut a soap cake sized piece of this, placing it upon the disk she had found. She hastily tucked away her special keep-sake underneath her dress again, then made her way into the house, toward her bedroom. She passed the others loitering around in the foyer, who spoke not a single word but only watched curiously. She hid the keep-sake inside the mattress tick, and the lard by the washbowl. Women often used lard as skin soft-ener, so noticing it would not arouse any type of suspicion, she reasoned with herself.

Her delicate mind was filled with clear, vivid visions as her heart hammered away with anticipation. Her breathing picked up as she anxiously awaited for the fall of night.

"Is something bothering you, June?" they all would ask. "You appear troubled."

Her mother walked up, glaring directly into her eyes as her own eyes narrowed in deep thought. Out of all her family, however, April was the one giving her the most reason for concern.

When the fire was finally going in the hearth place, and the sun was fading away behind the treeline, the house quieted when Papa smoked his pipe and took shots of whiskey, and mother drank her new wine in the parlor area. While June was inside her room, April suddenly eased inside through the half opened bed-chamber door, closing it tightly behind her.

"I know your dark naughty secret, June!," she whispered as she harshly spoke.

"What secret? What are you speaking of?" June replied in a muffled voice tone.

"You well know what secret. I saw it all. The other day I found the dark stoneware bowl. I filled it with rain water from the oak wood barrel outside underneath the roof eave. I placed it on the night stand inside my bed room. I lit a candle on either side of the bowl last night, then gazed directly into the reflection until I fell into a trance. The water became cloudy as the mist tumbled, but it finally cleared, and I witnessed the whole affair. I saw it all, June, for heaven's sake! You can't hide anything, sis," April spoke as she shook her head from side to side, almost coming to tears. "The spirits of the woods see it all, and tell it to those qualified to listen and observe."

"You're crazy, April. I don't know what you speak of," June snapped in a nervous breath, as she snatched her body around, with her back to April.

"You listen to me, and you listen well, June Ludlow. I see your secret forays to Blue Stone Manor. I see your activities in the woods all around us. I know of your tarnished secret in the woods, your dark midnight fantasies, even your innermost private, debauched desires. I know what you hid in the tick. It's all been going on for nearly sixteen months now. It must stop, sis, now!" April screamed, then caught herself, fearing her noises were heard.

"What have you been into, April? Have you sipped too large a drought from Papa's whiskey bottle? What on earth are you speaking of?" June spouted uncomfortably.

"You must stop these activities, June. They are all in violation of God's will. You heard the preacher last Sunday. He said the young were most susceptible to forces of darkness. The minds of youth are constantly overrun by scenes of debauchery, blood, theft, and violence."

"Oh please, sis!," spouted June.

April's face snapped around, wearing only an expression of anger. She clenched her teeth hard.

"Stop it now, or else!" April replied.

"What am I doing? Stop what? Or else what? What in the name of The Eternal are you speaking of?" June asked, with a spoiled blank gaze upon her face.

"Just stop it! I was told to pass on this warning. I've done my part," April snapped, as she whispered.

"You've already brought enough curses into this house and farm. Where do you think this disease originated from? Why do you think we are having to do all of this work around here?

What about all of this questionable activity from Mama and Papa's business associate, eh? I'm certain you are very familiar with that side of this equation, June! Don't you dare attempt to lie your way out of this one?"

"Oh yeah? Well, what about you, April?," fired June in a muffled explosion of anger. "Witchcraft is still a sin, and punishable by law. It may not be as strict here as in those Puritan areas of the country, but it may still fetch a fine or jail time, not to mention a public record for being a witch."

"You heard me, June!," April fired. "I have spoken. I seldom speak twice."

She quickly turned, huffing out of June's bed chamber, pushing the door closed behind her.

CHAPTER TWO

THE DARK BECKONING

Night time arrived seemingly fast. Mother and Father settled down almost immediately. Father read the scriptures until the light faded.

"Give no heed to the viceroy of evil, so says the scripture," father quoted aloud. "The earth abounds with his wicked minions. Spare not the thief, the adulterer, the fornicator, nor the murder, or the witch; for all stem from the same trunk, so says the Holy Word! I trust that the graces of God will go with us tomorrow and remain with us once we are in town. Good Lord, please remain on the home front to protect these girls. Please see us all through the night safely, Amen and Amen, in the name of your son, Jesus Christ."

June could hear their footsteps as each sister, her mother, and father made their way toward their bed chambers. The doors audibly pulled tightly shut behind them.

The house was slowly growing now. Their second great grandfather began with a simple box style dog trot cabin. Now the opened area transformed into an immaculate foyer, with the two living quarters on either side. The extra attic space was transformed into additional rooms for the girls and their anticipated families, always assumed to include male heirs of the grand estate. Outside where the foyer is, a small step shelter extends outward from the house. Father was in the process of building a nice porch area on the front and back side of the big house for lounging during the hot season. All of these details flashed through June's mind as she lay there motionless on the bed. Other unsettling thoughts crept in to disturb this comfortable idyllic scene, however.

A nude, well-conditioned, male form flashed through her mind, like streaks of searing lightning. She tried to fight it, but this singeing scene always returned. She felt his warm wet kisses upon her delicate youthful yearning neck. She felt his hands upon her thighs, then gracefully glide upward upon her breasts, as he skillfully pinched her nipples in ways instantly arousing her. She felt the sensation as he unbuttoned the cleavage of her nightgown. She tossed as she attempted to cast this vision from her mind, but she couldn't, since her body deeply yearned for the total penetrating, throbbing sensation. She breathed heavily as the thought prevailed, tossing and turning continuously, battling with herself until she simply couldn't resist the urge anymore.

She lit a candle upon her night stand with a flint and steel. It helped to light the wicks when honey very thinly covered them and gun powder was sprinkled sparingly. She prided herself on making this unique discovery. She took a measure of the lard in the amount of a teaspoon. Her hands trembled as she reached into the mattress tick, retrieving her recently crafted item. She held the teaspoon filled with lard over the candle flame until it melted into grease. Her trembling hands poured the grease over her item, this inch and one half by eight inch, round wooden shaft, bearing highly noticeably delicately carved, yet specific decorations. She panted heavily as she spread the oil by stroking the wooden shaft with her right hand. There was once a day when all she was familiar with were animals and young male children, whom she cared for as a method of earning an income. Later mental visions of these observations made an indelible depression upon her gentle, but ripening adolescent mind at the time.

Her hands, stomach, and breasts trembled in great anticipation, as she slowly pulled up her cotton night gown. She placed the well-crafted tip right where she craved for it most. She pushed it back and forth slowly and gently until the superbly craft-ed tip hit the perfect spot with expert exactness. She gasped when it did, desperately desiring to push harder and faster, but having to do so carefully, so as not to injure herself. She knew she was doing herself right when she felt she needed to go in deeper, until a wave of emotion surged inside her body, feeling as though it would explode her entire torso from the inside out. She breathed in deep, heavy breaths when it did happen at long last, finally collapsing back upon the bed. When her mind settled, she always worried that she had made a mess on the sheets. A few times she did, but luckily if it left stains her mother hadn't noticed anything, as far as she knew.

She noticed her breasts growing larger, much more so than the average girl or woman her age, she felt. She could only wonder as to why. Often when she would use a tool for her pleasure, she would pull her breast around and stimulate the nipple with her tongue. Maybe her active secret life was the reason why they were growing, eh? At age twelve, she was an adult, according to her father, who constantly reminded her. In her thirteenth year, she reached the age of marriage. There were many men inside the community whom father proposed in speech to her, but never made the effort to arrange any meeting with. Mother in-stinctively feared leaving her alone during the past three years.

The last time she crafted a tool, her youngest sister discovered it, tossing it carelessly into the fireplace. Another time, it was strangely missing. She hoped her parents had not discovered the thing. Surely they would have said something by now, if they had. As she lay still and her eyes became blanketed by the mist of insecurities, she heard the sermon of the preacher from the Sunday before, almost loudly, as if it were being spoken at that very moment.

"But I am afraid that, as the serpent deceived Eve by his craftiness, your minds will be led astray from the simplicity and purity of devotion to Christ, 2 Corinthians 11:3.

For the desires of the flesh are against the Spirit, and the desires of the Spirit are against the flesh, for these are opposed to each other, to keep you from doing the things you want to do, Galations 5:17.

"For I know that nothing good dwells in me, that is, in my flesh. For I have the desire to do what is right, but not the ability to carry it out, Romans 7:18."

She opened her eyes. The sun peaked in through a bay window beside her bed. She never heard a single thing. She figured it was maybe seven in the morning, and not much later. She picked up a nice pocket watch she had found while walking the two rut wagon road awhile back, but unfortunately, she had forgotten to wind it. She arose from the bed feeling energetic. She sauntered out the bedroom door still yet dressed in her night gown. No person was in the house.

She opened the front door of the house, stepping outside, glancing to the right where the garden was. The wagon was parked beside the garden space, while the others were loading it up with vegetables, cured meats, and crafts of various sorts. She closed the door, then made it back into her room, where she pulled her gown up above her head, putting on her plain tartan working dress. Quickly, she raced out the front door and into the field where the others dutifully labored.

"It's about time you made it out," snapped April.

"Yes dear, the good book says; early to bed, early to rise, makes one healthy, wealthy, and wise," quoted her father.

"You should have gotten up and made it out here, June," spoke her mother. "We don't have the time, and the work is almost done."

"Daddy or the others should have awakened me," June replied as she began to assist in loading the wagon.

"You're a grown adult now. You should be aware of your responsibilities. A marriageable man of means will expect it," her mother curtly informed. "Your short comings will reflect on us, your parents, and your family at large. We have our family honor to maintain."

"I hate having to live my life based on what mankind expects or wants. Why can't I live out my own life for myself? I have needs and expectations for the future," June replied. "Why can't I get an education at Chapel Hill, or over in the College Of Charleston, or still better yet, at William & Mary?"

"You hush that nonsense, woman!" suddenly fired her father. "You'll get all the education you need right here at home. College is for self-fulfillment, and we don't have time here for sitting around reading poetry, or wasting our good energy pondering some dead man's philosophy. I went only to the third grade, woman. I learned to read and to cipher. I have a doctorate in practical terms gained right here at Drunken Run. I've done my part for Ludlow Quarter here. I have added land and structure to the family estate. I have upgraded what your second great grandfather, Ebeneezer Ludlow, started years ago.

"You see that chimney yonder, woman?" Reuben fired, as he pointed.

"Yes, Father," replied June with a sigh.

"The brick in that chimney came all the way from Aberdeen-shire, Scotland. There in that chimney is the best brick crafted by man. Everything here on Drunken Run is like that, the best; not any scrub brush, driftwood, and hyff-iced scum in this mansion house. You hear me now, woman? Clan Ludlow deserves it, and nothing less! Don't you or anybody ever forget that now?"

"Yes, Father," June meekly replied, since her father's temper could be raging when incited.

Soon, the last of the materials were loaded upon the wagon. Reuben turned toward June again without smiling.

"Now you listen, and you listen well to what I have to say, woman. Your Mama and me are riding into Mount Horeb Village, as of this moment. It'll be at least a two-day trip, maybe three, I don't rightly know yet. We are going to peddle these wares, vegetables, and such. I have some business to investigate as well. I am going to take the money and buy some paint and marble for the counter tops inside the estate, and in our tenements. It's a newfangled idea, I know, marble on counter tops, but I spent time in Italy back during my younger days. I like the way they do things. I like being the first, which is what'll set Drunken Run Estate apart from all the others around here. You got me on this?"

"Yes sir," replied June meekly.

Reuben and Ruth loaded up onto the fully packed wagon. The two horses were already yoked up. He grabbed the reins in both labor scarred hands, glancing around.

"All you children wish us well. Godspeed, and we'll be on our way," the farmer said.

"Good bye mother and father," the girls said as they rushed up to the wagon, hugging them both and waving goodbye. Soon, the wagon cluttered toward the backside of the landed estate. There was a narrow two rut road running all the way over to the Cape Fear River. Soon they would be making their way toward town. June feared bandits might be laying in the wood, but Papa had his double-barreled shot gun and a brace of pistols he kept handy and ready. There should be no need to worry.

The wagon rode off until it vanished into the woods to the distant right. June turned back around, facing the horse stable. Only one remained, the plow-horse, who also made a good saddle horse in a pinch. He was nibbling grass nonchalantly, and casually walked out from the stable into a small fenced in area. June walked closer, over toward the fence. As she did so, an appendage eased downward beneath him, then grew until it swelled into what she silently labeled as being a monstrous proportion. She gasped heavily as her breathing suddenly picked up pace.

"If only he were a man," she whispered underneath her breath. "Do such men even exist?

She shuttered as she tried to shake the thought from her mind, but it simply wouldn't leave. Her eyes were fixated. Every time she attempted to turn away, she found herself staring again. The size of that thing, and oh, his huge swinging testicles, moving almost gracefully in a natural sense. She caught herself standing there gawking by the stable fence as she grasped its wooden edge for dear life, then abruptly snapped around with her back toward the horse, walking in jerky movements out toward the garden area.

"I must battle with the forces of Satan," she whispered. "I can overcome them, if I only fight."

Her sisters labored out in the garden, gathering food for themselves later on. She proceeded to assist, laboring as she stooped until she felt strained, then standing up again. She stood up, gazing toward the livestock fence not far from the horse stable. Here there was a small goat herd, four does and one buck. She noticed the doze was behaving strangely for the past day or so, and the buck would sniff them all over, as he was doing now. Suddenly, his appendage eased out of its flesh sheath. It wasn't large as the horses, but it was still large enough for her to silently wonder if any man could have as much. The doe moved around, facing her, as the buck rose up to mount her from behind. The expression on the does face was one of sheer ecstasy, June told herself underneath her breath. June's breathing heaved as she watched. Though she battled desperately with the thought, deep down she wished she could have as much, as casually as did this Nannie goat.

"What on earth are you gawking at so?" suddenly inquired Savanna, the youngest, as she silently eased up from behind, startling June from her examination and deep, trance-like thought.

"Nothing girl," June snapped. "You get back to work," she said as she gazed intensively around toward the woods' edge across the fields, and nearby.

"You're acting funny," said Savannah.

April walked up from laboring out in the garden, standing directly before June without cracking a smile.

"She's acting funny alright, Savannah," April said, as she glared June directly in the face. "You remember what I told you, June? The devil lurks about, and is working hard on you, and I know it. I see much, sister, but say little, except what needs saying. I know what I see in the pond, the well, and inside the dark bowel. Wood spirits never lie, June."

"You're crazy!" angrily fired June.

"Crazy, you say? Well tell me something, sis? How crazy is it with these little tools you keep carving out? "

April turned and huffed back out into the garden where her sister was. The work was almost done, except the cooking. The two made their way back into the house with armloads of turnip tops, beet greens, and collards.

"I'll be glad when our bond-servants get well," said Savannah.

"You and me both," replied April, turning to gaze at her sister, seeming to be frozen into one place, staring across the field at the distant wood-line."

"When is the doctor coming?" Savannah asked.

"Today, I think," April replied, looking hard toward June, who was frozen into one place a ways out from them, still gazing blankly across the fields into the distant woods beyond.

"Maybe that's who June is looking for, so, April," said Savannah as she smiled warmly from underneath her homespun cloth bonnet.

"Yeah, maybe," April snapped. "Just maybe that much is it."

The three daughters made their way into the kitchen area, taking down a large cast iron cauldron. The pot was half filled with water while the greens, harvested roots, and slices of cured pork were packed inside. It seemed like much, but all of it would cook down nicely. Piles of stored and hulled oats, usually fed to the animals, also made a fine morning breakfast for humans simple to prepare. Two good pot loads should last three days for the three girls.

The light-wood kindling from old pine stumps out in the woods made outstanding starter wood. Splinters of it were stacked like a T-pee in the center of the kitchen hearth. Dried punk from inside mullein plants made fine material for striking fire into. A small handful of this was tucked underneath the T-pee, then the flint and steel struck. Almost instantly a fire began to arise inside the T-pee. When it consumed the kindling, larger limb rounds were placed over the T-pee. When this caught, the rounds were replaced by split stove-wood neatly stacked underneath the eaves of the kitchen unit. The entire process didn't take nearly as much time as it seemed. Soon the girls were warming by the fire, and the cauldron was hanged on the hook inside the fire place.

An hour might have passed. The day before, when the sun was directly overhead, June wound up the old pocket watch she found a few days earlier out on the wagon rut road. She pulled it from her apron pocket. It was ten O'clock sharp. The food would be ready by eleven. They didn't eat, but twice in a day. There was no evening meal. She breathed heavily as she glanced nervously toward the window in the kitchen unit.

"The doctor should be here anytime, right June?" Savannah asked in a shy child's voice.

"Yeah, anytime," June replied as she turned toward the girl, then glanced back around toward the window slightly behind her.

"You sure act like you are dying to see him, June," Savannah said as she narrowed her eyes and smiled.

April glared at June with an angry face, yet said nothing.

When the vegetables and meat finished cooking, the three girls took the pot from its hook, struggling to transport it out the door, then poured the water onto the dew damp earth outside, while carefully retaining its contents. While the material yet remained inside the pot, the girls salted, peppered, and added a variety of spice condiments to it, such as bay leaves gathered from the woods, wild onions, and a sprinkle of dried powdered hot peppers. All of their stomachs growled as they anticipated consuming this extraordinarily healthy dish. Large spoon fulls were ladled out onto three tin plates by April. The girls preferred to stand with the plates resting on the food preparation table, eating until they filled. Cool fresh milk gathered from the stream house in large tin cups, served to wash the food down perfectly.

When they finished eating, June glanced back down at her pocket watch. It was twelve O'clock sharp. When she glanced back out the window, the sun appeared to be directly above. Suddenly the chickens began to cackle, and the porch hound barked from the opposite side of the big house.

"Somebody is here now," spoke Savannah.

A few minutes passed, and a heavy knock thundered upon the closed door of the kitchen unit. June carefully peaked through a nail hole in the door. A muscular man, maybe thirty years of age, stood outside the door, waiting patiently. He carried a big black leather bag in his right hand.

"I'm the doctor from way out on Ramah Plantation, who was summonsed a couple of days or so ago. Is anybody present on these premises?" he announced.

June carefully opened the door latch to welcome him.

"Tis so good to see you, sir," she stepped backward toward her sisters and said.

As the man stood there at a distance, he wore faded white, thin but snug, cotton work pants, a white long-sleeved shirt made of thin cotton such as doctors wear, and a dark brown corduroy vest, with a beaver hair felt tricorne the same color. His complexion was pale, his thick mustachio coal black, as was his greased hair combed neatly backward upon his head. He smiled slightly with a broad, friendly smile as all three girls stood frozen, staring, and not saying a word.

24

June's breathing instinctively increased as her eyes moved gradually from his face, to his loosely buttoned but very neat blouselike shirt, down to his somewhat snug pants, then froze solidly upon a very noticeable nearly large bulge in his pants above the right thigh, immediately below his belt. She tried to ignore it, but couldn't shake the sight from her mind. Butterflies formed inside her stomach as she feared he noticed her gawking, but nothing inside his demeanor indicated that he did. Maybe this man was intelligent enough to anticipate her glares, and cunning enough to feign ignorance, she thought to herself. Her sister, April, glared hard at June, but made no comment.

"My understanding is that the bond-servants are down with the ague?" the doctor asked.

"Yes, they are down, sir, but we know not of what," cautiously replied June. "We call it the plague."

"I was instructed only to speak with the eldest, should the master, Reuben Ludlow, not be home, and you are her, eh?" the man asked in polite jest.

"I am her. My name is June Ludlow. I am Master Ruben's eldest in his second marriage. His first wife died in childbirth, you know, and the child never lived past the ninth day. Even his second wife, Ruth, and my dear mother, fear the ninth of December for this reason, I have always presumed; although Father seldom speaks much of this horrible experience."

"Could you show me to the bond-servant's living quarters, please?" asked the doctor in a pleasant, soothing voice.

"Sure, follow me this way, sir," said June with an inviting smile. She paused at the door threshold, glancing backward toward her two sisters.

"You two clean up, and make sure those vittles have been placed into proper sealing stoneware containers. Both of you know your chore duties, so get to them while I am out with this kind gentleman here," she fired with an unusual authoritative harshness in her voice, then casually turned, smiling pleasantly back toward the doctor; as her sister, April glared hard without saying a single word, although she nearly exploded with desire to do so.

The doctor and June then turned, moving out toward the animal corals and horse stable.

"So tell me, June, when did the servants first come down with this plague, as you label it?" the doctor asked.

"Maybe a fortnight ago, or a week longer," she replied.

"What were the symptoms?" asked the doctor as they walked.

"Weakness, stomach upset, fever, and puss laden sores that cover the skin," June promptly replied.

"Were there any deaths?" inquired the doctor.

"Uncle Boes died, the elder, but he was already sixty-five years old. The family hated to lose him. He served us very well," replied June. "He worked in the big house, and Papa even allowed him to sit at the family table, which is very rare in these parts, I hear."

The doctor laughed.

"I agree totally. Good folks should always be treated accordingly." the doctor replied.

"Papa offered Uncle Boes total liberation at age fifty, but he politely refused, declaring he could never live as well anywhere else on his own," informed June. "Papa still told him he could come and go as he pleased, but he seldom ventured outside the estate, except when in Papa's company."

"What were Uncle Boe's job duties?" the doctor asked.

"Mainly he was a butler, but he also helped break-in the new servants. He was always dressed in a new suit and tie mother bought him at Christmas Time," June said.

"Has any effort been made to replace him?" asked the doctor.

"Not until this scourge passes, sir," June replied.

"I agree. Makes perfect sense. I have some bad news, however. Many plantations are affected by this sickness. I also have some good news. Some of the sores I have scratched with a prick. I scratch a normal healthy individual, and he becomes slightly sick, then heals, never to sicken again from this specific scourge. I have all faith we can work a cure for your plantation here."

As the two walked along, June's eyes glanced downward involuntarily, again spotting the rather noticeable, if not large, bulge in the doctor's thin pants. She glanced back up, nervously smiling while attempting to feign ignorance and innocence. She tried to maintain her breathing, but it heaved instinctively, in spite of her best efforts. This feeling of hunger swelled from deep inside, this gnawing starvation for penetration, by flesh of the flesh. She nervously hoped the kind doctor hadn't noticed and was not intuitive enough to anticipate her precarious situation.

As she walked along, she compelled herself into gazing forward, toward the bond-servant cabins immediately ahead. There were four of them. The day before, she had walked out in that general direction on the break of morning toward the livestock area, where the goats were. She noticed a Nannie goat casually licking the fully extended flesh shaft and testicles of a certain dominant buck in the herd. The male became excited to the point of honking loudly in a series of piercing bleats. She heard this identical bleat since then from afar on many occasions, when the goats were not in sight.

The thought disgusted her, but excited her in ways she simply could not explain, as she glanced downward again at what appeared as a rather large, now pulsating bulge in the doctor's pants. This bulge appeared to have swollen, but was this all in her imagination? She wondered if this doctor might be a human version of the horse, but chucked silently at her own question. Before she could deduce any answers to either question, they both were standing before the first cabin door. Her day-dreaming had caused time to pass quickly, she thought in silence to herself.

The cabins were comfortable twenty by forty-foot structures. There were nice central fireplaces, and four spacious rooms in each one, with plenty of closet space to go with it. Many yeoman farmers in the surrounding area would be greatly envious if only they cared enough to know. Each cabin had a spacious seventy by seventy-foot garden area located in the rear. Each year, these house born bondsmen were issued a fresh change of clothing, while the field hands received one every fourth month due to excessive sweating and accompanying dry rot.

The high dollar investment required to own bond-servants demanded nothing less than the best accommodation owners could afford, from a business perspective. The farmer even taught certain carefully selected individuals to read and write, contrary to the efforts of many others in the area. The farmer's unique biblical endorsed policy of care and concern for the chattel, and its wellbeing, always granted top amounts per acre, at superior quality. His every undertaking was considered among the best, and in high demand by numerous business enterprises, to include the surrounding plantations. The appreciative bond-servants assisted in this conviction of chief quality, by going to great lengths in bringing out the best in the estate at large.

"Who's cabin is this?" the doctor asked warmly.

"We call him Skeeter, but the other bond-servants call him Crow-Marty," informed June. "I don't know why they call him that. I ask, but most politely skirt on, giving a direct answer. We think he might have been raised up in the old Rich Cromarty place. You know, way out on Windsor Bridge, overlooking the Cape Fear River, so everybody describes it, although I can't tell it overlooks the river when I've been there. Everything only looks like deep woods to me. We really don't know the answer to the question of why he is called Crow-Marty, to speak the truth."

"I've heard the tale of that place. I may have done some work out that way, on pigs and cows, rather than people, however," replied the smiling doctor with a slight chuckle.

The doctor smiled warmly as June raised her right hand, knocking three solid times on the cabin door. The wooden door eased open, revealing a sun baked male donned in old cotton, tartan patterned, patched over pants held up by homemade rope suspenders, with a worn a shirt of the same sort underneath. He bore a serious, solemn appearance on his scraggly bearded face. His extremely dark skin appeared as perfectly tanned, broken in molasses colored leather. He nodded politely as he gazed deeply into both faces.

"So you must be Skeeter?" warmly asked the doctor.

"Yes sir, I'm him. What can I do fer ya?," Skeeter replied firmly, as his dark eyes glanced back and forth, almost nervously.

"Well, my name is Jim Dyson. I hail from Mount Horeb Village, sir. I am the doctor, and I am employed way over on Ramah Plantation. I understand you and your household have been sick, as of late?"

"Yes sir, we've all been sick, mighty sick round here. I'm most well, myself, however. The women folk is sick, but maybe healing up," Skeeter informed. "The young ones are very sick still, sir."

"I think I can work a cure. Ramah and Blue Stone Plantations have been saved by my unique cure, and I think I can cure you and this plantation as well, if you don't mind me doing so," spoke the doctor.

"No!, not at all. Go ahead, go ahead, please! Anything you can do will be fine by all of us. Anything around here is better than nothing at all."

The doctor stepped on inside. June stood by the door, glancing down at her pocket watch. The watch showed two O'clock in the evening. She carefully rewound it as she patiently waited by the door. The doctor opened up his black leather bag with the triangle shaped top. He pulled out a bottle filled with a root tonic of various sorts, giving a tin cup full to each servant. He also pricked the recovering sores of those who appeared to be healing up for the scourge. Some time passed, then the doctor glanced up from his duties toward June.

"You are free to go on back home. I thank you for your wonderful escort, your warm hospitality, and your enduring patience."

"Not a problem. Then I'll be on my way, if you can find your way back," June replied with an inviting smile.

"You feel comfortable walking back to the kitchen and big house through the wood stand, then I trust?" the doctor asked with concern.

"I do it all the time, but then I probably need to head on back before darkness settles in on us, to be on the safe side," June replied. "So, until next time, sir."

"When I complete my duties here, I'll leave a note on your kitchen door saying so before heading out. Give it to your father when he returns," the doctor said. "Until we meet again."

"You know there is a cabin only a hundred yards or so from the two rut wagon road going out of here, like you came in. Stay there for the night, if you would like, good sir," June informed with an inviting smile. "The door is nearly always ajar."

"We'll do, and thank you ever so much again," the calm doctor replied, with a smile somehow conveying a sense of manly innocence underneath a thick black mustachio.

Still smiling, her eyes instinctively flicked back down to the remaining bulge in the doctor's pants, as the forbidden vision refused to exit her mind. She suddenly closed the door to the servant's cabin, then turned and walked away.

Still, the questions weighed heavily on her mind as she walked along. She fought, searching for an answer, but always returned to standing before the question. She ambled down the two rut road, passed the clearing in which the servant's cabins were located, on into a wood-stand beyond. The two rut wagon road passed through a rolling thirty acre tract before ending at the clearing in which sat the big house, the kitchen unit, the horse stable, and livestock fence.

By now, according to her pocket watch, it was only three o'clock in the evening. Down in the woods, darkness was already settling in. As she casually ambled down the hill where the old cypress wood bridge crossed a tinkling bourbon tinted creek, her breathing began to heave all by itself. Flashing surges of heat raced through her body, like shocks of lightning zipping through her blood. She was instinctively aware of an unseen presence lurking at the bottom of the hill, a presence she utterly despised, but yet simultaneously deeply craved, for reasons she couldn't fully explain.

31

Before the bridge stood a six-foot diameter live oak tree, maybe eighty feet in height. She hesitated to walk past, but forced herself to do so anyway. When she walked past, stepping onto the wooden bridge, she heard a movement behind her. She turned to see a somewhat slim but well-toned male figure wearing snug fitting, thin, off-white cotton pants. He wore a doctor's white shirt covered with what appeared to be a dark brown leather vest. He also wore an almost amusing pointed white cloth hood, with holes cut out for eyes on a mask. Then she beheld it from way out on the bridge, that almost slithering serpent-like bulge in his pants. Her breathing heaved as a powerful magnetism drew her ever nearer, in spite of all the potential for personal danger.

She battled with herself, fighting the urge, then suddenly turned and ran with all the might she had to give. The hooded figure quickly followed her, moving with great stag-like strength ever nearer from behind. She made it across the bridge to the sharp curb, then raced off abruptly to the right, being swallowed up into the woods. A hill stood between the creek, her, and the pursuing figure. Soon she approached another hill on the opposite side. She glanced backward, and the hooded figure was immediately behind her. She turned suddenly in a panic, racing over the top of the hill to the left, while hoping to lose the hooded figure; but when she made it over the hill crest down on the other side, he grabbed her solidly from behind.

Once he had her stabilized, he gradually moved his hands from her thighs to her breasts from behind. He commenced softly, squeezing them both as he gently messaged her swelling nipples. She desperately wanted to fight, but somehow found herself holding back, while slowly giving in to his aggression. Her breathing was totally erratic. She could feel his sudden warm kisses and wet licks on her bare, tender neck.

"I've been watching you carefully for some time now, June,"

the hooded man said in a hoarse whisper.

"I know," she replied as she panted.

"I saw you looking at the horse and the goats. I know all about your little carvings. Do you know that?" asked the hooded man.

"Yes, I could feel that you were nearby," she struggled to reply.

"I know all about your little charms that you carve out, and what you do with them at night. Often I stand right there at your bedroom window and watch. I give you credit. You are very talented," the hooded man rumbled. June made no reply, yet breathed heavily as her stomach knotted nervously.

He suddenly grabbed her right hand, gently placing it directly on the bulge in his pants.

"You like that, don't you?" he asked her in a low, rumbling whisper.

She allowed her hand to caress it up and down. It seemed to snake along his thigh as it swelled more. She moved her hand slightly downward and felt what she visualized as being horse sized testicles. He began kissing her heavily on her neck and behind her ears. Her breath heaved to the point she felt her heart would stop.

"I saw you watching the Nannie goat and what she was doing," the man said as he licked and kissed her neck with more passion.

"Yes," replied June as she struggled to breathe, "I saw everything," she spoke as her breathing heaved.

"Do you know who I am?" the heavy male voice asked her from behind her neck as he kissed. Gently she unbuttoned his pants, pulling them down with her right hand, as she seized the

33

man's body with her left. She grabbed hold of his rigid organ that seemed three inches larger than her toy. She began gently messaging the shaft, reaching down periodically to skillfully pleasure the testicles with her right hand. She was amazed at how well-endowed this man was.

"Do you know who I am?" the male voice asked again.

"Yes," June very nervously replied, as virtual knots formed inside her stomach.

"Look down at it," the hooded male voice asked her in a grunting rumbling whisper.

She turned her head downward to stare at it as her breathing began to heave more.

"Move closer to it, and keep your eyes wide open," the hooded man spoke in a muffled rumble. "I know you like surprises. That's why I wore this hood. You love for me to be aggressive with you like this. I already know it, my dear delicate farmland Angel."

She moved her innocent appearing face almost immediately upon this rigid, throbbing tower of pulsating flesh.

"I want what the Nannie goat did for the billy," the rumbling male voice told her.

"It's not right. None of this is right, or ever has been from the very first time," she said as she glanced upward into the hooded man's face. "The preacher gave a sermon on all of this recently. The devil is on the loose in these parts, and on our estate in particular, it seems. I have told you no every time. When are you ever going to learn that no means no?" she barely said as she struggled to breathe. Now she could have her raging, searing appetite quenched for a three or four days spell. At long last, she thought in silence, but would never say aloud. For some reason, she felt she needed to resist, yet desperately craved what she anticipated receiving.

"You always say that, June, but it certainly will not be the first time, by far and away. You always wind up willingly submitting. I know I can't be here enough for you, but I have been coming around here visiting you on the sly like this for a year and a half now."

"My father wants me married, and only married people are supposed to engage like this," she told the hooded man.

"Well, at least you'll know how to please your man when the time comes. Now doll baby. I can't say that he'll be able to please you, however, but you are always welcome to visit the likes of me; or I just might drop by and pay you an unexpected visit like I know you like," the hooded man growled as he gasped.

The urge totally overwhelmed her as she eagerly and hungrily commenced granting the man oral gratification like a well-honed professional, without farther hesitation. Time had taught her all the needed skills, determined by his reactions. Only performing the act, while being aware that her own gracious gift from him would follow, generated an exhilaration bordering on sheer erotic ecstasy. The man was hungry and almost viscous, but deep down she loved it when he was like that with her.

As she went down, he seemed to thrust himself reflexively. At first, this bothered her, but she had trained herself over time to absorb the shaft all the way down to the very hilt, licking her unnaturally long tongue out like a poisonous viper to caress his testicles on the front, bottom, and backside. Sometimes this would happen where a hand-held mirror was laying beneath them. When she would cut her eyes down at the reflection, the man seemed almost feminine, since she had taken him down so far, even to the point of totally absorbing his rather large testicles. For reasons far beyond any explanation, she often felt to gain more pleasure from doing this than he did from receiving it in the initiative.

"Awe yeah, lady, that's right. Move up and down. Yeah, like that! You pleasure me like I love, baby, and I'll give you everything I know you so desperately want," the hooded man said, as he clenched his teeth in raw excitement. She would visualize him shattering his teeth suddenly, when she even bothered to give the matter any thought.

They both quickly removed what remained of their clothes, with the exception of his white hood. She lay backward on the dried leaves against the hill, while he skillfully thrust in and out, striking the perfect spot with every near violent stab. She hated the person behind the hood with all of her heart, but loved what ole Tom Cat-Daddy could do for her, as she playfully referred to him when glancing backward while he was caught up in the fierce heat of battle. He held back on nothing, which made her love what he did even more.

"Slap my cow bags!," she would growl while slinging her head from side to side as she snarled at him, when he got crazy, hogwild on her, as if he wanted to cause her pain or even kill her with his actions, as he violently stabbed with his mighty sword of flesh. "Bite down on my nipples, you filthy rotten pig!" she raged through tightly clenched teeth, when she was maxed out on carnal excitement. When he did this for a spell of time, as he continued to thrash her madly with his rigid shaft, she soon felt the hot ooze of her own body juices down her inner thighs.

He continued for what felt like thirty minutes, then backed away. She turned her back to him, raising upon her knees, spread wide, while placing her head sideways down upon the leaves, allowing him to mount up from behind like the billy goat did on the Nannie. She loved it when he began moving slowly and gently, then gradually picked up speed, until he was going hog wild with all the strength he had to give her, trying to hurt her she often thought, though he never could. If anybody was nearby, they could hear the sounds of their lovemaking for miles in any direction, she imagined.

After what felt like long twenty minute spans, at the final moment he would back off from her body, part her buttocks, spit in there several times, then mount back up to shove in his massive organ where she would never have to worry, until both reached a second glorious climax.

The first time he ever did this she thought he might split her up the back, and the pain was nearly unbearable, but at the same time it complimented a certain type of erotic pleasure that when combined with the pain, really aroused her into a hard, energy sapping climax. Now she was well lubricated by him always and was conditioned by time and consistency to totally absorb his endowed organ in that one special area of her body. By this time the act had highly craved, while being shear erotic pleasure to her, and nothing less. When he finally backed away, both lay backward on the leaves and could hardly breathe, as the muscles in their stomachs twitched violently. They finally rolled over, trading directions as they simultaneously finished each other off orally for a third and last time. All the time she imagined the hood would be a hindrance to the man, but he skillfully managed somehow, to her own astonishment. She switched back around, rolling over onto the dried leaves beside him.

"I hate you with all of my heart, you sick bastard," she gasped as she yelled. "You dirty, filthy, rotten dog! Yet somehow, I can't shake the thought of you from my head," June roared at him in a panting voice, as they both lay back nude upon the hillside in the crispy fall leaves.

37

"I would come around more often, but for obvious reasons, I can't," the hooded man informed in a muffled rumble that seemed almost like a demented purr.

"It's completely dark now, at least down in these woods, anyway. I know the way home, however," June struggled to say as they lay on the leaves.

Finally, they both slowly replaced their clothes. As they did so, the man told her.

"I'll be around for the next three days or so. Feel free to come back down here again, as the urge dictates. You know, when your father returns, it will be much more difficult for you to sneak outside again, let alone be like this with me here in the leaves," the hooded man continued.

"I know," she nervously replied. "I'll be back here tomorrow at around the same time," June told the hooded man, "if I can live up to it and nothing happens."

CHAPTER THREE

THE SHAKEDOWN

In Mount Horeb Village, Ruth and Reuben made their way to a bed-and-breakfast they had reconditioned from an aging hotel establishment. Their plan was only to serve coffee and cured ham sandwiches primarily. A nearby bakery sold some splendid loaf bread. Egg whites, mustard, and freshly prepared cucumber pickles made an excellent dressing for the ham sandwiches.

A friend of Ruth's was managing the place. His name was John Coleman. He was a thin, but strong twenty-five-year-old* man, clean cut with sharp facial features. He possessed an entrepreneurial disposition. Reuben, through his dear wife, made a fine choice in him. He was dressed in a lace decorated shirt, brown suede vest, and tie, with a dark felt tricorne dress hat. He had big plans of his own, and was seeking to make a career from property management, and maybe one day have his own establishment. Reuben was proud to offer him the opportunity. Reuben and Ruth entered into the establishment, walking over toward the shiny wooden counter top, behind which John dutifully stood.

"Well hello, John, it's so good to see you again," Reuben said as he reached over-the-counter top to shake John's right hand.

"Fancy seeing the both of you again," John solemnly replied.

"We had a number of reasons for riding out into town hereabouts, and vising with you was one of them," Reuben said.

"Yes, and I am so glad that you did, frankly we have much to discuss," John firmly replied.

"The establishment looks good. I mean really good around here. You keep the place up very well, I see," Ruth intimated with a pleasant smile of satisfaction.

"Yes, it's all a work in progress, but there are problems you must be made aware of, Reuben," John firmly informed.

"Like what?" Reuben asked with direction in his voice and a steady glare in his eye.

"I manage this establishment, and am here virtually seven days a week until late, sometimes all night long. I know how many customers we have, exactly how much this establishment takes in, and can calculate to the single pence-cent how much we have laid up in our vault, at any given time. I do all the book work around here, and I manage everything to the last cent. Nothing around here makes it past me. Should we need more food, drink, to pay our employees, more paint or wallpaper, I record the amounts and deductions. I always ask for written receipts. People don't like to make the effort to give them out, and won't in numerous instances, but I still ask so that I might make the record in our bill book," John replied adamantly.

Reuben gazed with firm conviction directly into John's face.

"So what, specifically, is the problem?" Reuben asked in a low angering rumble.

"This man who you are partnered with, Clark, Jarlan Clark, I think he is, is the source of all our problems, Reuben," John curtly informed.

"What problems?" Reuben spouted as he narrowed his eyes.

"He saunters in here with an attitude like he carries a golden chip on his shoulders. He swaggers over to the bar in our lounge over there, drinking in the house until he can hardly stand. He talks trash to our customers, especially the females, with his rude winks and crude shenanigans. He especially does this toward the young girls, and their fathers don't like it one single bit."

"Oh yeah? Keep on talking, John," Reuben rumbled in a low angering voice, as he leaned forward.

"Several men have called his hand on this, and demanded for him to shut his trap, or else. You know, neither one of us intended to run or own an establishment catering to riffraff. We want to attract a higher caliber of customer around here, Reuben. Clan Ludlow has been an associate of the Clark clan for generations now. I am hoping you have experience in knowing how to deal with this man."

"The Clark elders before him were some mighty fine people, I tell you. We would never have had these problems in the past. His fore-bearers ran a highly successful plantation estate. Many held high positions in government," Reuben informed.

"So Jarlan must be the spoiled brat dimwit lout, who inherited the family fortune, I suppose," John spouted.

"I reckon you could put it that way," Reuben somewhat chuckled as he spoke.

"Somebody else is going to inherit it all if he doesn't change soon. I don't want it to happen on these premises, however," John replied, with a look of serious concern on his face.

"Is there anything else you need to inform me of today, John?" Reuben asked.

"Yes, it's the money, Reuben."

"What money?," Reuben firmly asked.

"On a daily basis, we average thirty British pounds around here. That's minus all expenses. This establishment is doing well, to say the least," John spouted.

"Keep on talking, John," Ruben said with a sigh.

"Every third day, like clockwork, Clark comes in here to the vault and wipes it completely clean. I know how much we take in, and precisely how much cost is for everything, Reuben. When time arrives to pay out, he doesn't even have enough to pay for the food, the drink, wages owed to include my own, etc. What you are seeing here is coming directly from my own purse pocket, Reuben."

"I take it he's pocketing the rest, eh?" Reuben asked.

"Exactly! Money is like water, it never simply vanishes. It either goes back up in the air, in the ground, or somewhere, but there is more, Reuben."

"Keep on talking, John. I need to know all of this," Reuben asked, as his smoldering anger swelled.

"The banker-man, Andy, arrived asking for the other half of the mortgage down payment, and the accompanying installment payments. He whispered of foreclosure if arrangements are not soon made, Reuben."

"So you are saying Clark is double-crossing me all the way around, John?" Reuben asked.

John only gazed into Reuben's face with hard, narrowed eyes.

"I get it, John. I think I'll order the wife and myself a cup of coffee from the hearth there. By the time we finish, Andy, the banker-man, will be over in his office. We need to pay him a visit, I think."

"I hate to be the one to inform you, Reuben, but as an honest friend and businessman, Jarlan Clark is a lout, and you mistakenly misjudged his character terribly, based on the character of his past elder fore-fathers," concluded John.

Reuben placed his half-pence coin on the countertop, sighing deeply from disappointment, as he turned and sauntered slowly over to the hearth-side at the large central fireplace. He poured himself and his wife a cup of steaming coal black coffee. It felt good only to ease backward and sip it every time the front door of the establishment opened, and a whiff of cool fall air over passed. Fifteen minutes later, Reuben and Ruth arose from their wooden tie bottom chairs, heading toward the front door.

"Keep up the good work, John, and we'll see ya in a bit," Reuben said as he forced himself to smile.

"I anticipate kinks in your project, and I wish you all the best in ironing them out," John replied.

"They all will be. They'll be ironed out well, John. Keep an eye on my wagon tied out front here, while I do what I have to do across the street."

"No problem here, Reuben. Not a problem at all."

As John spoke, Reuben and Ruth passed through the front door and out into the dusty street beyond. Across the main street, and down half a block away, was the elegant bank building crafted from marble, with grand Doric columns in the front supporting a neat foyer, its expensive crystal pane lantern swinging over the entranceway, with all the trimmings no other establishment could ever afford? These bank buildings, office buildings of the most successful lawyers, and those East India insurance companies always seem to be the grandest virtually anywhere Reuben ever traveled to.

Carefully he pulled apart the wooden doors, stepping inside, making a right to the office of Andy Shylock, the chief loan officer and partial bank owner on duty. He paused behind the tightly closed, heavy wooden door. He knocked. A cheerful, low-pitched voice with a slightly foreign east European accent answered;

"Come on inside! We're always glad to have you here at Shylock & Hockstaple Incorporated," the voice announced as the door was opening. "Ah, I see, it's Mr. Reuben Ludlow. Just the man I've been seeking for a day or five around here. It's so good to see you again, sir," Said Andy with a large smile on a rather broad face and body.

Behind a desk flanked on either side by two pistol and sword bearing uniformed guards, sat a middle sized, bearded man, with shoulder length hair wearing a fine dress coat, and black stove-pipe hat.

"I was only recently informed of my shortcomings, although I have anticipated negative possibilities for some time. Please forgive me, sir," Reuben said as he took a seat before this man.

The man behind the counter smiled, then said.

"But let us be honest with ourselves, Mr. Ludlow. These short-comings are not your own. I am fully aware. I only want you to know."

"What's your own take, Mr. Shylock?"

"I know Clan Clark is made up of highly responsible, trust-worthy people. Your partner is simply not one of them, how-ever."

Shylock sighed deeply, then leaned back in his seat, leaning up again toward Reuben from across the desk.

"To put the matter bluntly, Mr. Ludlow, your partner has simply not lived up to his half of the bargain. He failed to pay down his half on the mortgage, and he is failing to pay his half of the installment payments on the loan, while always saying he'll fetch them to us on later notice. I'm still waiting, Mr. Ludlow."

"How much is owed to you presently, Mr. Shylock?" Reuben asked politely.

"Five hundred pounds for his half of the down payment, and two hundred for the installments he hasn't paid on."

"How late are you going to be in for today, Mr. Shylock?" Reuben humbly asked as he slowly arose.

"I am always in until sundown, five days a week, sir," Shylock replied.

Reuben and his wife turned to step out the door.

"Mr. Ludlow!" Shylock snapped suddenly.

Reuben turned back around to face him.

"I tell you what. You pay me half today, and I'll drop the other half. I know you are intending to pay me something today, and we'll pick up the pieces from there, sir."

"I don't know how to thank you enough, sir," Reuben replied.

"Don't worry about it. Sir, you have much to accomplish today and so do I, now adieu."

"Be back before sundown today," Reuben replied, "until then, sir."

"Until then, sir," Shylock said as Reuben opened the door.

Reuben pushed the door closed until it snapped. When they both were back out into the street, his wife suddenly angered, grabbing Reuben by the arm.

"And how, pray tell, are you aiming to fetch him that money today?"

"Selling our wares and produce," Reuben replied in a muffled voice.

"That's not going to be enough. I can tell you that right now," his wife fired.

"We may have let your horses and wagon go with it," Reuben said with a confident air in his voice.

"What! Are you out of your mind, Reuben? It's a twenty-mile walk back home, for crying out loud," Ruth fired.

"Well, mother, Mary, done it back in her day, and so can we here in ours," replied Reuben in a voice of seriousness. "It's only a day and a half walk back, Ruth."

"She, being a young pregnant woman, may well have been escorted the ninety miles from Nazareth by Zechariah's or her father's caravan too, but where on earth is ours?" Ruth snapped in a combination of frustration and anger. "A day and half walking will kill my aging feet."

"So we'll rest for half a day," Reuben politely informed.

Ruth glared hard at him, speaking nary a word.

They both made it back to the wagon hitched out in front of their bed-and-breakfast establishment. A simple tug on a rope released the hitch, and soon both were heading northbound on Mount Hoarb Village main-street. In the center of the main was the Market House. The Market House covered two acres. It was square shaped, with four openings directly facing each incoming street. The upper area held a jail cell, multiple rooms and a rather large bell tower, since the establishment also functioned as an academy and rented office areas for city hall.

Old man Richard Gillespi, chief patron and owner of the Gillespi Plantation, Marble Ridge, located on the opposite side of the river between the British militia borough of Cedar Creek and the Harmony Hall plantation woods, was a big time local speculator. Mr. Gillespi also owned the Market House, an established landmark in the broad area. He drew a percentage amount from every transaction, rent, or sale made on the premises. He was known as being warm heart-ed, but very shrewd, however.

By now it was near noon and a crowd was gathering at the market house. An auctioneer was present who would fetch top dollar, or hold on making any sale. Farmers for miles around came to buy and sell items from deer hides, salted and smoked pig and bear meat, farm animals to occasional bond-servants, and sometimes expensive high classed household prostitutes locals politely referred to as concubines, when city hall allowed it. Every farmer had to book a position, secured by a hand written note signed by the city constable or his handy-dandy assistant, with ten percent of the asking price as prompt down payment for the license to sell, going to none other than Mr. Gillespi, of course.

Reuben walked up to the auctioneer, showing him the wagon, his vegetables, and his wares. The auctioneer asked him how much in total he wanted, and he told the man four hundred pounds in British coin.

"Well, all we can do is try to see what happens. You owe me ten percent, regardless, however, payable at this very moment."

Forty pounds was asking much from Reuben, but he tossed his payment for, thereby promptly receiving a hand written place holder note, signed by none other than Boss Shipman, the county commissioner, and local booze peddler. Of course, it was his personal assistant standing there doing the actual signing, hired and legally certified to perform such specific tasks, among others.

Reuben and Ruth stood in line with twelve others peddling their wares as well. They were at the back. When their time finally arrived, their items sold more quickly than they figured. Problem was, they only netted three hundred pounds. Reuben asked about his wagon very reluctantly. The auctioneer stated where he felt the wagon and one horse would round out the amount in needed coin. There again, an additional ten percent was to be collected from the sale by the Market House. Reuben's shot gun conveniently covered that bill. Now he and Ruth were free with the needed cash to cover payment on their personal property investment.

Reuben glanced up into the sky as he and his dear wife walked, pulling the horse down Main Street, back toward the fancy bank building where Shylock's office was. The time must have been around five in the evening. When he entered inside, Shylock sat behind his desk, leaning way backward in his newfangled swivel seat, smiling broadly.

"Well Mr. Ludlow, usually I am saddling up at this time of day, but I remained dutifully in place, knowing well you were certain to return," Shylock said with his characteristic smile and a slight cuckle.

"Yes, here I am, in the flesh, sir, and here are your funds," Reuben said, as he politely tossed the four hundred pounds up onto Shylock's desk. Quickly, Shylock counted them out.

"Outstanding sir, outstanding, and congratulations on your grand accomplishment," Shylock replied.

"As of this moment, you are the proud owner of 112 Liberty Street, Mount Horeb Village, NC. What are you naming your establishment, sir?"

"The Rooster's Den, we think," Reuben replied.

"A fine-sounding name for a bed-and-breakfast, and catchy enough I might say," Shylock replied in a slight chuckle with his characteristic wide smile on his broad face. "Should sufficiently lure the working men inside who are laboring to expand this village settlement on a day-to-day basis. Most are of admirable character, I should say."

"I have another question before I go," said Reuben. "Jarlan always paid me my share of the rents in Spanish Doubloons. We function at British Pounds still around here. Our Continental has not stabilized yet, unfortunately. What might you reckon is the explanation for this?"

"Why, he is collecting exchange fees on Spanish Doubloons, of course! The exchange rate is twenty percent. The rate is the same for the French Franc, especially if it is made of solid silver or gold, which they are in virtually every consideration. Many plantation stores and village enterprises still yet collect coin in Spanish Doubloon or Franc at this very moment. Solid gold and silver are very valuable, regardless of its origin, and may be readily exchanged back into currency. A currency exchange business does well, to be honest. Now you might consider taking his share of the rent, and making the same wise investment!" Shylock cheerfully announced.

Reuben smiled as Shylock spoke his last words for the evening. He nodded his head as he turned around, gently closing the man's door. It was almost dark, and he needed to find a place for the night. Reuben, his wife, and his horse walked back across the road to his own establishment. Luckily, there was a small back room remaining vacant. He and Ruth gladly paid the rent for that, so no gaps would exist in the record books and total calculations. John had enough irregularities to deal with already.

When they finally laid down for the night, his wife began staring upward at the ceiling.

"Reuben, I have this sickening feeling about the girls, especially June. I hate that we are going to be a day later getting home. I anticipate where it will be evening by the time we make it there."

"Try not to mull over this," Reuben replied, "replied. will be an active, long day. We need to save our good energy for the best that we can."

CHAPTER FOUR

A DISCRETE RENDEZVOUS

As the sun went down, April eased into her sister's bedchamber. Her inflexible figure stood before her sister in the flickering candlelight.

"I was down at the creek yesterday, June. Where the water puddles near the cypress bridge, I gazed into the puddle during the early morning immediately before dawn. The water spirits showed me everything." There was a pause in time as she gasped while speaking, nearly coming to tears. "I saw it all. I saw what you did, and with who. Knowing the truth about you would rip the very heart of mother and Papa from their breasts. They wanted a marriageable lady of high quality, not some fornicating cur- hound harlot!"

"Leave my room with your crazy physic garbage and pathetic lies!" June screamed.

"You will pay for this gross dishonor of the family name and its reputation. Clan Ludlow has been known for more than seven generations as being very dependable and respectable. It's so sad that one single floozy such as you can potentially shatter what took hundreds of years to build into a thousand tarnished fragments! Papa will be furious, and you can care less what you are doing to him or mother, or what the final outcome of all this courtyard dance with Satan you are engaged in might be."

"I told you, leave! Now!" June fired as she pointed toward the door.

"I've told you once, sister, and I shall say it again. The horned hunter's curse from the deep woods is upon you," April spoke in an eerily calm voice. "He appeared to me last night as I gazed into the dark bowl, consumed totally in the spirit. You'll reap what you sow in blood, June, only to be damned to walking the estate of Drunken Run as a lost soul, forevermore."

April then turned, opening the heavy wooden door, then huffing out, almost slamming the door as she exited. June lay backwards on the bed, nearly collapsing. She stared blankly at the ceiling, pondering the past year and a half, not knowing exactly how to quantify the veiled but dramatic events she had experienced. She could sense where something wasn't quite right with her. She missed her issue last month. Now, in the early morning, she was feeling nauseated, to an ever-increasing extent. These days, she nearly always felt as if she were losing her mind, and didn't know precisely what to make of it.

This surge of passionate heat flashed through her body with much more intensity now, she thought in silence to herself. The compulsion to satisfy an innate animal appetite was far too much for her to resist. She simply couldn't ever have her special itch scratched enough. She wished she could. The first time she ever tried, she fantasized where doing so would help solve her problem, but her itch only worsened. She deeply wished she were married, as Papa wanted, but he never actually made the effort to arrange such an event. He talked about doing it all the time, yet never motivated himself to make the arrangement happen.

The heat waves flashed as she lay on her back on the bed until her breathing increased into heavy gasps. She hated her backdoor lover, but at the same time, wished desperately he or somebody more talented, if not much more endowed in fact, would mysteriously appear. They must be men of means and positive reputation, however. Only the best of the best would ever do for her. The tool completely lost its magic appeal by now. Absolutely nothing at all could ever replace the real thing. She placed her hand up her gown and began touching herself, allowing her right middle finger to ease back and forth slowly inside. If she continued for enough time, this could be better than the tool anyway, when no other options existed.

She glanced at her head to the right side as she lay on her back, still engaged in her delicate activity. The curtain was pulled back on the bed-chamber window. The moon was full, and it's embracing soft glow, beautiful in the nighttime gloom. As she continued on in her questionable activity, she thought she heard a rustle in the thick azalea bushes growing beside the big house. Suddenly, a hooded face appeared before the bedroom window in the moonlight. She was deeply startled at first, but found herself gradually turned on as she resumed in her delicate activities, intentionally moving her body on the bed where he could clearly watch everything as it was being done. Now something about the hooded figure watching added to the allurement all together. She had no answer to the question of why.

She hated herself. She desperately hated the man in the hood for compelling her, yet she was heavily addicted to the sword he carried, and the splendid tricks he could do with it. Though the hooded man was her first, she had tried a few other men since. One was the thirty-five-year-old preacher back in Mount Horeb Village. He couldn't last long enough, nor was he violent enough in stabbing with his sword of flesh to suit her tastes. He refused to satisfy her special oral needs as well. On top of it all, he wasn't nowhere near endowed enough for her tastes, yet if he would pay special attention to her unique oral needs, she might overlook all his other faults, if he was good enough.

Her math tutor, who traveled to the plantation every Wednesday from over on Widow Moore's Creek, was another one she tried on and off for a while now. While Papa loved him to death and probably wanted her matched with him, truth be known, he simply didn't measure up to her special expectations either. She loved both of these men as people, but they simply didn't have the skills or body to satisfy her deeply held longings. Maybe if these men were loaded with mega millions, she could overlook their shortcomings, but their estates stood only on the bottom level of the top end economic bracket. At this point, only the man in the hood, who she despised to the point of nauseating herself, with all of her heart, mind, body, and soul, could cook up the numerous deserts like she so graciously adored having them served out.

Her breathing heaved in heavy breaths while her body trembled as her hands unlocked the windows. Her heart raced as she opened the window with great anticipation on the inside. She stepped up closely, sliding over the wall, then taking care to reach back over the wall and gently pull the window closed. She turned around, sensing an unseen presence. In the soft glow of moonlight, she saw nothing but the azalea bushes swaying in the light night breeze, the horse stable, the open areas, and the distant wooded darkness on the opposite side of the fields. As she stood there, the horse snorted and grunted in the stable across the yard.

She began easing down the driveway, leading toward the wagon road. Right beside the road, in front of the horse stable, stood the hay barn. She desperately wanted to turn and run back toward the big house, but some satanic magnetism mysteriously drew her toward the hay barn. The doors were never locked, being always slightly ajar. There was absolutely no movement other than a very light night breeze. The only sounds were of distant bull frogs, night crickets, and an occasional hoot owl. A shrill Whip-Poor-Will suddenly started up from the five or six large live oaks standing past the hay barn forty yards or so out. A sensation of terror generated a witch's potion, preventing her from stepping inside that barn. She fought it due to an overwhelming passionate desire, doing so in spite of her every inner warning.

Upon stepping inside, a heavy odor of curing hay heavily assaulted her nose. It was pitch black darkness inside the barn, save a bar of moon-light glowing in through the slightly opened barn door. When she stepped into the wall of thick darkness beside the moon-light bar, a powerful male hand seized her delicate left arm. She felt his body push itself upon her from behind, and a powerful right hand seize her arm below the opposite shoulder. As he kissed and licked her neck from the shoulder to her ears, she could feel his heavy hot breath and the canvas of his hood.

"I knew you would find me in here. I've never seen the likes of a farmer's daughter such as you," he said in an all too familiar wheezy muffled voice as he gasped, licking her neck and the insides of her ears.. "I saw what you were doing in the bed as I watched through the window. You liked letting me watch like that, didn't you?"

She hesitated with a response, finally forcing herself into making one.

"Yes," she gasped as she tossed back her head, deeply anticipating forthcoming complete gratification.

She felt both hands move upward from her thighs toward her breasts, massaging them and pinching her nipples in ways heightening the already overheating flashes of seething desire. She felt his right hand move down upon her buttocks, gently rubbing the crack, and her most tender erotic areas, all the way around toward her front. This action aroused her. She bent over, allowing him easy access. He knew how to stimulate her in ways, causing her body to reflexively thrust back and forth until she felt like screaming with ecstasy.

"That's right," the raspy voice in the hood whispered, "you love what Cat-Daddy can do, don't you?"

He kissed and licked her neck from the shoulders up to the ears. He smacked her on the buttocks through her silk night time clothing.

"Yes," she gasped as she leaned back her head.

"Take off your nightgown," the voice commanded her.

"No," she gasped.

"I said take off your gown now!" the raspy voice commanded again in a firm muffled voice.

Her trembling hands reached down toward her hips, pulling until the thin gown eased over her head.

The man snatched off his hood, and continued kissing and licking her neck, going down past her shoulder, down her back with his tongue. As he commenced kissing her nude buttocks, she leaned forward, granting him much better access to all she had to give. His skillful, unhesitating talents thrilled her beyond all retention. He continued licking, tonguing, and skillfully kissing until all her innocent inhibitions were totally released, and her mind was motivated only by raw animal desire. Finally, he moved back up her back, licking with his hot tongue as he did so. He grabbed her large left breast with his left hand, then reached up, seizing her chin with his right, snatching her head backward until the top rested upon his ripped nude chest.

"Now you are going to do what I ask, right?" the raspy voice said. She cut her eyes around, attempting to seize a glimpse of his face, but the darkness was too thick. She nodded her head up and down, saying;

"Uh, huh?"

His right hand seized hers, then placed it upon the swollen bulge she well knew was in his thin cotton pants. She gently rubbed it up and down until it swelled more, and she could feel every curvature and shape.

"Now take it out," the raspy voice commanded.

She fumbled with his buttons as she did so with her right hand, and it felt massive and completely rigid to the point her hand couldn't completely fit around it. In the darkness, his organ seemed to be a foot long as it stood totally erect. Or was this only her lusting imagination? Was he the horseman she had long fantasized about? He began kissing and licking her on the neck again as she massaged the entire length of his flesh piece. Every now and again, her hand would drop down to gently massage and lightly tug upon his testicles.

"How I love it so much when you do that," the raspy voice panted and whispered, "the way you glide your hand, and the creative moves you make. There is not a harlot anywhere in all Bath County who can do anything like you can, even when good money is spent on it." Some time passed as she continued massaging him, heating both of them up as she did. "I have another surprise for you," the rumbling voice whispered.

"What surprise?," June gasped as she panted and struggled to speak.

A powerful male hand abruptly seized her free left hand, placing it upon a firm, but massive bulge inside thin pants. She massaged as it swelled more quickly, snaking along his thigh beneath his pants, into seemingly larger proportions than that of the raspy voice.

"Who is it?," she asked.

"A friend," the heavy breathing raspy voice informed her in the pitch black darkness. "Unbutton his pants and do him like you've done for me. He'll love you for it, I promise."

She slowly did as the raspy voice commanded, though inside she hated herself for giving in. She could have long stopped all of this in its very tracks, but did she really want to?

"Do you like it?" the raspy voice asked.

"My word, I've never felt anything like this on a man any-where," she gasped heavily out of heart, racing with fear and sheer excitement.

She heard him ripping his clothes from his body in the dark-ness, including his canvas hood. Soon he stepped up beside her and the other man, as she massaged them both. Both men breathed heavily in the darkness, yet she could not discern ei-ther face. While she well knew who one was, she only thought she recognized the other, since he had yet to speak a single word.

"Now you are going to do something for both of us. I want you to do both of us like the Nannie did the billy, and you have done for me and all the others so many countless times before."

Her breathing heaved, and she panted deeply as she gasped the word, "no!"

"You know you love doing this as much as I love receiving it," the raspy voice snarled.

She desperately wanted to turn and run away, but she deeply craved the action she knew would follow. What the man had done for her earlier had now overwhelmed her mind with raw passion. She hated herself for it, but wilted to her knees as she totally gave into the domineering white hot urge. When she started the action, she began to enjoy it, though still she hated herself on the inside for allowing such things to occur. Hungrily, she kissed the rigid organ of both men, as though she were possessed by some bewitching demon of lust. She even totally swallowed them both all the way down to the skin on their bodies, a special talent she instinctively developed many long months ago to pleasure the man with the raspy voice and a few carefully selected others throughout the community. Both men were about to lose their minds as her mouth retracted and her unnaturally long tongue flicked like a poisonous timber rattler all over their testicles and the head of their rigid appendages.

Suddenly she felt the hands of the unknown man, snatching her body around with his back toward the moon-light bar shining into the hay barn. She kneeled on all fours, as he began thrusting his massive flesh-spear like a half-mad demon possessed beast. She felt he would rip her apart at the thighs, especially when he slammed the erotic spot where she knew she would never have any worries. As he stood behind her, slamming his mighty flesh staff with near raging violence, she glanced behind her and upward, catching a glint of his narrow chiseled, thick black mustachioed face with coal colored hair combed backward in the moon-light bar shining into the barn through the slightly ajar door, as he struggled to throw his mighty spear and strike that certain magic spot precisely with an unerring consistency.

The man with the raspy voice stepped around in front of her, and she pleasured him orally, while the mustachioed man continued on until the act completed, and when she glanced backward, her tender buttocks now glistened in the moon-light with new luster. The men traded places, and the action continued on for what felt like an hour more to the young woman. By the time he completed the act, she did so as well, and all three fell backward upon the hay bales, gasping heavily for breath.

59

"I hate you with all my heart. You filthy, dirty bastard! You pig!" she raged through her tightly clenched teeth at the man with the raspy voice as she suddenly commenced to sob.

The man with the raspy voice arose to his feet, then stepped to the side of the barn to urinate.

"Yeah? Well, I know better," he said as he glanced backward toward her as she lay. He turned, then walked back over to where she and the other man still lay. The man lying beside her arose to his feet.

She couldn't help but glare at his huge billiard ball sized testicles underneath his now retracting shaft. She began to sob heavily as the two men replaced their clothing.

"We both shall return, maybe with more pleasant surprises next time," he grinned as he chuckled, slapping the silent man upon his bare back.

She continued sobbing as the man with the raspy voice spoke. The other said absolutely nothing.

"No, don't either of you ever come back around here again. I never want to see the likes of you!" she screamed as she wept, while still sitting nude on the hay.

Both men were finally fully clothed.

"We'll only come back around again when the time is right," the man with the raspy, almost cat-like purring voice informed her. "We both know how much you'll be dying to see us then. We can see it in your wildest midnight fantasies." They both chuckled as they replaced their hoods, clothing, and boots, striding out the barn door into the thick darkness beyond.

She thought she recognized the silent man's peculiar chuckle when she reflected on what she saw in the moonlight while inside the barn, but couldn't quite match a name up with the face she recalled. She plodded back over toward the stacked hay bales, sitting down on two laying out from the stack on the barn floor, hating herself again for her weakness, and weeping bitterly as she held her face in the palms of her hands.

CHAPTER FIVE

THE CONTEST

The following morning, June arose early to assist her sisters in preparing food for the sunrise meal, and food for their parents so they could welcome them back home. Scenes almost vivid as reality from the night before weighed in upon her heavily as the girls labored. She labored dutifully as she attempted to forget all of it. She suddenly felt nauseated and soon stepped out the front door. When she stepped back inside, walking over to the food preparation area, April was standing close by, while Savannah labored on the opposite end of the food preparation counter.

"My, oh my, dear sis, what have we here now?" April stood frozen, bearing a composure of rigid sarcasm as she gazed hard upon June.

"What do you mean, April? What have you been into of late?" June replied.

"You know what I'm talking about!" April suddenly snarled as she lowered her eyes.

"April please, not so early in the morning, especially not on this morning!" June replied.

"Why not, when one may clearly see where Satan's spawn is kicking?" April continued to snarl.

"April... enough!" June spouted.

"Or might I say, which demon is responsible? In my crystal ball, June, I beheld a dear Ludlow angel smoking two great big pipes at the same time last night, and loving every minute of it!"

"April! Please, and not in front of Savannah. Have respect, for crying out loud," June roared out of frustration and disgust at what she knew to be the truth.

"Savannah doesn't know what is being said here," April sneered, "so leave her name out of this."

"I do know too! I know what an angel is and a smoking pipe. I do know what you are talking about," Savannah emphatically informed.

April smiled back toward June with jesting sarcasm, with both hands on her hips.

"See what you've gone and done now? You should be ashamed of yourself, June Ludlow," April said.

June threw all the vegetables and meat she held on her tin plate down, racing hysterically out the door of the kitchen extension back toward the big house.

"You may run, but you may never hide from this demon you have awakened and given birth to!" April yelled as June raced out.

"Why did you do that? Why did you scare sissy off like that?" Savannah asked.

"It'll be alright. June will be back," she informed her younger sister.

June raced into her bedroom, slamming the door tightly shut as she did. For what felt like the next hour, she fell face down on the bed, weeping. What was she going to do? Who of any means would ever marry her, with her being obviously spoiled merchandise now? Mother and Father only wanted what was best for her. They tried their best with everything they possessed to give. She had only taken advantage of their generosity at every opportunity. She didn't deserve any peace, or even half of the material effects she possessed. In all honesty, she didn't deserve to be a part of Clan Ludlow.

If father knew the truth, what would he do? How might he react? If he knew who the hooded man with the raspy voice was and what he had done, his rage would be unquenchable. He would probably challenge him to a duel. Her daddy had fought three duels already and won. His bullet and knife scars proved it. Problem is, her Father was older now. This time around, things might not go down so well. Regardless of what happens, it all would be her fault.

Finally she arose from the bed, stepping out from the big house, walking toward the horse stable simply to get her mind off everything. The horse stood still in the middle of the corral with his appendage fully extended, but June didn't pay it any attention. Her depression was far too great for her to occupy her mind with such matters.

She missed lunch. She pulled her watch from her apron pocket, glancing at it, then shoved it back inside. It was two forty-five. She saw no sign of the others when she glanced around. She walked back over to the kitchen house. The food was already prepared, but her sisters were gone. Soon she heard a horse snort, and the sounds of shuffling outside. She turns around and opens the door to the kitchen house to see her parents walk up with her mother on the horse, and pause before the horse stable. June races out to meet them.

"I'm so glad to see you both again. I am so happy you both made it back home safely."

Her parents made no immediate reply, as her father helped her mother down from the horse's back.

"It's good to be here," finally replied her father, "but there is much to attend."

"Where is the wagon?," June asked her father as he pulled the horse toward the stable area.

"Couldn't keep it," he replied.

"Why not? What imposing situation forced you to separate from it?" June asked.

"The situation was either he sell the wagon or lose his tenement," replied Ruth.

"I can make another wagon from the scrap lying around here. Steel for the axial may be replaced with iron wood in a pinch," Ruben said. "It won't last as long, but one may replace it every fourth month until he happens upon some scrap steel."

"What event thrust this situation upon you?" asked June, with a sound of urgency in her voice.

Ruben and Ruth made no reply as her father began splitting dried hearth-wood beside the front door of the horse stable. He took a wedge headed hatchet, splitting the foot diameter log rounds in a single stroke. He picked up the two halves, splitting them in a single stroke. Now he had fine burnable wood cuts.

"See, oak wood has lines in it, June. It's can be almost tough as steel, yet if one hits it along the grain lines, its weakest point, it splits with little effort. It's all about knowledge, knowing how to function, and specifically what to do," he spoke with patience as he labored.

"Yes, I see," replied June.

"You see, strong bonds between people may split in the same manner, once one strikes solidly along the weak connecting lines," her father said.

June gasped, saying nothing in reply.

"And it doesn't take much effort at all to sever a bond that built over generations," replied Reuben.

"I grew up around Clan Clark. We were close friends, like family, I say. Ebeneezer Clark, John Grimsely, Riley McPherson, Abe McDowell, and many other local clans related with the Clarks, had a solid foot on these grounds, freely giving assistance to your great-great-grandfather in laying the first cornerstone of this plantation here on Drunken Run. If these elders were alive today, Jarlan would pay dearly, I tell you! Back in the past, June, families didn't tolerate dishonor, nor disrespect. Even their own blood would pay the ultimate price, depending on the degree of their guilt."

"I don't understand," replied June.

Her father began to tremble in mounting rage.

"If Westley Clark should refuse to hand him over, I tell you come first moon on the twelfth-striking. I behold the flaming cross moving across this landscape, planting itself in the ground firmly before the front door on Blue Stone Estate."

"Is it really that bad?" asked June, as she shuddered with mounting fear.

"I tell you, a bad moon is rising on this land, June. Like your sister, April, keeps on saying, Satan and his demons are moving all about unfettered," Reuben replied.

"We never inter-married with the Clan Clark, June. We were not on the same social standing, and intimate associations mean everything. While Clan Clark adored us, they did not always get along with everybody on such quiet terms, often taking roguish directions in their relationships. Many have been jailed or even executed, here and in our Scottish homeland. They were very shrewd in their business undertakings, however. If they liked a family, they could also be very loyal. Such is why we associated with them at all. Clan Clark is very creative, industrious, and business minded, minus their weaknesses. Their personal business was and is their business, unless it concerns me or my family."

"I understand," June trembled as she spoke.

"I honestly couldn't take anything else Jarlan might have schemed in, directing it toward this family,"

Ruben spoke as he paused, trembling with rage as he also battled to conceal the fact.

June spoke little as her father continued splitting the wood. She only pondered everything she had been through, fully realizing now the wickedness of Jarlan. She walked with her father back to the big house, stepping inside, sitting down in the parlor. Her father placed several split sections of wood into the large fire place. Her mother soon sat across from June. Thoughts filled June's mind to the point she could no longer emotionally contain them. She exploded into tears suddenly.

"What on earth, child? Whats the matter?" asked her concerned mother.

"I didn't want to tell it, but I have no other choice," June sobbed as she spoke.

"What do you have to tell us?" asked her mother.

June began to weep bitterly.

"Speak to your mother, girl!," her father demanded, instantly pausing in his work, "tell us everything, now!"

"I knew something was amiss, Reuben," her mother gasped in great distress. "I knew we should never have left her alone."

"I was raped," sobbed June. "I didn't want to, but he demanded so harshly."

"Who! Who woman, my daughter, did this to you?" asked Ruben.

"Jarlan Clark,"June said underneath heavy sobs.

"By the eternal, this is it," roared Ruben, as he threw down his armload of wood into the floor. "I will follow in the footsteps of the elders. This family has been insulted enough by the likes of good for nothing, Jarlan Clark! First light tomorrow I'm sending for him. He still owes us some work around here that I allowed him to put off until later, yet paid in his share of the monthly mortgage installments. He owes me, and he will pay for so much more!"

June wept in bitter unending heaves. She had done it all now; she thought to herself in silence. Who knows what kind of Pandora's Box she has opened?

Reuben drank more whiskey than usual that night, June noticed. He spends more time than usual carefully sharpening his knives. When morning came, Reuben skipped breakfast, heading directly over to Skeeter's cabin. On the way there, he met his favorite servant boy, Juba. Juba was special, having a very pleasing, pleasant, loving personality. Juba truly wanted to perform well on the plantation. Reuben went to great lengths to show the boy special affection, such as buying him expensive knickers, shirts, and felt tricorn hats, not to mention leather shoes with solid silver buckles. Reuben even hired a tutor who taught Juba to read, write, and figure. One day, he intended to allow Juba total liberty at will, on and off the plantation. Doing this was unheard of in any plantation, anywhere around Drunken Run, or the entire state, for that matter. Reuben liked being different, and done this simply because doing it was his own prerogative, and he felt like doing it.

"My little Juba, seeing you makes me feel so happy, and I need to feel that way right now."

"I'm glad to see you, sir," Juba said. "Where have you been for so long, sir?"

"I need you to do me a favor, if you can, Juba," Ruben said.

"Sure, just ask, and it shall be done, sir," Juba replied.

"Do you know where Blue Stone Plantation is?" Reuben asked him.

"I sure do. I go there all the time to fish, and to run errands for the misses."

"Can you make it there safely?" Reuben asked with great concern.

"No problem, sir, you can count on me," Juba said. "I even know a shortcut way there."

"Do you know Jarlen Clark?" Reuben asked.

"Yes sir, I know Mars Clark, and know him well," Juba replied.

"Go over there quickly as you can, Juba. Tell Jarlan I need him to help me split some wood today," Reuben said. "When do you think you might make it here with him today?"

"Maybe by two."

"It's twenty miles, Juba. How could that be?"

"Not the way I go. I go through the swamp, off the roads."

Reuben took a notepad from his pocket, tearing off a piece of paper. Quickly, he scribbled a permission slip in case Juba was apprehended and questioned along the way. He handed it to him.

"Here, take this, and should anybody stop you and give you a hard time, tell them I sent you out and show them this."

"Yes sir, and I will be out and on my way directly, sir," Juba replied with his characteristic large happy smile.

Reuben ambled on back out toward his horse stable. He began curry combing his two horses out, and thinking about where he was going to fetch scrap for building the wagon. He had four planks to form the sides right now. He was certain if he searched hard enough, he might find beam wood for wagon timbers, iron wood for the axles, and such. The entire wagon could be held together with wooden pegs. He didn't see where he would need to ride back into town for anything at all.

All morning he walked about, picking up this old board or that one. He took a one man crosscut saw, stepping into the woods cutting the timbers to be later crafted into wagon beams. Doing this work was therapeutic in its effect upon Reuben's psychology. His mind momentarily forgot all about the negative situation he and his family were in. Finally, all of his parts were virtually assembled before him.

He would use old metal barrel hoops for tire rims. Once he crafted the wooden tires, the hoops would be heated up until they were red hot, fitting carefully over the wooden tire, then cold water poured over them. When the metal rim cooled, the wooden tire would be solid and tough to crack. He glanced up toward the sun, which had passed from being directly over, into the first notch of heading down. He heard crunching

70

footsteps in the dry leaves, moving down the wagon road in his direction. He glanced up, catching sight of Juba and Jarlan walking down the wagon road. Soon they were standing beside him, both wearing large smiles.

"See sir, I told you I can be depended on," little Juba said with a smile.

"I never had any doubt about you," Reuben said. He instinctively glanced hard at Jarlan. "I wish I could say that about everybody."

Jarlan smiled in a sarcastic, sadistic manner.

"Now, now, Reuben, let's not go off on a tangent here."

Reuben glanced hard without smiling.

"Me? On a tangent? I would never do such a thing."

Jarlan continued smiling as if he sought to intimidate Ruben.

"So what's on for today, mate?"

"Well, I'm building a wagon here. It's in pieces right now," Reuben told him. "Juba, you can go on back to Skeeter's place, and thank you for your services, my wonderful son."

"No, thank you. It's my pleasure, sir," Juba replied.

He took off running down the wagon road until he was out of sight, turning sharply to the left and vanishing among the distant oak and pine trees.

Jarlan stood smiling, his grin of intimidation.

"So what happened to your old wagon, Mr. Ludlow?" he asked, "or do you need an extra one?"

Both men picked up wood, moving it toward the stable, which also served as a periodic work shop.

"No Jarlan, I had to get shed of my old wagon."

"What on earth? Was it money problems, or what, Reuben?"

"Jarlan, don't you dare play dumb with me about this matter," Reuben fired.

"What are you speaking of here, Ludlow?" Jarlan said as his grin transformed into a snarl. He never referred to Reuben as Ludlow or Mr. Ludlow. Before he always addressed Reuben by his first name. Something isn't right, Ruben thought in silence.

"I'll just be frank with you, Jarlan. You didn't pay your half down as you promised. You kept my half of the rents and lied to me outright."

"Oh my, Mr. Ludlow, what crass accusations here do we have? I can't believe it. I am so insulted!"

"No Jarlan, I spoke with the banker-man, Mr. Shylock. It's not an accusation, it's fact, he knows and so do I. I know all about how you took the rents, changing them into Spanish Doubloons, then traded them out for twenty percent in exchange fees. Good job, Jarlan. Even Mr. Shylock thought it was a wise idea."

Jarlan stood glaring, with an open-mouthed grin, saying nothing.

"You have offended generations of close camaraderie between our two clans. That association garnished adoration from prominent clans in the broad area, such as the McDowell clan, the McPhersons, the Bryants, the Brissons, the Clan Shaw, and numerous others. Feet from every family I just named have trodden right here on this soil, donating blood, sweat, and complete loyalty from every individual. Doesn't any of this mean anything to you, Jarlan?"

Jarlan's eyes suddenly opened wide.

"Now wait a minute here, Reuben. This story is not what it appears now. Damned Shylock is a dirty rotten shiest-er, I tell you! When I went to pay my half of the mortgage installments, he came up with a hundred different fees, not giving me credit for paying my half when I couldn't afford the extortionist fees. I did my part in this deal."

Reuben's breathing increased as he almost appeared to cry. He gave no immediate reply, only continuing to labor with increased energy.

"The elders wouldn't have taken it," Reuben spoke as he labored along, gritting his teeth. "The flaming cross would now be standing tall in your yard. Your grand pappy, Claiborn Clark, would have had no choice but to hand you over; but then, I know it would have been a willing move on his part. He fully comprehended the conviction of family honor."

"What do you mean by telling me this? I told you I am a victim of treachery myself here, Reuben!"

"I've heard enough of your lies, Jarlan Clark! You're gonna do some work around here, as you promised."

"No problem, Reuben, no problem here on my part," Jarlan said as he gave his characteristic grin, holding both hands up with the palms out.

He and Reuben stepped over toward the wood pile. One round was turned up on its end.

"Here, Jarlan, take that hatchet sticking in the upturned round there, and start cutting me some hearth wood. Can you do at least that much for the Ludlow family, after we have done so much for you?" Reuben asked him as he clenched his teeth in gnawing anger.

"Now, Reuben, that's not nice of you to act as you have. Look, I know life is stressful. I know how it all is. Trust me on this one. Level off with me, Reuben, man to man, out here where its only is us. What's bothering you?"

Reuben was nearly beside himself with rage, trembling, as he fought the urge to say what was weighing heavily on his mind.

"First, you double cross me in our business dealings. Then you lie to me as you have!"

Jarlen cocked his head sideways as his jaw dropped.

"Reuben, I explained all of that, now didn't I? I was a victim of fraud myself. Now, listen here, I am man enough to accept this tangle was a result of a big misunderstanding." he shrugged his shoulders as he spoke. "No problem on my part. I can forgive. Here," he said, as he stuck out his hand to shake on it.

Reuben was panting with rage, and he refused to look at him.

"Look at you now, Reuben. I ask forgiveness and you ain't too forgiving. What's up with you, Reuben? Be out with it, man."

"You want me to be out with it? I'll be out with it. First, you will never have to worry about our business, because it's all mine now. I took it over and you are on your own, Jarlan."

"Whoa ho ho now, wait a minute here! You mean I am all out, just like that, Reuben?"

"That's right, Jarlan, out of my affairs just like that."

Jarlan glanced up into the sky, which had begun to darken heavily. In the distance loomed a low roll of fall thunder.

"Hmm, thunder is unusual for this time of the year, Reuben. It must be an omen of some sort, don't you think?"

"The elders told me growing up that fall thunder was a sign of early ice and snow. I stepped down to the pond to fish. I was going to use the worms on the Catawba tree next to it. They already spun their silk," Reuben panted with mounting anger as he said. "Certainly the signs are true."

"You know what, Reuben? I always heard fall thunder was a sign of evil soon to come. You are so right, the omens are always dead on."

"You raped my daughter, Jarlan!" Reuben suddenly spouted with exploding rage. "She informed us all about it."

"Wait, a minute here! Hold up on that one, please! Now say that again to me. I am not sure I heard right," Jarlan said.

"You raped June, Jarlan."

"Me? Raped June, or any woman? I never have!"

"Jarlan, my daughter would never lie about such matters."

"Look, look, now Reuben. I'll fess up here. Me and June had a little, shall we say, association going on for a bit here, but associations don't translate into rape. I mean, come on, Reuben, June is a grown adult old enough to choose her own candy. I can tell you very bluntly here, sir, she certainly chose her own candy!"

"Rape doesn't mean choice. Last time I checked," Reuben growled.

"I mean, Reuben, you need to get real with her here. Why, I was by far and away wasn't her first. I mean, the preacher even sliced her cake with his knife, for crying out loud here! Come on with all of this rape garbage, man."

Reuben suddenly shot out his left fist, striking Jarlan dead on the jaw, knocking him flat of his back upon the ground. Reuben quickly pulled his razor sharp shop made a pocketknife from his overall bib pocket, crafted from a worn out saw blade.

"Your head is mine, son of a bitch!" he growled as he moved toward him.

Jarlan rolled, barely escaping him, moving toward the upright splitting round.

Reuben paused, searching the ground for a wooden staff or an ax handle he recalled lying around. He turned his back for a split second on Jarlan as he searched the ground.

Jarlan snatched the hatchet from the wood round suddenly, quickly stepping up behind Reuben, striking him solidly with the blade, spitting the back of his skull completely open, and exposing his brain. Reuben sank to his knees with his head completely turned upward, until he faced Jarlan standing behind him, gazing directly into the eyes.

"Why, after all we've done?" he gasped in ending heaving breaths. "Curses be to you and all of your descendants! May you and yours die in your own blood, four times over what I am paying in mine," Reuben struggled to speak, as blood and brains gushed from the gaping split back of his head.

Jarlan raised the hatchet again, striking Ruben in the forehead, stabbing the hatchet blade deep inside between his eyes, knocking him to the ground face up, into a standing pool of blood. This time it was all over with for good. Once Jarlan saw his final conclusive act, a flash of lightning brilliantly lit up the scene.

"Fall thunder and lightning also means the dark spirits abound, and Ludlow, the dark spirits have certainly trod upon your precious soil today," Jarlan spoke aloud into the scene surrounding him, gazing at Ruben with the hatchet buried solidly between his eyes...

Rolling thunder nearer by generated an atmosphere of heavy apprehension. Jarlan knew he must act fast and develop a workable plan. With all of his might, he struggled to drag the dead weight corpse of Reuben Ludlow into the horse stable as the lightning flashed and the crashing thunder rolled. He seized a round nosed shovel leaning against the wall Reuben used to shovel manure, as the horses snorted and screamed from time to time. Quickly he pulled back the one foot thick layer of manure, digging a hole in the soft soil eight feet, three by three, by five feet deep.

The wind picked up pace as Jarlan heaved the dead weight body of Reuben Ludlow's corpse inside the hole with all of his might. Across the edge of a top board in the side wall of the horse stable were bundles of scorching hot cherry peppers and tomatoes Ludlow kept hanging up to dry. These peppers. He sifted between his hands until the powder covered the corpse. He then buried it underneath the damp spoil. He reapplied the manure layer until it appeared as if it was never been disturbed..

On the outside by the wood splitting area, he dutifully cleaned up the blood trail, dragging a dogwood branch over the tracks and body marks on the earth. The soon coming rain would help out even more, he thought as he labored. In short order, all scent and sign of Reuben Ludlow would be purged from the earth forever. Once Jarlan was confident in the quality of his wicked labor, as the lightening flashed, the thunder rolled, and the rains finally commenced, he eased away into the tall standing woods, walking back home through the trees into the pouring rain, intentionally avoiding the roads or any type of established trails.

The girls and their mother, Ruth, were inside the kitchen extension preparing food. The hours passed, and it was nearing evening.

"Have you seen Papa, mother?" asked June.

"Did he even say where he was going this morning?" asked April.

"He said he was sending for Jarlan, if you remember. He left out not long after first light. I glanced out around noon, noticing him splitting hearth-wood by the horse stable. Beyond that much, I have no idea, except I do know he was highly upset about this business with Jarlan Clark," Ruth replied. "Jarlan should be the person in question if we have a reason to question anything.

"But Jarlan wasn't here, was he?" asked April.

"Maybe Papa'll come in after nightfall, eh?" Ruth replied in a hopeful voice. "Jarlan wasn't around anywhere, to my knowledge."

The girls glanced at one another with widened, unsettled eyes, as the lightning flashed and the thunder rolled. Darkness quickly covered the land.

"My, it sure is strange for thunder and lightning this late in the fall," Ruth said, as she glanced uneasily out the windows. "Surely your Papa is taking cover somewhere by now."

"Papa said it was a sign of a cold winter," little Savannah said.

"Wickedness is afoot in the land," April suddenly spouted without smiling. "Dark spirits are walking about."

"Oh, come on with that!" fired her mother, Ruth.

"No, mother, I can sense it. I know what I am speaking of," April replied.

As she spoke her words, lightning flashed again, and the thunder rolled heavily.

"I can feel it in air, the atmosphere surrounding me, the flash of the lightening, and the rolling sound of the thunder. Somehow Papa is not coming back. I don't know how, but somehow Papa isn't making it back home tonight."

"You hush that fuss, child!," fired her mother, Ruth. "Enough of that. We are going to walk in the ways of light in this house, not darkness! Papa is taking cover somewhere, that's all. He'll be back soon as this rain stops. There is an explanation for all of this. If he misses tomorrow and tomorrow night, I'll ride out to the old man, Kracken Shaw's elegant estate, over on Mars Hill. He is a close friend of the constable, and often raises blood hounds for the Sheriff. Nothing escapes the nose of a well-trained Blue Tick, and Kracken raises the best. Should Reuben fail to show, Kracken's Blue Tick will walk us directly to him, and the truth, wherever it lies," Ruth announced with an uneasy sigh.

The cold windswept walk in the rain from the kitchen extension to the big house bore a sensation of apprehension. The family habit of hanging rain slickers in every building saved the day, however. All night long the wind howled, the lightning flashed, as the thunder clashed and rolled. When bed time arrived, the girls went to their bed chambers consumed in a sensation of uneasiness. Ruth went to bed alone, feeling intimidated by the very walls and the darkness within. April lit her candle. The candle flame burned, leaning over. April gazed around, searching for more indications. A leaning candle flame was a sign of a spirit's passing.

Lightning flashed, and in the sudden blue flame, she thought she saw a silhouette standing by her dresser. When she lifted her candle, she saw nothing, save the bare wall and the dresser.

The thunder rolled again, and a ceramic figurine of a British chimney sweep suddenly over turned on the smooth dresser top. She fully realized an unseen presence was inside the room accompanying her. Maybe this entity had a message for her.

She set her dark ceramic bowl filled with water on her nightstand, placing her candle beside it, then placed another on the opposite side, lighting both. She gazed intensively into the reflection on the water, yet saw nothing indicating communication with the spirit realm. She sat on her bed side gazing for what felt to be long drawn out hours, yet still there was no mysterious revelation in the water.

CHAPTER SIX

THE SEARCH

All night long, the rains poured as the big house creaked and moaned in the howling wind. Sleep finally settled in upon the family. When they awoke, the sun was already above the tree line on the horizon. The sky was sweet baby blue and crystal clear. Breakfast time came and went. Noontime arrived and there was no informing message. In no time at all it seemed, nightfall fell again, and sadly no Reuben Ludlow.

"I feel the worst," spoke Ruth in tears as she mumbled prayers. "When this rain ceased, there was no doubt in my mind that my dear Reuben would return. I could understand him not wanting to walk in the rain, but today the skis were crystal clear, and still no Reuben. Tomorrow, girls, we are walking over to Mars Hill. I pray dearly your father soon returns."

When the sun came up on the following morning, the skies were clear again. The girls and Ruth broke a pan of recently cooked cornbread, eating it with cured salt pork, washing it down with black coffee. Soon they were walking down the wagon road. The road wound up and down hills, passing through deep thick woods, through natural meadows, passing an occasional time ruined by long abandoned cabin homestead. After maybe two hours, the wagon road forked, and the three took the left fork over the same terrain, until it finally arrived at large, open, broken fields. The road ran along the edge of the field until the ground elevation suddenly raised. They paused, gazing forward toward the topmost section of the hill, where a magnificent Doric mansion sat tucked away among well placed live oak trees, azalea and yaupon hedge bushes. From the distance, for inexplicable reasons, the estate bore an almost oriental atmosphere.

"Well, at long last we've reached it girls, the famous Mars Hill Plantation. Old man, Kracken Shaw, can find your father. He has a nose himself as sharp as his hounds. If mischief has occurred, he will know where to place the responsibility."

"Tell us about Mr. Kracken Shaw mother," asked Savannah as she gazed upward through squinting eyes in the rising sunlight.

"Mr. Shaw is a veteran of three wars. He won metals during the Revolutionary era. He is wise as an owl, and rough as a bear. Bad men don't want to mess with him," Ruth said. "His father was Gardrow Shaw. His grandfather was Slam Deck Shaw. Slam Deck Shaw was a sailor, and the terror of the seas. He sailed with Captain Morgan, became governor of some Caribbean Island, then turned into sea policemen and terrorized the pirates. He lived to be more than a hundred years old, so they claim. In all fairness, he was the one who secured the family fortune."

"Wow, he sounds interesting!," said Savannah.

"I hope he can help out," said April. "Did father know him?"

"Your Father knew him well. Most people do all around here," replied Ruth.

As they walked up the slope, the two rut wagon road transformed into a beautiful tree and early fall flowering shrubbery lined driveway, with the columned front of this astonishing mansion facing them. The porch hounds barked as the women neared the steps. A horse tied onto a nearby tree grunted, jerking his head. A servant dressed in a shining bleached white sailor's dress uniform stepped forward from the door to greet them.

"Hello mam, what might all of us here on Mars Hill Estate do fur ya today?" he greeted.

"We're here to see Mr. Kracken Shaw, if he is in, sir," Ruth replied.

"Give me a minute and I'll fetch him if he is," replied the servant. "Might I ask who wants to know?"

"Tell him it's Ruth Ludlow, wife of Reuben Ludlow from Drunken Run, and let him know it's an emergency."

"I sure will. Wait jest a minute, and I'll be back directly mam," the servant replied.

Three minutes passed, and out stepped a rather large old man, donning a dark blue sailor dress uniform. He wore a huge smile on his face, with both arms opened wide.

"It's so cheerful to see you again, Mrs. Ludlow. I was just asking about you and Reuben the other day. It's been such a long time!"

The girls walked up the stairway meeting him, as he hugged Ruth at the top, and she hugged him likewise. The girls knew this man must be very important, since Ruth almost never hugged anybody who wasn't an immediate family.

"Well, I do declare, Mrs. Ludlow, it's so good to see you again," Kracken said with a smile. "So please tell me what brings you out of my way."

Ruth hung her head, glancing back up, cracking a smile.

"Reuben has vanished on me, Mr. Shaw."

"Well? Now I don't know how to take that. What do you

mean?," Shaw said to Ruth.

"There was a problem. Harlan Clark stiffed him in a business deal. Clark also raped our eldest daughter, June. Reuben was going to confront him. I don't know if he did or not, but when he walked out our front door, we haven't seen him since," Ruth replied, glancing up toward Shaw through squinting eyes.

"I see," Shaw sighed, "and that much is certainly a horse of a different color we are dealing with here," Shaw replied. "How long has Reuben been gone now?" Shaw asked her as he took a drag on a pipe he packed and lit during the conversation.

"Two days," Ruth replied.

Shaw casually turned toward his door servant.

"Could you fetch Cassidy for me?"

"I sure can, sir," the door servant replied.

"Have him brought a brace of our best hounds when he comes. Probably Rock and Jupiter are the best out of that crowd we have at the present time."

"Yes sir, I'll tell him soon as I can make it out of his way, sir," the servant replied.

"Thank you Dexter," Shaw replied. He turned to face Ruth. "Look here now, Mrs. Ruth. We'll escort you back to your place. It's not that far out to Drunken Run. I'll have Nu Nu and Papa-Dew to load up the wagons, so we all may ride back in relative comfort."

"What do I owe you for your kind services, sir?" Ruth asked in a polite, humble voice.

"Considering the magnitude of your possible loss, a decent plate of beans, rice, and hog backs might suffice," Shaw replied.

"Let me know what I can do to repay your losses in helping me," Ruth intimated.

"Look Mrs. Ludlow, I've known Clan Ludlow all my life. I am also a man of my word. All I want is what I have already requested, mam,"

Ruth never said a word. She only cut her eyes his way. To the left by the staircase, two male servants brought two elegant wagons hitched with two horses a piece. When each wagon was fully prepared for the journey, the male servants presented them to Ruth and Mr. Shaw. Mr. Shaw arose from his porch swing, stepped down the stairway until he was center, and then extended his right hand to Ruth.

"The buggy is ours and the wagon is for Cassidy and the two hound dogs," Shaw informed Ruth and the girls.

Shaw helped Ruth and the girls up into the buggy, then he himself climbed up, sitting across from them inside the buggy. Papa-Dew, a skilled, well dressed buggy driver, climbed onto the outside seat.

"I hear people pay big money just to take a ride around the area in your buggy, Mr. Shaw," Ruth said.

"It's a service that helps pay the bills, Mrs. Ludlow, but for you, it's all on the house."

"Thank you so much, Mr. Shaw."

"My pleasure, Mrs. Ludlow. It's the least that a true knight could do for three damsels in great distress," Shaw replied.

"I'm sure when all of these end well, Reuben shall thank you dearly for your willingness to assist," Ruth replied with a slight smile.

As Shaw and Ruth engaged in conversation, the dogs and the servants were boarded, and the call to pull out was struck with a flick of the leather reins. The buggy and the wagon pulled out. Now the three-hour walk was cut in half. June pulled out her handy pocket-watch she was keeping wound up nowadays. The time was one o'clock.

"I know it's lunchtime. Here is some fresh jerky and cornbread in the food box underneath the seat. There is a freshly corked bottle of water," Mr. Shaw said.

The girls reached down, pulling out the wooden drawer, nibbling on the food, while Ruth didn't.

"Not hungry, Mrs. Ludlow?" Shaw asked.

"Not much of an appetite right now. I am apprehensive about what we might find, to be honest. My stomach has a knot forming in it."

"You and the girls have a right to be apprehensive, frankly," Shaw replied. "I well understand."

"It will be a blessing if Reuben is at home waiting on us when we arrive," Ruth came to tears as she spoke.

"We'll all have a big party then," Shaw replied with his characteristic broad smile. "I'll tell ya what. Those dogs'll be starved before hunting. When we arrive, give me a piece of Reuben's clothing, his boots, an old hat; anything he wore regularly, and they'll go after him in hot pursuit."

"It's amazing how they can find somebody like that, anywhere he may go," April said.

"Yes, it is. Matter of fact, there is only one way to throw them off a scent. Raccoon uses it all the time.

"Most folks who don't coon hunt with dogs don't know about it, however," Shaw said as they rode along.

"What way is that?" asked Savannah through squinting eyes.

"When the dogs are after a wise big ole boar coon, he'll seek out a run, preferably a large one. They'll go down in the water and swim upstream maybe two hundred yards without touching anything, then get out on the other side. They try to walk in places where the ground is hard, so they don't leave tracks. This will throw the dogs off, causing them to run up and down the stream from the place where the coon went in the water. Sometimes an experienced dog will realize what the coon has done, then he'll cross the run, searching out the scent on the other side. Often the coon is long gone by the time he picks it up," Shaw said. "People on the run who are wise often make the same move."

"Wow, a coon is a smart animal," Savannah said with her young smile.

"Wise dog handlers, which most people aren't, have developed an effective strategy for neutralizing this move, however," Shaw said as the buggy continued moving along.

"What is that?" asked Savannah.

"They have a leash on one or two dogs, holding them back from the others. When the others commence running up and down the stream, he'll follow the dogs on the leash, leading them to the water and across," Shaw informed. "He then leads them up and down the stream until they pick the scent up on the other side, then the pack follows, going on ahead in the direction of the target."

"Is there any way around them?" asked April.

"Wise criminals, which only very few are, have developed a

method of neutralizing the dogs. If the pursuit using dogs is anticipated, pieces of fat may be stuffed with glass splinters, and left along the trail," Mr. Shaw explained. "Any dog on the trail will instantly pick it up. When he does, the dog will sicken in maybe two hours' time, then lay down, creating a burden and distraction for the owner. In a day or so, the dog will virtually always die."

"Is there any methodology for countering that?" asked April inquisitively.

"Wow, what large words you use, Miss April!" Shaw laughed. "Thankfully, most criminals are not intelligent people. Sometimes we may surround a large area ahead of the dogs, where the criminal is deductively anticipated as being, if we have a posse large enough. This strategy usually works. Nine out of ten criminals may be herded like sacrificial goats for the evil sins committed, but then there is always this one."

"If anybody has done anything to Papa, I hope he is not smart," said Savannah.

"You hush that fuss, girl!" suddenly spouted Ruth. "Nothing has happened to your father. Stop saying that it has."

"If anybody has Miss Savannah, I'll bet it was somebody your Pap knew and we'll nail him, but we will not expect the worst. Pap is only lost out in the woods or something, and we're gonna find him still today," Shaw said.

The wagon road transformed into familiar woods, then the woods opened up into a meadow and a freshly broken field. Ahead, by a stream and a finger of woods branching from a much larger densely wooded area, were the servant cabins. The narrow road moved on passed, over a hill and through a thirty acres or so patch, then into another opening. Next to a pleasant stand live oak trees stood the horse stable and the big house.

"Home at last!" said Savannah.

"We're home at last, but still no sign of your Papa," Ruth nervously announced.

By the big house door stood a well-worn pair of leather boots. Reuben kept three pairs on hand, in case one wore out and he couldn't make it back into town. Ruth stepped down from the buggy and over to the steps, picking up the boots. She walked toward Shaw, who received the boots, then tossed them before the barking, hungrily sniffing hound dogs.

"Nothing makes it past Rock there. Wherever Reuben is, Rock will lead us to him."

Rock tossed up his head, barking deeply and very loudly, indicating he was picking up the scent. The servant released him, and off he went, directly toward the wood splitting area and the horse stable. He barked insanely as he sniffed the hatchet, and split logs, and the surrounding area.

"Reuben was splitting wood, and definitely inside the area," Shaw announced.

Rock headed over toward the horse stable, circling around it wildly multiple times while barking insanely loud.

"Let's all of us head over toward the sable and see what we have," Shaw said.

Every person boarded up, offloaded, then headed toward the horse stable. When they arrived, Rock was sniffing the ground and manure all over, barking, and running around in circles throughout the stables. The two startled horses pranced to their feet while occasionally snorting and grunting. Soon he zipped outside, circling the stable, sneezing several times, running back inside sniffing the manure, sneezing a few more times, then eventually moving back outside and laying down.

"I don't know what to make of this," Shaw said. "Usually I can read Rock like a book. Go find him, boy!," Shaw said. "Lead us over to him like I know you can. Find him for us!"

This routine maintained for what felt like hours until sundown.

"I've never seen anything like this in my whole life. I don't know exactly what to make of this, but there is something about that hatchet sticking in that log round there, the wood splitting area, and that horse stable. That dog has never behaved exactly like this, however," Shaw informed.

When nightfall arrived, Mr. Shaw was allowed to sleep over in the guest room. First light the next morning, the dogs were released again. Rock made the same moves, except this time he ran down in the woods for an hour, then returned to the wood splitting area and into the stable, behaving in the same manner.

"Which way do you reckon the dogs' barking was coming from when he was out, Mrs. Ruth?" Shaw asked.

"Southwest, I would suppose? I am not sure, Mr. Shaw," Ruth replied.

"I thought so too. What is the nearest estate in that direction, Mrs. Ruth?" Shaw asked.

"The nearest one is Blue Stone Manor, I will presume, but that one may be some fifteen miles out," Ruth replied.

"Blue Stone Manor? I've never heard of it."

"Well, people identify it by different names," Ruth informed, "I don't know why, but they do."

"What family owns it?" Shaw asked.

"Why, the Clark family, of course," Ruth replied.

"Was Reuben's business associate one of the Clarks?" asked Shaw.

"Yes he was. Jarlan Clark was his name," replied Ruth.

"Hmm, this is interesting. Old Rock never lies nor misleads. " Shaw paused as he pondered. " He always has the absolute truth to say when he speaks at all. Only this time I don't know what to make of his message, but I can clearly see where he keeps repeating the same one."

Kracken Shaw spent the night again, repeating the same process, as did his famous hound dog, Rock. Rock continued to send the same identical message, behaving in the same manner. After three more days, Shaw decided he and Ruth would pay the Clark residence a visit. Jarlan was the person meeting them at the door. Contrary to Ruth's anticipation, Jarlan was pleasant and very cooperative. He admitted going to Drunken Hill, helping Reuben split hearth-wood, and spending time with him on the day of his disappearance. Otherwise, he had no idea what might have happened. All the time he stood before them at the door speaking, Rock was going crazy with howling and barking.

"Something is not right. Rock is telling me so. I think Jarlan is lying, but without hard proof, I can't say so in honestly, Mrs. Ruth. You are aware that the body of your husband could well turn up from this investigation, aren't you?"

"Yes, I am," she replied to Shaw as tears began welling up in her eyes.

"Honestly, without that, Mrs. Ruth, we have nothing to build a case on."

"I know, sir." Ruth hung her head and commenced weeping bitterly.

For weeks and months thereafter, Kracken Shaw returned to search, with everything being the same. Old Rock would always behave in exactly the same manner, giving the identical message every time, while the humans never comprehended what he was saying. Finally, the search was called off, closed, and eventually recorded as being unsolvable.

It was spring time two years later when the case of the Reuben Ludlow disappearance was closed. His daughter, April, sought an alternative means of discovering her father, however. The first stormy night provided a perfect atmosphere. Upon her nightstand stood the dark stoneware bowl filled with water. As the lightning flashed, two candles were lit on either side of the bowl. A blotter of ink provided an eye focus point. She held her gaze fixed, attempting to peer directly into the reflection itself, rather than the water. Soon the water was filled by swirling clouds, then after a while, the clouds cleared. The horned green man of the woods appeared in a startling vision before her as she sat gazing into the bowl.

"Tell me, oh ancient spirit of the woods, where is the location of Reuben Ludlow, my father?" spoke April aloud above the vision in the bowl.

"Try to try, though the elder wise man may. He shall never find Ludlow on any future day. Though, dear one, the thought may send a chill, the body of Reuben Ludlow lies forever still," the vision replied in unsettling whispers echoing throughout the room.

"Who is his murder?" April asked.

"The wise hound did rage and bark, yet no human saw where Reuben's murder was Jarlan Clark. With the banker's beautiful daughter, Jarlan has forcefully laid, and Shylock's hired assassin shall soon have his way," replied the vision.

"So there will be no justice," April gasped. "What be the future in all of this, if there is any at all?" asked April in a disturbed voice, nearing tears.

"For three seventy year generations, Clan Clark was honest and true, then in three seventy year generations, the curse of Reuben Ludow shall come unglued. When the ghost of the elder shall unto a Clark reveal his bones. Then his terrible curse shall right the wrong."

"What do you speak of, wise spirit of the woods? What curse?" screamed April in desperations, as the lightning flashed and the rolling thunder crashed.

"When the two clans have merged into one, the possession of June shall be undone. The spouses of two sisters shall lay in her bed, then all four shall soon be dead. This tarnished queen of Clark and Ludlow meld shall make out splendidly in the end, riding astonishingly high above mortality in her dark world of greed, lust, and horrible sin."

CHAPTER SEVEN

MOUNT HOERB VILLAGE, NC 1993

A baby blue Toyota Torricelli made its way down highway 78, running directly passed the center of Mount Horeb Village. An exit to the right would take a person around the old Market House. Inside the car, the driver was an unusually attractive woman, maybe twenty-three at the time. She wore a lavender net type business skirt. The sultry summers made such subtle, revealing attire most necessary. She was employed in the Urban Planning department of the village town.

Her name was Brenda Ludlow. Her mother was Scarlet Bridger by birth, hailing from Clan Bridger. She married Kieth Ludlow, a direct male descendant of the original estate founders. Both families were well established residents of the area, going backward three hundred fifty years. These elder families, in general, were pure Scotch-Irish to the bone, some with a generous sprinkling of Norman or Danish blood, but all gilded in their lavish inheritance, and very proud to say so. She was making her way to a family reunion down on the old Drunken Run Estate. She couldn't wait to see her relations for the first time in a while.

She tapped the brakes sharply while on the paved road, making her way down to a narrow two rut gravel road in the dense woods to the left that was once the wagon road. She eased along as the gravel and sand crunched and popped while she drove. The general scenery was absolutely beautiful, with the winding road being shaded by massive overhanging live oaks, some dating backward in time five hundred years before the plantation was developed. As the road wound along, to the left was the family cemetery surrounded by a black iron gate.

The Iron Gate seemed to be made of swirls with flowers and faces in them, she always thought as a child. It was ageless family tradition for members to pause and toss a white carnation flower with one's own personal handwritten note, upon a founding mother's grave on March first; by old tradition, the first day of the year since it heralded the dawn of the planting season. Brenda always wanted to do her part. At the end of the family meeting, all would gather at the grave, while the notes were plucked up to be read aloud by the present day family elder, William Edward Ludlow III. She eased the car into the now opened grave entrance way, parking it to the right of the road in case others pulling up might want to pay their own respects.

Twelve carnations were plucked from a huge bush near the apartment where Brenda lived in town. Twelve carnations were significant since they represented the twelve most prominent founding mothers in Clan Ludlow. The first mother was Rahab Ludlow, a strong fierce woman who battled with rifle and sword against rival clans, natives, criminals, and straggling interlopers, somewhere around the year 1650. The last mother held in reverence was Gretchin Ludlow, in the year 1830.

The year 1830 was significant to Clan Ludlow, since this was the year individuals could no longer legally lay claim to land holdings without placing targeted tracts under survey, otherwise granting wealthy individuals, banks, and corporate entities a right to seize the tract for their own holding, even if people did lay claim. This was Andrew Jackson's gift to the family dynasties who financed the central bank of the day, since clandestine agents of the bankers threatened to remove all gold from the backing of issued currency, crashing the economy should he refuse. Such covert facts were the true reason Jackson made an all-out war with the central bank of 1830, the elders were fond of saying. The family also stood at its greatest apex from every avenue of consideration during this golden era of 1830.

Brenda gently kissed each white carnation while whispering a prayer as she laid them gently upon each proper grave stone, or by the door of a molding, aging mausoleum. Tied upon each flower stem by a thread of gold was her own note reading; to a mother well deserving, from a future daughter lucky enough to bear your precious endowment. Her mind raced as she gently laid the flowers down. She imagined each woman performing the grand deeds she was informed of since early childhood.

As she moved along, she paused before the grave stones of Ruth and June Ludlow, among many others. For some reason, here she always felt a deeper connection, and much more so toward June. Reuben Ludlow, Ruth's husband and June's father, was still yet missing. One day his bones were sure to be discovered, and his grave would at long last receive its own stone, so the family legend declares.

June was a woman caught up in her own personal passions. She was always informed. Her unbridled desires wound up destroying her, proving all warnings to young adolescents so freely given by the elders of every age since. In time she birthed Jarlan Clark's child, but her own father, and the father of her babe, were dead by then.

The child was a man-child, who was a successful planter, intellectual man of letters, and business-man. He carried the Ludlow name, however. Over time, a granddaughter married into the Bridger Clan. This was the name of her own mother's people, who were part of that clan. Since the relationship was rather distant in her own time, the family saw no harm in allowing sixth cousins to marry when they possessed gilded connections with an endowment justifying it. After all, the children of Issac and Jacob married first cousins back in their time, so holy law certainly didn't forbid the bond.

Thus, when her mother married Kieth Ludlow, her own father, there was no problem with it among the elders, who actually cheerfully applauded. Anything was better than some laboring, yet penniless, nameless, ne'er-do-well genetic amalgamation hailing from within the mysterious out-lands somewhere, without any endowment or family connections, marrying into theirs. The last thing any family elder desired for was some pathetic dim-witted lout with no heritage of entitlement, to inherit a family fortune, only to squander it in future time.

An ultimate response from the elders was indeed not off the books, should such concerns ever actually materialize. They never did, since parents among these wealthy chief clans always arrange marriages of their children. This fact is a modern day secret held tightly in the area, simultaneously preserving virginity, blood patrimony, position, and estate inheritance.

The baby blue Toyota pulled into the live oak lined driveway of the Drunken Run mansion estate. Many cars were already parked outside, maybe seventy five in total. These cars were Lamborghini, BMW, new Ford F150 pickup trucks, on down to the most basic vehicle, domestic and foreign models. The family enterprises tended to do well inside their home areas. Possible expansion was a subject of discussion this evening. These notices and thoughts passed through Brenda's mind as she stepped from her car and into the doorway.

The ball room area was already buzzing with company. Maybe two hundred people in all were gathered inside. The smell of easily recognizable home cooked food, such as collards, roasting sugar cured ham, roasting venison, roasting ear corn, butter beans, and scratch made biscuits filled the air. Almost everybody present commented on how pleasantly the food scents saturated the air inside the room.

"Well, who is doing the cooking?" one unidentified relative asked.

"Some of the Lessanes, employed in Jay Burney's catering service over in Bridger-town. What's better than that and fitting for our particular occasion is where these kind folks are directly descended from servants who once lived right here on this estate from day one," another lady replied.

This lady was a distant cousin from the McDaniel family, but Brenda couldn't recall which one. She weaved in and out among the gathered people, smiling, curtsying, and saying hello. She finally stood to face a short, slightly balding man with a broad smile, though he must have been somewhere around her own age. He possessed a rather feminine mannerism; she thought to herself. She thought she should recognize him, but couldn't quite match a name with the face.

"Hello girl, how are you after all these long years?" the smiling man asked her. Brenda smiled back.

"Very well, thank you," she replied in a cheerful voice.

"You don't recall who I am?" the man asked her. "I'll offer you a hint. I am a friend of your sister, Sheila. We've been off and on for years now."

"Don't tell me now, let me guess. You must be Bennie, Bennie McNeil, eh?" she smiled as she replied with a gasp.

"You got it!" the man replied as he moved toward her with opening arms.

They both smiled, laughing heartily, talking about times passed, and recent life events. Running a business and professional work seemed to take up far too much of a person's time. They both agreed.

The McNeil clan owned numerous farm estates. Renting farm land out was a best move in the present time, since the government was appearing to overtake the business of managing American agriculture. The family consequently owned a series of jewelry and pawn shops financed via farm rents, providing needed funds to patrons from an office over in Dillon, South Carolina, where one's right to lend out his own money was semi-allowed. The McNeil family also had an interesting history.

James McNeil, the famous painter, hailed from nearby Breezy Oaks plantation. He was also an adventurous friend of Edgar Allen Poe, accompanying him to New York, and both nearly freezing to death in the process. These were McNeil family secrets often told at yearly reunions, and not found in any books, however. Brenda always loved recalling these types of secrets best.

Many in the McNeil family were also active in North and South Carolina politics. Sheila Ludlow had made a wise choice. Brenda smiled as she secretly thought. This was a good note in regard to Ludlow's family reunions. Long time close clan allies were also allowed inside. The reunion was a great stage for wise parents to arrange marriages. Much more was occurring inside the grand manor house that untrained eyes failed to notice. The family elder walked up to a somewhat thick podium positioned in the center of the room, gently leaning his cane to the side, then seizing up the microphone with his right hand.

The elder donned a genuine mid-night black Eermenegildo Zegna double-breasted silk suit, with matching pants. He wore a velvet top hat and almost glittering black leather shoes. His perfectly combed gray hair covered his ears. A lengthy beard fell spread out upon his breast. He stooped, poised in educated, wise splendor. His name was George Ebeneezer III.

"Ladies and gentlemen, may I have everyone's attention on the scene here? We have much to speak of. There need to be no distractions. Our armed guards standing by the door and positioned in various places throughout the estate today have all our backs. Let's give them all a huge Ludlow thank you applause!"

The gathered crowd clapped enthusiastically. The applause subsided gradually.

"Our kind cooks have our backs today. That food smells right. Drinks will be served soon. We couldn't have made a better choice, so let's give them all a big Ludlow thank you applause!," the elder announced.

The roaring applause eventually subsided.

"Today is also my eighty forth birthday. I can't believe it! Where did all o' that time flit off to? It's been a ride on an ocean of high waves, but please wish me well today, if you feel moved to."

There was another applause.

"We have much to speak of today, Clan Ludlow and associates, so please stick around. The orchestra music shall commence in a moment."

As the elder completed his address, several youths clad in suit and ties opened cases up, retrieving violin, Dobro, and various other stringed instruments. There were flutes and saxophones.

The songs played were traditional chamber music and a few ageless tunes familiar to the family. Conversation buzzed. Finally, the elder grabbed the microphone again.

"Ladies and gentleman may I have your attention again?"

The music ceased, and the conversation gradually faded.

"As drinks are being served, the good food is being placed upon our grand banquet table in the manor dining hall. As we make our way inside underneath these highly decorated archways, let us keep our minds focused on those who have gone on. Drunken Run was founded in 1650. The founders originated from Aberdeen-shire, Scotland, and Northern Ireland. The Scots from the coast are also heavily saturated in Norman blood, originating from Norway. From day one, ever since our military predecessors, the Vikings, seized Normandy, in France, allowing ambitious settlers from Norway to assume positions of high office, we, Clan Ludlow, have been proud right hand agents of the crown."

The gathered family crowd clapped in hearty applause.

"In 1066 William The Conqueror seized the United Kingdom, claiming it for Normandy, bringing in Norman settlers and allowing them to assume chief positions in Norman Government. Clan Ludlow, though half remained in Normandy, was part of that spectacular moment!"

The family clapped in grand applause.

"To this day, we still have family in Norman and the British government. When America's land mass was seized and claimed by England, Clan Ludlow stood among the Lord Proprietors, receiving twenty thousand acres as a grant. From that original grant and tract was carved Ludlow Estate, upon which a modest cabin was founded, and a simple farm. This farm eventually developed into a prosperous tobacco and food crop plantation. As that plantation estate grew here on Drunken Run Creek, so did this manor house you now stand inside. By 1740 Drunken Run stood among the most prosperous tobacco plantations in the Carolina's."

The family enthusiastically clapped in cheerful applause.

"We were active in government, both at the state and the national levels. These chandeliers are original, solid gold and crystal. Our silverware, locked away inside the China Cabinets, is among the finest from the era to be obtained in Britain. Most of it was given by various British dignitaries over the years.

"When the Revolution occurred, Clan Ludlow chose to stand beside the Patriots, unfortunately separating ourselves from our guardian British brethren. Later, we paid the ultimate price for that choice in position, when our own government turned against us and our grand achievements. We lost our status and wealth, like so many others from our social plateau in the Southern half of the US; but not our land, nor our pride in excellent patrimonial heritage, or individual personal achievements."

There was a long hearty applause.

"Today I sit before you and I am proud to say that we, Clan Ludlow, have successfully reclaimed that loss. We still retain Drunken Run Estate, although the NC Historical Society now conveniently manages the estate for us. We are listed on the state historical register of sites. Isn't that nice?"

There was another long applause.

"We bear that distinction, since part of our estate was where the battle for control occurred on the Cape Fear River. We also owned the sheltered landing where the great battle of Mount Hoarb Village took place between the Tories and the Patriots."

The gathered family applauded.

"During the Civil War, our estate was a center for continuing partisan guerrilla resistance, when Fort Fisher, the Gibraltar of the South, finally fell. Because of our position and facilitation of partisan resistance, Mount Hoarb Village and its surrounding areas were spared the ruthless devastation, plundering, and merciless murder accompanying it, via a fierce reputation of the fighting forces we entertained."

Another applause followed.

"In a few months, we will be allowed to facilitate estate tours. While the state reaps seventy-five percent, since hosting for these tours will fall primarily upon their shoulders, we, among Clan Ludlow, shall reap our tax free twenty-five percent. This is payment for us allowing the great State of North Carolina to manage Drunken Run Estate for us, and our past efforts in the name of preserving liberty. I am proud to announce here today that we own a running estate vineyard, gift shop, dining area, vegetable farm, and heritage museum, with much more being planned courtesy of the state, myself, and other family elders. Our greatest venture on the table as yet may well be a small casino being planned, soon as we can convince the State House to vote it in. Regardless of one's stance perspective on the consideration, examine the potential fine paying jobs to be generated for the local population. Look at the growth contributions facilitated by this planned casino. All is positive, right? Indeed!, so why not, if we win state congressional allowance?

There was another long applause.

"The State Of North Carolina will benefit, and so shall Clan Ludlow, with each direct member receiving a stipend. So again, why not, eh?"

There was another drawn out, eventually fading applause. Soon the crowd began to mill, becoming anxious.

"I can see everybody anxiously awaits our noontime dinner here on Drunken Run Estate. Let us all gravitate into the manor dining hall at this time, since the air is so full of the wonderful aroma," announced the elder.

The chatter became intense as the people moved from inside the foyer and the parlor area into the grand dining hall. The grand estate was preserved into a dazzling display of time-honored pieces and collections. The couch and most estate furniture originated from Tryon Palace, way down on the coast in New Bern, with relatives who once served there in the state senate. There were portraits hanging on the wall of governors from the Tryon era, and family members who served underneath them. There were also hunting scenes of young boys from Clan Ludlow, wearing tight thin brown pants and off white blouse type shirts, posed beside a flint-lock rifle and seven rabbits laying on a fallen log out in the woods somewhere on the estate lands.

The crowd moved underneath a huge archway, with a large carved face in the center, and swirls containing leaves, flowers, and vines. A large shining table of oak some fifteen feet across stood in the center of the room. On the walls were the heads of large deer, cougars, bears, and various animals said to have been taken over a course of time from the woods all around. The food sat steaming, while the well-dressed cooks and servers stood proudly against all four walls, smiling broadly. Conversation between the family members resumed.

A smiling early middle-aged man walked up dressed in a black suit and tie, with perfectly groomed blond hair parted in the center and neatly combed on the sides.

"I know you have to be Brenda Ludlow, right?" he said

"I'm her. I can't quite match a name with your face, however. I apologize," Brenda said.

"My name is Donald Grimesly. I run the local christian academy, Angel Institute."

"Now I have you pegged," Brenda Smiled. "Your name and face couldn't quite connect at the moment I first laid eyes on you."

"I am rather astonished," Grimesly gasped. "I am also a close associate of your sister, Emogene. We've associated for years."

"I am so sorry, sir. I do apologize," Brenda said, briefly hanging her head. "My life has surely been a long ride on a broad sea filled with high waves."

"This is strange," the man continued. "While I've spoken regularly with your other sisters, I've only heard them mention your name in casual passing. I recognize the family resemblance in you, and I've also seen pictures over a course of time."

"I've been gone since my school days back in the old Mount Hoarb Village High School. I hated to see that time-honored academic building go. Some of the happiest times of my life were living there. This new contemporary styled building now replacing it utterly disgusts me. I've always despised contemporary art, architecture, and the socialist ideology accompanying it, since I am well aware that contemporary design always veils a subtle social command, all dipped heavily in appeal to emotion, for individual persons to embrace their own destruction. Such has announced the end of great empires since time immemorial," Brenda stated with a confident intellectual air.

"A feign of progress, eh?" Donald said with a smile. "Wow, you sure are knowledgeable about history,"

"I don't know much about Clan Grimesly, however," Brenda retorted.

"While I am chief agent at Angel Institute Academy, the Grimesly family also owns it. The state allows us, as owners, to select who we want to attend. We only allow those with the cleanest behavioral, medical, and academic records to enter in. Our students hail from accomplished families, with ultra-high academic achievement records, the best both physically, mentally, and academically among the best. No others are granted access by intentional design. People of achievement deserve such options, right? Allow the social misfits, criminals, and nonfunctional dead heads to remain in the state supported public schools system, as they are indoctrinated to embrace their own social and heritage destruction. Must we conglomerate our elegant patrimony with their tainted ones? Forebear the order, please!"

Brenda commenced laughing.

"We, among the excellent and accomplished, deserve so much better. I sincerely hope the state of North Carolina continues to allow us, the property owners, this special liberty of selective choice," Donald continued.

"Tell me more," Brenda asked.

"We own the Queen's Riverside Deli here in town. We also own the apartment complex, Golden States, off Ben-Street there. We own the complex over in Brunswick by the same name, along with several office buildings near the university. I like it, personally, because Grimesly family members don't have to worry about finding great, well-paying jobs, as so many others are and have been for a long time now. We go to university for the purpose it was originally intended, self-enrichment rather than job security, as the disgusting commercialization has falsely led a majority into believing."

"I like that," Brenda announced with a glittering smile.

The servings of mashed potatoes smothered in chicken gravy, the almost sweet dark eared butter beans, corn, venison, turkey, and freshly cured farm raised ham was so good going down, absolutely no conversation could stand against it. As the plates were being loaded, the gilded elder assumed the podium again.

"Ladies and gentlemen of the house, please grant me your undivided attention here for a moment. Let us bow in humble gratefulness for the food, and for the great mortal fortune of being born into an accomplished, well-connected family such as we have."

A gradual hush fell over the entire dining hall. Every head bowed.

"Good Lord in heaven above, please bless this food to the nourishment of our bodies. Please, oh Lord, grant us more powers of creativity and entrepreneurship. Bless our endeavors and continue to make us all prosperous, in the name of bringing souls closer to you. We ask this in the name of Jesus Christ, Amen."

The heads picked back up, and the feasting continued. The libation of choice at the moment was iced tea. Coffee would generally accompany the desert rounds. Then the final libation was freshly uncorked by wild grape wine. People began mixing back and forth. Soon Brenda's two sisters dropped by with several female accomplices.

"So I understand you and Bennie have already met, eh, sis?" Sheila spoke up and announced. She wore a gorgeous ankle length lace dress, complete with elbow length white gloves.

"Yes," Brenda announced as her eyes widened, "and I can't believe it's been so long since we were in one another's company!" Her eyes ran up and down. "How nice you are there, sis! My, how you have such fine tastes."

"Clan Ludlow expects nothing but the best. I make my selections based upon that grand expectation," Sheila laughed as she said.

"I can see," Brenda replied.

"Otherwise I might be caught uptown this time of year in tropical business attire, if not down on the beach somewhere in a bikini," Sheila replied.

"I'm right there with you, sis," Brenda laughed as she grabbed her sister's left arm.

"Well, Brenda, allow me to introduce you to my accomplices here, who are actually relatives, as you might have guessed by now."

Sheila pointed to a young, seemingly empty headed, sandy blonde, who giggled rather sheepishly.

"This is Clair Bellemore. She's the secretary in The Plantation Realtor uptown here. Her father was the town mayor maybe twenty years ago. She isn't married, but let me tell you honey, she is all wide eyed and a lookin'!" all three women suddenly gasped, dropped jawed, falling out with laughter.

They all stood back up, then Sheila pointed to the lady immediately beside her.

"This is Louise Gore. She's the intellectual in the crowd. She's working on her MA. Isn't that so nice?"

"Yes, it is," Brenda replied. "Congratulations," she said as the dirty blonde, Louise, turned a rather solemn face, seemingly forcing a smile.

"Her father is the town constable, active in the JC's, and at the local Shriner's mason lodge."

All three women smiled, embracing one another.

"And lastly, but certainly not among the least, is Kathy Inscoe here," she announced, pointing toward a lady with reddish brown hair tied tightly into a bun, standing toward the rear somewhat. "She is a business mind in the making, you know, but between all of us, she's the wildest one among us all!"

All five women fell out laughing and hugging for what seemed like many long minutes. Finally, they regained their composure.

"Her father is Leroy Inscoe and owns the horse ranch outside of town. He is also part owner of the prison camp over at Crystal Lake up the road there. Her father says while it might cost twenty thousand dollars to support every inmate for a year, every inmate in his prison pulls his own weight until he turns seventy, or else! None of us have figured out what else means yet, but it must be working out lavishly well for him," Sheila announced.

All the ladies hugged and laughed loudly.

"So let's talk a bit about you, sis. What have you been doing for all these long months since I saw you last?" Sheila asked with a smile.

Brenda laughed in apparent astonishment.

"I lived at Duart for a while. I worked as a city hall receptionist. Now I moved into an apartment in Mount Horeb Village, on the edge of town," Brenda replied.

"I heard you were closer by," Sheila snapped.

"Yeah, well, you might say that I'm around," Brenda shrugged and smiled.

"Who's the man on the hook?" smiled, then laughing Lousie

Gore, with a childlike shrug.

"I never said I had one," firmly replied Brenda.

"But we all know better, don't we girls?" Laughed Kathy Inscoe, as the others chimed in.

"I might have one or two jumping around on a hook, but I can't decide for the life of me if they are worth reeling in. I'm simply not so lucky as my two sisters are in the male department, now," Brenda smiled, saying as she pretended to slap out at Kathy as she spoke.

The elder assumed the podium again, seizing up the microphone.

"Ladies and gentlemen, I know the food and the conversations have been good, but we have a few items for discussion regarding Clan Ludlow's business agendas. We've assisted in opening The Queen's Riverside Deli and opened The Belle's Bakery recently. All is going well. Our associates, the MacDonald's and the Campbells, are in with us full swing, seeking to open an extension of the already well known Plantation Advertising Agency all the way from Wilmington, on the edge of Mount Horeb Village here. They've been kind enough to offer Clan Ludlow this share of local ownership."

The seated crowd applauds.

"Isn't that nice of them?"

The applause picks up in energy.

"The elders here kindly accepted."

The seated crowd applauds again, energetically.

"There is talk of a toll road going up on Interstate 78, our main thoroughfare. Since the road expanded on Ludlow soil, a deal is being negotiated with the governor to allow Clan Ludlow a garnished share."

The seated crowd applauds with more energy.

"It's only right, is it not?" stated the elder sarcastically as the crowd continued to applaud.

"Boy, having time-honored family influence in the State House here and down in South Carolina, sure is nice, is it not?" the elder smiled as the crowd clapped in agreement, with raw, energetic enthusiasm. "Nobody has true freedom without proper connections, I tell ya," the elder continued. "What Clan anywhere could ever excel paying in these extortionist levels of tax being charged to those not knowing where the Grand Master's back room is, and not being able to tolerate the sweet scent of fresh cigar smoke, eh? I tell ya, we all must sip a mite O' wine, and slap a solid back, every now and again. At the least, we can assist in passing out a few campaign fliers here and there, take a voter down to the booth, or we might even be kind enough to carry the ballot in for him!"

A deep sighing wave fell over the gathered crowd as they smiled enthusiastically, applauding sporadically.

"Clan Ludlow is always, and always has been, open-minded to what e'er we must do, as we are flexible, rolling with any following punches. This information is all important for you young-ones to recollect, if indeed the Clan is to continue being successful and prosperous."

The gathered crowd claps energetically on a wave of laughter gradually filling the room. It gradually fades.

"After all, what all of this enterprise means is that all of you, each and every member, shall draw a portion? While the elders may garnish a chief portion, what remains is allotted back out to all of you."

There was an energetic applause.

"Consequently, all of our children may now attend the local Angel Institute Academy, with the MacDonalds, Campbells, McDowell, McPherson's, and the other time-honored noble clans. We do not have to attend the public institute of government indoctrination, where true established religious belief systems are replaced with poisonous Darwin and Marxist ideologies of social-communism. Instead, our children are taught forward, thinking of positive virtues of investment and entrepreneurship! Our children are instructed to possess true character and personality, since those who were born via superior noble blood should noticeably stand out from an ever eroding, downward morphing crowd at large."

There was an energetic applause.

"We adamantly reject the deceptively false ideology being proselytized among today's masses, that by embracing our own patrimonial, social, and economic destruction, we as a society may somehow achieve a higher plateau of success. Are they going to wave a magic wand?"

There was another extending applause. Minutes transpired.

"But such a muddy truck is being taught in our public school system today. In other words my lovely brethren, with that financing, Clan Ludlow, our children and family, may access the very best life has to offer, living a live that shines forward in a dawning sun, rather than inverts timidly into an imposed bleakness."

When the family reunion concluded, Brenda, Sheila, Emoleta, Louise, Clair, Kathy, Donald, and Bennie stood before the front door of the estate manor house. The others made their way past, many yearning to walk about over the estate, while more family members loaded up in their vehicles.

"You know," Clair said as the wind tossed her sandy brown hair, "I was thinking during this reunion about all of us getting together, maybe next weekend? What do all of you say?"

"Sounds fine by us," the others chimed in.

"Where could we meet?" Kathy asked enthusiastically.

"What about over in the Tory Landing Park uptown there? There is a nice building we could gather in out there. We could walk the many trails in the park there later on. We could make a real day of it, spending long missed time in one another's company again," Clare replied.

"Does everybody agree with one o'clock next Saturday, then?" Brenda asked.

Everybody chimed in with a cheerful "yes" reply.

"Then come one o'clock next Saturday. May we all meet at the Tory Landing Park?" Brenda concluded.

CHAPTER EIGHT

THE TORY LANDING PARK

The following weekend seemed to arrive quickly. Brenda found herself hesitating for reasons she couldn't comfortably explain. There was much to do in the Urban Planning department even in after hours, negotiated contracts to be signed, agreements needing official endorsement, signature letter replies, etc. Brenda really didn't have much time for play. She knew her sisters would be disappointed, and she hadn't seen them in a long while. Something undefined was weighing down upon her, causing her to have knots in her stomach regarding this meeting. Maybe she was becoming antisocial? She most certainly didn't want that!

The true value for her attending this rendezvous, however, when she deliberated the matter over in her mind, would be in reviewing the bond formed between her sisters and these men they were courting. From an outside perspective, it might be possible to conclude whether these men, their patrimonial endowment, and their blood, were factual or merely charlatan, done so in pursuit of their own personal opportunity.

The park stood on the edge of town, down by the river flowing on the backside. During the battle of Mount Horeb Village, the site became infamous. The old landing once ran from the city store fronts on the hill, down to the river in a ditch. A masonry archway once covered the ditch, providing shelter to shipments of supplies coming in from the river, forming a tunnel of sorts. Constantly maintained hanging lanterns lit the passageway on the inside.

The firefight, a type of Civil War between sympathizers calling themselves Patriots, with the English crown government allies known as Tories, commenced in town, where the Tories wound up hotfooting it away from the combat zone down through this tunnel. As they loaded onto a number of Jon-boats docked by the landing on the river front, small arms and light six-pound cannon opened fire, killing many while creating a virtual death trap where no retreat was possible. For reasons never clear, the masonry tunnel eventually collapsed, with all signs of it and the landing vanished, save the old ditch barely existing to this day.

A wave of nostalgia during the early 1980s caused town civic leaders to conceive this park. The park had grown from a mere opening in the woods to now containing a stage area for play productions, and a spacious community meeting house constructed in classical style. There were also smaller shelter structures all up and down carefully marked wood trails. After 1700 hours and on the weekends, the community building was locked up. Brenda knew a secret way in from the backside, however. She let the proper people in Town Hall know of this rendezvous ahead of time, in case trouble came from them being found out. Family name and reputation carry a long way anywhere in the eastern parts of North and South Carolina.

When she pulled her baby blue Toyota down the hill from the main road into the parking lot, three other vehicles were already present. The wine colored Ford Mustang Boss was her sister Emoleta's, so she certainly must have arrived on time. She eased out of the car, down the winding dirt footpath, toward the meetinghouse. The others standing before the meeting house, smiling broadly with opened arms, welcomed her cheerfully.

"We were not sure you were going to make it here, Brenda," Sheila said in a voice of mixed astonishment and elation. "This meeting wouldn't be the same without you, girl!"

"The park area here appears interesting," said Brenda. "I wonder what the history of this place has been in much more recent times."

"Before the day of this park," Donald continued, "this was a favorite abode of outlaw fur trappers and meat hunters."

"And marijuana smugglers coming in from the river," laughed Bennie. "I honestly think these are the true reasons this park was built, to hedge away this kind of activity."

"Now all of them come here to smoke their hash and consume their side-meat, since there is no gate to block their way inside," snickered Kathy.

"Security is definitely something the city must work on here," replied Brenda in a serious tone, breaking the playful ice. "I am going to make a proposal sometime next week."

"Doesn't Clan Clark own part of this landscape here?" asked Claire with a cheerful tone in her voice as the group slowly ambled along.

"Yes, I'm afraid so," Brenda replied. "There has been talk in City Hall of charging admission to this park. Clan Clark would reap a nice steady percentage. Since Ludlow and others are part Clark, how would we access the recipient pool? These types of questioning have consequently put any plans to charge admission on hold."

"Where are we going from here?," Clare asked.

"If you would all kindly follow me, I have any anticipated questions regarding infrastructural concerns already answered,"

Brenda replied with a confident smile.

Soon, the group stood on the front porch of the community building in the park. Brenda reached into her purse producing an antique styled key.

"Benefits of being in the Urban Planning League and on the town council," she announced as she held the key up, winking at her right eye.

The group made their way over to a large folding table positioned in the middle of the central room area. Each individual took a comfortable seat in one of the many folding metal chairs.

"Why is there this observable disconnect between you and the family, Brenda?" Kathy asked inquisitively.

"Disconnect? Well, I've been busy for more than a while now. I'm out of town often visiting other municipalities, seeking to discover how they solve common problems.

Emogene and Sheila glanced hard at one another, then back over toward Brenda. The others took notice.

"Well," sighed Claire, noticing the hard glances, "what do you do in your free time? You are not married, right?"

"I've been invited a few times to the military ballroom social over at the old Cross Creek banquet hall. In my case, the situation was a Halloween masquerade. Another was a Christmas social."

"That's great!" smiled and laughed Kathy and Claire on the same note, "only the top brass enters into that hall. So who offered you the invitation, if you don't mind us asking?"

Brenda smiled and hesitated.

"Come on here now, girl, you can tell us we're all family!" Kathy and Claire chimed in.

"O.K. then," Brenda hesitated, "I can reveal my secrets. It was Colonel Longstreet."

"My, oh my, won't you listen to that!" Kathy continued. "Colonel Longstreet is not only one of the youngest posted at Cross Creek, he is also one of the wealthiest. He owns Longstreet Residential, a complex with plans to develop across America. He is into general real-estate development, reaching from Brunswick, to Sneeds Ferry, down to New Bern, then back over to Asheville. His company is also expanding into South Carolina."

"You'll be walking in high cotton, cuz, while you're rolling in satin sheets," smiled Claire. "Tell us all about it here now. Has he proposed yet?"

Emogene and Sheila glanced hard at one another, without smiling.

"No, not exactly," Brenda sheepishly replied, cutting her eyes downward.

"Why don't you just be out with it, Brenda, here and now," Emogene snapped while Sheila smiled broadly. "You have your hand in his cookie jar, we can all be rested assured of that."

Brenda laughed slightly.

"I don't follow what you are driving at there, sis."

"Oh yes you do sis, you know exactly what I am speaking of here," Emogene snarled. "You haven't changed one iota, sis. You're paying his price in flesh, but we can believe you made him sweat all to hell for it. You certainly insured you were going to get your payment in gold five times over the value of your used up flesh. I know he must have signed over at least a fifth of his business venture to you, sis, you smooth devil you."

"And that was not before you had him over a barrel by the balls," Sheila growled in concert with her sister Emogene. "What did you threaten him with, turning him into the top brass for refusing to accept your signature?"

Brenda sighed astonishingly, nearing tears.

"I'm not sure I am following what you are speaking in regard to here."

"I know you, Brenda," snarled Sheila. "We have two male outsiders in our presence. I give you credit for having enough class not to speak out, but both of these men will soon be part of Clan Ludlow, and they might as well know who their sister-in-law really is."

Brenda gasped in astonishment.

"I know they have not said anything, but they might as well be made aware," Emogene continued.

"I am a full believer in the virtue of listening, rather than being heard," Donald laughed slightly.

"I second that," replied Bennie with a broad smile, glancing downward.

"Well!" Claire sighed, "me thinks we've already seen enough of this community gathering place. It certainly reflects our rich local heritage. The building embraces the artistic soul of classical architecture, as it courts the spirit of our natural environment. Kudos to the city planners! All of these are positive attributes, but I think we've seen already enough. A breath of fresh air shall do us all well. Let's take a stroll through the park here on this bright and sunny day. I've not been through here but twice myself, in the ten years since the park was first established."

Claire opened the heavy wooden door of the building as the group stepped outside onto the porch. Emogene, Sheila, and Brenda glared at one another through tense eyes, without saying a single word. Brenda turned as the door pulled shut, shoving in the key to lock it tightly, spinning back around and stepping down the stairway without speaking a single word. The group soon caught up.

"It sure is nice walking along this narrow dirt footpath. I think the stage area might be two or three bends up," Kathy spoke as she smiled. "That will be a nice area to lounge around outside in."

Sheila sighed deeply.

"We are heading toward the ditch where the landing was. I vividly recall walking here with grandpa long before the park was ever conceived. Outside of a few cypress pylons, there is no evidence of a landing, a tunnel, or anything remarkable ever being here."

"I think the state cleaned all of it up when they hard-surfaced the roads. I don't know why they didn't save any of it," Donald said.

"I found a few old homemade bricks in the ditch as a lad," said Bennie, "but that is all I ever heard of anybody finding."

Emogene glared hard at Brenda without adding anything to the conversation.

"No brass, silver, or golden buttons, no knives, no bayonets, no swords. I've always wanted to find a sword myself. Haven't you been there, sister Emogene?" Brenda spoke with a rather long sigh.

"I'm sure if one was required by circumstance to do the sword a noble favor for receiving a gold or silver button, you would be first in line allowing it to have its share of pricks into your supple flesh, dear sis," Emogene harshly replied.

Brenda gasped in heavy astonishment.

"Why must you speak such insulting statements, sis?" Brenda gasped, laying her opened palms flat upon her chest. "I'm your sister, for heaven's sake, here!" she announced, gasping heavily for breath.

"Don't play dumb with us here," Sheila snarled through clenched teeth. "We know your foolish acts. You've been rehearsing them all of your life before us!"

"Speaking to both sisters now, what am I guilty of? I'm a highly successful lady-in-waiting," gasped Brenda. "I'll have you to know that I am part owner of the local laundry mat uptown. I own the movie house. I too am advancing into real-estate. I'm no lout nor a loser, honey. So what is your problem?

"All of Clan Ludlow will glitter one day in the future, hailing me as their anointed divine daughter, you'll see! I can't wait until the next honored Ludlow maiden festival. I'll be the one receiving that crown, not another, as I bear witness to each and every year. I will be the one blessed by the family elder to carry on the gilded heritage tradition. My name shall be the one going down with exceptional note inside the ageless Ludlow Chronicle Of Unblemished Patrimony And Achievement and be the one blessed at every family reunion forward from the day. Every Clan mother shall go to great lengths arranging marriages for their sons and daughters seeking to preserve my genetic patrimony, and all the others from within the out-lands be desperately desiring a bond for a gate to their own precious inheritance via mine."

"We all bet it will, and you'll stop at nothing to set your place on that ageless page," spouted Emogene in a near rage.

"Well, explain to all of us what is wrong with having ambition and desiring excellence, sis?" returned Brenda. "Explain that much to all of us, here and now!"

"Ladies now," interceded Bennie with a smug smile, "let jettison aside personal differences and opinions as we enter this beautiful outdoor stage area. I forget the name, if I might be casually reminded. I wonder what types of outdoor drama occur herein. Who is the performing association?"

"Officially, the place is called The Tory Landing Amphitheater on paper," replied Claire with cheer in her voice. "However, among the proletariat masses, it is locally known as The Climax Amphitheater, but we won't delve into that pot of witch's brew."

All the women laughed, save Brenda.

"Why not?," all the group, save Brenda, asked in cheerful laughter. "We're all adults here."

"Do you really want to hear this tale?" Claire continued. "O.K., here goes all. The primary performing association here is Alien Lakes Players. According to native Waccamaw legend, meteors directed by strange flying machines more than ten thousand years ago formed every lake here in all of Bath County, NC, down into eastern South Carolina. These mysterious flaying machines landed all around here. Strange pale beings seven to eight feet tall, bearing piercing radiating ice-blue eyes, donning hooded cloaks, very muscular and with horns from their upper foreheads, exited from these machines. They interacted with the Waccamaw, giving them wisdom in every area of consideration. They bred with the most attractive local native women, so claim the Waccamaw, informing them they were the creators of all mankind, hailing from the Solar System Ares in the constellation Pieces, to put the specifics into English dictation. Hence, the area and play company name, Alien Lakes Players."

"Alright," laughed the sisters and the two men in astonished disbelief, "we all get that. Now tell us the good part."

"I heard about that part of the tale where the aliens bred with the native women," Kathy laughed. "They claimed the women could twist the alien's ears, adjust the size of his sword and the intensity of his stabbing thrash."

All the women, save Brenda, laughed heartily and loudly.

"Well," Claire finally continued, "Alien Lake Players once were a rather rowdy bunch themselves. Like many artists, they were given to shocking lecherous conduct backstage and after performances."

"Wow, really?," asked Kate in astonishment, seeming to be more a feign, "like orgies and such stuff?"

The group chuckled among themselves, save Brenda, who neither smiled nor made any reply.

"Exactly, exactly, doing the thing right out here on this very stage, as entertainment for their own intoxication, according to local legend," Claire continued, announcing in low, mysterious tones.

Sheila laughed in astonishment, shaking her head.

"I just don't know about all of this," she kept saying, cutting her steely eyes over toward Brenda as she spoke.

"I've heard about it," chimed Emogene. "So this fine tale of debauchery goes. They supposedly filmed themselves in action, right? Out here on this very stage, eh?"

"So where's the film at, then?" Sheila inquired. "I am curious to have a peek, since I know virtually every person in it, more than likely. Watching such a thing would be funny, I think, don't all of you?" she struggled to say as he laughed.

"Nobody knows," Claire intimated. "This sole piece of evidence would prove the account, but it's never been found yet."

"It only goes to show one simply can't believe everything he hears, now doesn't it?" slurred Brenda.

"People certainly hear what they want to, that's for sure," replied Sheila, suddenly catching herself as she spoke, glaring through narrowing eyes hard again at Brenda.

Donald, who said little, suddenly burst into laughter.

"Whatever the truth is, this wooden amphitheater certainly is a nice, and well built. The city planners done well to conceive of constructing it here, in this place. Wouldn't you agree, Ben?," he said.

"Maybe if this wood could speak, we would know the truth then, eh?" He patted the stage with his right hand as he spoke.

"Kudos to the city planners! Aye, let's hoist all cheers. If only we had some," replied Ben.

"You know," suddenly giggled Kathy, "I thought about doing the local sack-cloth thing, and smuggling in some party cups and cans of beer into my purse here."

"Yeah, the local sack-cloth class is not too bad all the time!," cheered Claire.

The others neither smiled nor made any direct comment.

"I casually forgot about the beer, but I brought in an oversized bottle of Hay Counti's best muscadine. This should rip the sack cloth right off of our affair here!" Claire laughed. "What about it now?" cheered Claire.

"O.K. I'm in for kicks. What's a gathering of friends without it?" finally replied Emogene with a sigh, who seemed to force a smile, while glancing hard over at Brenda, displaying no emotion nor expression, let alone making any comment.

She opened up her purse, taking out seven plastic wine glasses. One was placed before each person was present. The bottle was tipped, filling each glass two-thirds of the way full.

"A bit of aristocratic meridian ingenuity shall see us all through every time," Sheila chuckled as she picked up her own glass. "Cheers to divine Minerva!"

"I find your family enterprises interesting," spoke Brenda suddenly toward Donald.

Donald chuckled.

"Clan Ludlow and Grimesly have worked closely together for many long generations. We've all shared in the fortunes and misfortunes of one another for a long time now."

"Really? Somehow I was never aware, Donald," spoke Brenda with a smile and a sudden twinkle in her eye.

"It was only natural for me to tie in with your sister, here," Donald smiled again as he made a reply.

"I find all of this very interesting," Brenda said. "Its good to have the blood of ambition entering into our veins from a multiplicity of family directions, eh?"

Donald chuckled.

"Our families are related, but from a far distance. It's been a mighty long time since there was a cross between our two bloods."

"It seems like all the old established families are related for miles around in these parts," Brenda said.

"Well, families try to keep fortunes within families. Considering how everything is, I can't really blame them at all. If I had children, I would be the same way," the thin, somewhat awkward Donald spoke as his spectacles slid down upon his nose. Quickly, he pushed them back up, then burst into a smile again. It was strange how at first he seemed somewhat macho, rather than as he was when she gradually felt she was coming to know him.

"There is this old saying," Sheila spoke with a wry smile, "cousins make dozens, you know."

"Wait, a minute here. That's speaking rather serious, don't you think?" Donald announced with a gasp and a light chuckle.

"My sister there wouldn't think anything about it," Sheila sneered, nodding toward Brenda.

"What?" Brenda gasped.

"I'll give her credit where it's due, however. She always said no man could ever lay a hand on her unless he was swinging at least a rock hard twelve inches of solid golden shaft, and she would have to see it and know it, rather than hear a tale about it, let me inform all of you. "

"Now Sheila, don't you think your crass insulting has gone far enough for today? You have no right to say what you just did. I'm your own blood sister, for crying out loud here!" Brenda spoke with a heavy gasp in her voice.

"My hat is off to you, Brenda. You held to your word religiously. Your first affair was with a man whose family owned a chain of jewelry stores. You made him crawl first. I'll give you due credit, having him literally eating out of your hand," Sheila snarled.

"Sheila!" Brenda snapped, "please."

"That's right, he gave you a brand new Mustang GT one Christmas morning, tied with a red ribbon, if I am right!" Emogene chimed in.

"I've said, enough is enough!" Brenda suddenly spouted.

"You men don't believe such a true life vixen of the dark divide exists in our own time, sitting right here before you, do you?" Emogene continued on in her snarl.

"Please!" she appeared to be on the verge of weeping.

"Well, let me tell all of you something. You haven't heard the half of it," Emogene continued.

"The lady asked both of you to lay off. Give her some breathing room here, give her some breathing room for heaven's sake!" Donald and Bennie spoke with a gasp and a forced smile at the same time.

"You know all of this accomplishment she claims she has, the businesses she owns, and all of this?" growled Sheila in spite of the pleas.

"Please, enough!," raged Brenda.

"Well, at a young age, she learned all she could about Ludlow enterprises. If there were any secret back door deals or under the table money being passed, she wanted to know all about it," Sheila continued.

"Please!"

Brenda burst into tears.

"Then she approaches the Clan elders, threatening to turn them in if they did not grant her an owner share. I kid you not. She was like this by her own family as a lass," Emogene chimed as she raged.

Brenda burst into tears, hanging her head.

"Ladies, enough is enough here!" spoke Bennie with firmness in his voice, raising from his seat. "I personally think it's time we make our way back home now. I feel some of the elders need to know about all of this pent up family animosity between you sisters."

"But let us be honest," Donald replied, "all the animosity appears to be directed toward Brenda here, from her two sisters. I honestly don't understand. I've been watching Brenda closely, and she appears to be a well-mannered, educated, ambitious lady."

"I see a lot of class in Brenda myself, personally," interjected Bennie, "and I feel such a perception is specifically what you are alluding to there, Donald."

"Precisely," Donald returned.

Emogene gasped, staring hard at Donald, then Brenda, and her sister Sheila, who gazed back in utter dismay at what was revealing itself before them.

"Personally, and I'll just tell it as it all is, what we are witnessing is a case of family envy and resentment being directed toward one who, in reality, is a true born success," Donald announced.

"And I fully agree," Bennie replied in affirmation as he likewise arose from his seat. "Matter of fact, I feel on this note, we all need to head on back out. Before we go, I desperately want to inform the parents in regard to all of this negative observation. Maybe they might propose a cure for the ill, don't you think?"

"I agree, so let's make our way back out of here," Donald replied.

CHAPTER NINE

THE SOLUTION

Emogene and Sheila were very apprehensive, and rather disappointed at the two men. Brenda had no feelings either way. Kathy and Claire didn't know precisely how to quantify what they were observing in the actions and reactions of the group and its members. Soon as the group exited the park, they headed out to the home of the three sister's parents. The parents listened intensively as the men led the conversation, then politely informed them of the family's inner conflict.

Before settling in on any answer or listening to many more questions, the parents offered small plates of rice pudding, fried squash, or recently made banana pudding, with a fresh round of black coffee to the gathering. In the end, only Uncle Benet, a bookish, long bearded family elder who wore denim coveralls everywhere, known as the Bootlegger Monk, or simply The Monk back in his day, held a motion near to any conviction resembling a resolution to this inner sibling conflict.

"The holidays are nearing. All of you have time off for nearly the duration of next month. It's been so long since we have all been in the company of one another. Why don't we all move back into the house here, and live together until sometime after the New Year celebration, eh? Being in company again has been known to work magic at healing deeply festering soul wounds."

"That's a fine idea!" gasped their mother. "We could all relive the time of you-all being children, back when we were a close knit family. You'll be surprised at how many long suppressed memories will re-surface once we get to moving around again inside the house and throughout the estate grounds."

Brenda glanced all around. Indeed, it had been a while since she spent time underneath this roof or out on the estate. She could easily afford the time, since government employees didn't have to return to work until January forth. The modern classical styled cottage house she was raised in stood on the old Drunken Run Estate, but across the hill from the original manor house, now turned over to the state. The family held all rights, however, but the state done a marvelous job of maintaining the structure and the surrounding lands. Besides that, the cottage house was a relatively easy walking distance from the big house being across the hill from the old servant cabins.

As a child growing up, Brenda loved roaming around throughout the estate, in the fields, forests, and spending time at the manor house. The family graveyard held some type of special allure for her for reasons she could never fully explain. The fact of Reuben Ludlow's missing grave was a mystery she often vowed to solve as a child.

Once she discovered crumbling homemade brick columns and cypress building timbers underneath dried leaves, in the midst of which stood a rusted large heavy cast iron cauldron. She knew it was old, dating way back to the days when Drunken Run Estate was in its earlier stages. She asked Uncle Benet about these ruins.

Uncle Benet informed her that what she had found were the ruins of the old estate washroom, but was also a private hangout for the original founders, including Reuben Ludlow. According to family lore, nearly all the male founders may well have been what would be called woodshed alcoholics in later ages, sauntering over to the washroom to light fire and socialize privately, away from the women-folk. Here, stories abounded of how many virgin women each man once conquered it was long said, and how many imposing men on the outside feared them. The gathered men-folk regaled one another in regard to how many belligerent men each Ludlow man had beat up or cut all to pieces, or where, in some non-confrontational manner, Clan Ludlow maintained the upper hand.

This is not to say that the founders were bad people, on the contrary. Most were recorded as being very helpful people who would give the shirt off their backs to neighbors or even strangers in need. All anyone was required to do was humbly ask. Often Reuben Ludlow and numerous other founders were remembered on the outside for their great generosity to the surrounding community. Where people in the surrounding area went wrong, many times was when they attempted to throw their weight around with the family or their alliances. Clan Ludlow was known as being fierce when the situation call for it.

Her grandfather, Adonias Ludlow, and his brother, Andrew, made their way down into a deep backwoods community filled by rundown off the grid cabins referred to as Scuffle Town. They stumbled in by accident, at first not knowing where they were. This area was populated with known outlaws, and existed unto itself. The people therein were referred to negatively as trolls.

Seven of these hulking brutes jumped Brenda's grandfather, Adonias, and her Uncle Andrew, out of a sheer effort to intimidate them. There were three on her grandfather, and four on her uncle. Uncle Andrew was known for carrying a razor sharp pocket knife shop-fashioned from a worn out crosscut saw blade. He pulled his knife, cutting one twice across the stomach, causing him to double over, grasping his abdomen with both arms. Blood gushed out across the tops of his arms, covering the ground so thickly to a point one could not see the new spring grass underneath. The horrendous troll staggered fifteen feet, then collapsed, unconscious on the cold ground.

The other trolls ceased in their battle to pick the fallen troll up off the ground and transport him to the hospital. While they were heaving the dead weight of the fallen troll and struggling as they stuffed him into a parked fading green Mustang car, Brenda's grandfather and Uncle Andrew were hotfooting it out down through the thickets along an old railroad bed. They wound up spending the night out in the swamp, but at least they were in one piece, and free.

Deep down Brenda knew much once occurred on the Drunken Run Estate she or anybody alive was not aware of. There were certain deep, dark family secrets only released accidentally across her inquiring ears by elders engaging in what they thought were secret conversations. She heard about the intriguing legend of Sweet Mama Jean that way.

Mama Jean was a house servant known as a fabulous story teller down through the ages, since she loved to spin tales handed down from the Caribbean of pirate kings, treasure chests, and voodoo spirits. She is recorded as seldom being required to labor in the big house, except for only two host important guests. Mama Jean was known as being unusually attractive in a natural sense, and very well mannered, presenting herself exceedingly well in high classes' educated fashion to these valued guests when donning the accompanying dress. Why was this so? What might have been going on here nobody in our present day knows of?

Mama Jean was also once commanded to oversee the serving of more than one hundred important guests, when little in the way of needed food supplies were available, yet still she managed to accomplish the astonishing feat to a splendor in service to her master while he was away. She claimed the feat was accomplished by utilizing voodoo magic, and everybody concerned laughed back at that time. Seventy years later, elders who were then children claimed she fed the guests crow prepared as fried chicken.

Did she really? Did somebody figure out her secret, and did she "pay" him not to tell, as people later whispered, pointing to certain misfit family members who lived on the social fringes? Maybe she was all legit, somehow managing to find enough chicken and vegetables inside such a sparse environment of the time, eh? We'll more than likely never know the true answer.

Then there was the mystery of Reuben Ludlow's missing grave. What happened to him way back when? Why did he not make it back home? Did he fall? Was he attacked and eaten by wild pigs? Did his business associate, the wicked Jarlan Clark, have anything to do with it? Why couldn't Shaw's magnificent, infallible talking blood hounds, as the locals once referred to them, locate Reuben? Out of all the other mysteries throughout the estate's long history, this one remained with Brenda the most. She was determined to find the answer to it, when all the others had long since lost interest.

When her anger cooled, she agreed to move back into the cottage home she was raised in. Matter of fact, she was considering moving there for the next six months, since the ride to her place of work was not all that far away in the overall scheme of things. It would be fun roaming around in the old home place again as an adult, rather than a child. Would she view the place through the same set of eyes? Would the same secret spots still capture her vivid, if not overactive, imagination? She could hardly wait to find out. Maybe they're still yet lay family secrets buried, waiting for her to uncover.

Her two sisters still yet lived at home periodically. One was an elementary dance instructor, and the other was a nurse's assistant. They were quasi-attractive, yet contrary to the Ludlow tradition, tended to lack obvious class or business savvy. Brenda felt both deeply envied her status, career, beauty, aristocratic demeanor, and general suave mannerism, especially in the art of negotiation. These were the real reasons the family elders allowed her inside on business ventures.

Often she accompanied her cousin, Duchy, on her mother's side, to the governor's mansion in Raleigh, or to the mansion on Arsenal Hill in Columbia, South Carolina. The family owned a smaller estate in South Carolina, while owning numerous business enterprises there, such as a series of tenements, a liquor store, and a small distributorship. A casino establishment on Drunken Run Estate would be fabulous, but it would also do very well on Huckleberry Ridge Estate in South Carolina. Local economies would explode with positive possibilities. Offering touring services and charging modest admission to tour Drunken Run Estate and the big house would be outstanding for the family and its future. She was glad she could be a part of negotiating these manifestations, whether they were successful or not.

In spite of the cheer, for mysterious reasons a rather gloomy atmosphere pervaded over Drunken Run Estate, ever since she moved into her family cottage where she was raised up. In the nighttime all the way until late in the morning, an unusually heavy fog virtually always blanketed the entire landscape. Sometimes she had trouble sleeping. When she could glance out at her widow and view even a hazy half or full moon looming through the tumbling fog, she would often silently ease outside and walk.

She nearly always heard a hoot owl upon stepping out the door. Low-pitched croaking of bull frogs sounded from nearly everywhere all around her in the night air. In the far wooded distance, as she passed the big house to her right a hundred yards or so away, she heard a sound resembling a woman screaming in great distress. She knew this sound to be a wildcat on the prowl.

As she slowly ambled down the now graveled wagon road donned in her black lace ankle length night gown, nearing the family graveyard, she heard a repeating chime of the Whip-Poor-Will. She paused, watching the graveyard sitting on a slight hill from a distance. She gasped suddenly, thinking she saw a shadow figure moving around inside the black wrought-iron gate. She hesitated to approach, but forced herself to do so anyway.

When she cautiously made it to the graveyard, she saw absolutely nothing, yet strongly perceived a mysterious, if not unsettling, presence. In a burst of night air, she thought she heard the faint whisper of her own name. Her heart raced as if it would leap from inside her breast. She turned, hurriedly making it back to the cottage home, glancing behind her, seeing pursuing shadow movements among the trees. Was this all in her mind? Was she only terrified to a point of seeing things not really present in the night-time darkness?

Though she wanted to race back inside the cottage house, she fought with herself to remain quiet as she opened the back door. She kept glancing backward, seeing what she felt were faint movements in the darkness. Was it beast or human? She closed the door firmly without making any sound.

As she slowly made her way into the den area of the home, she glanced down to the left side, noticing an oaken coffee table with standing pictures of children and adults. One suddenly collapsed for no apparent reason after she passed by, heading toward her bedroom. She was startled with a gasp, then relaxing upon realizing the insignificance. Though she knew the heating system was on, still an eerie damp chill hung in the air.

Maybe her father turned it down or off, since most people sleep better when it's cold at night in the home. Something wasn't exactly right, yet she had no explanation for the reason why. Maybe it was all in her mind, she whispered as she made her way toward the bedroom.

Next morning she arose with the fresh smell of bacon and eggs. When she made her way into the kitchen area, her parents and her uncle, The Monk, were seated.

"Well, good morning, Brenda, there," her uncle greeted with a smile.

"Good morning, uncle," she replied with a yawn.

"I see you must have slept well last night," The Monk replied.

"I slept O.K. I guess," Brenda replied.

Brenda yawned as she paused, then said;

"Tell me more, uncle, about the history of this place."

"Well, what specifically do you want to know, gal?" Uncle replied, as he lifted his coffee cup to his lips.

"Tell me about June Ludlow, and her sister April. What happened to them after Reuben, their father, vanished?"

"Ah, there gal, now that's a fine question. June's child by Jarlan Clark grew into a fine young man, but his mother, June, never fared well thereafter. After her father's disappearance, she constantly struggled to find stability, silently blaming herself for a chain of negative events, to include the disappearance of her father. She was said to have lived out her entire life in the big house here, imprisoned by her own poor choices and her unfulfilled passions. She eventually perished from crippling, consuming arthritis, filled by intense longing and bitter regrets, so it has been said.

"Her sister, April, eventually opened an academy in town, being sometimes an instructor, sometimes only a business manager. From time to time she would drop by to check on her sister, exclaiming that if she had only listened, she could have avoided her horrible destiny. April went on, married, had a fine family who made valuable contributions to the Ludlow clan and estate, though she always had warnings to give out."

"Is there anymore? How might all of this affect us now, Uncle?"

The others said nothing as the food was passing around.

"It has been said that June's spirit haunts the house and grounds, still to this day. There have been reports of questionable occurrences," Uncle replied.

"Like what?" Brenda asked, smiling with the inquest.

"The sound of hounds on the pursuit in the areas where the old horse stable was, when there was none. The sounds of frustrated yelling voices coming from the same area. Sometimes a ladies' footsteps are heard coming through the big house, I have been told. One of the state workers there claims to have seen a sad female apparition, donned in attire from the late 1700s, and quit her job on account of it. The description resembled what we have always been told about June Ludlow. I don't know what to make of it myself."

"That's interesting," Brenda replied.

"It was prophesied first by April, June's sister, that one day in three seventy year generations we would know what happened to Reuben, and where to find his remains. To be honest, now is the time for that great revelation. Every member of the family is on the watch for some sort of sign. Most don't really believe it will happen, however. Even more, don't have much free time to give the matter any heavy thought," Uncle chuckled as he spoke.

"That is most interesting. Should anything ever be revealed to me, I'll surely let you know first," Brenda replied.

"And I shall hold that thought in mind, gal. When that time arrives, should it ever arrive, I'll know it may be fully trusted," her uncle smiled through his long beard and replied.

At times throughout the day, Brenda was left alone in the home. The others may be outside, or uptown buying groceries, or something. All through those times, she felt as if she were being watched. At times, she sensed an unseen presence in the room with her, as if it were standing immediately before her, gazing down upon her. The feeling was unsettling, to say the least.

At night late, she could hear a female child crying in the distance, when there was no child in the house or anywhere nearby. On another occasion she was sitting on the couch around 0900 drinking her coffee, and a shadow moved across the floor, pausing immediately before her. There were no windows behind the couch, only a bare wall. She arose, stepping outside, seeing nobody, yet still this shadow loomed. Then suddenly in simply moved on away. How might she explain this occurrence?

On other occasions, she saw an old woman's face appear in the patterns on the wood of her wall, and in the mirror of the bathroom as she primped. One day, she stepped outside for a few hours, only to return inside the house to find it filled with hundreds of house flies.

There was one unexplained phenomenon which disturbed her most of all. Late at night during a full moon, when the heavy fog seemed at its thinnest, she found herself not being able to sleep. She would gaze out the front window in the parlor room, toward a live oak tree with a wooden swing chair hanging. The form of an aging male with a long chest length brown and gray beard would saunter up to the swing chair, sitting down, gazing directly toward her as she cautiously peered through the window. Quickly she would snap backward with a gasp, covering the window with the curtain. She would eventually open the back door, only to find the swing empty. It was strange; she thought to herself, that no dogs barked at this mysterious figure. During the infrequent fall lightning storms at night, the same figure would often appear in the swing again, gazing directly toward her, as if it instinctively knew where she was.

Once a few days later, she heard the clear scratch of a fingernail on her window pane during one of these infrequent blue fire storms. She moved aside the curtain to see the same man standing immediately before her bedroom window. He appeared to be mouthing her name, but the sound of his voice was drowned out by the rolling thunder. She raced hysterically into her father's bedroom, who seized up his hand held spotlight and a thirty-eight Smith and Wesson revolver. Neither did the dogs bark, nor was the sign of anybody discovered. Was she losing her mind?

When she found herself on one of those rare occasions where she was alone on the estate, she carried her favorite puppy around with her, which was a particularly playful blue tick hound. Often she felt an unseen presence was nearby, and the puppy would growl and bark wildly. Her father had a smaller thirty-eight caliber hand gun. She began carrying this around with her in case she had trouble of some sort.

There were reports of thug-gangs hanging around underneath the river bridge a few miles upriver. Maybe some of these people were up to no good, since Clan Ludlow were perceived by the locals as being wealthy, exclusive unto themselves and those on their own economic standing. Often wealthy influential families in the area endured the wrath of tremendous envy from those of lower social and economic status. Maybe she was

140

being harassed due to such a phenomenon. When she made it back to the house, a smell of rotten eggs sometimes filled the home interior. What on earth was going on?

In early January that year, it had been raining hard. Although it wasn't a usual occurrence, electrical storms were frequent during late December and early January. The elders always said it indicated unusually cold weather and deep snow. A small number claimed it was a dark premonition of wickedness coming to the land.

Brenda was dozing in her soft canopy bed one midnight, not being able to sleep. She mysteriously felt full of energy and motivated to ease open the back door. When she did so, she noticed it was not raining, only frequent flashing lightning, and distant lengthy night-time rolling thunder. Fog thinly hung in the air when it was usually thick. Ahead, thirty yards away, she beheld a vague older male figure with a brown and gray chest length beard donning home crafted cotton overalls. He motioned energetically for her to follow. Her heart raced with fear, but she compelled herself to do so anyway.

Strangely, the man's feet never touched the ground as he walked, she thought. At times she felt as if he might be translucent as she ambled along, then at other times, a solid rank-and-file man. His boots were obviously shop crafted, and his homemade hat fashioned from straw. Such a sight was indeed rare in this day and time. She desperately wanted to turn and run in sheer terror back toward the house, but kept pushing herself to follow for reasons she couldn't readily explain.

The figure ambled or floated down the gravel path once a two rut wagon road. Ahead, over the hill, maybe two hundred yards away, stood the old Ludlow manor house. To the left, maybe three hundred yards away, still stood a few of the old servant cabins. Lightning flashed and distant thunder rolled, shaking the ground beneath her feet, she thought as they suddenly paused. The mysterious, unsettling figure faced her, pointing with an eerie dried finger to the right, in the distance from where they stood. He moved in that direction, and she followed as she shuddered with mounting terror. A cold, uncomfortable sensation saturated the air surrounding her.

They moved across the field a hundred yards to the other side. Behind them was the standing woods. They paused in the area that was once been the manor horse stable and animal coral. They were in easy walking distance of the manor house. Suddenly, the figure paused, turning and facing Brenda. He pointed down toward the ground upon which he stood. The wind suddenly burst.

"This is the old stable area," Brenda spoke in the wind to the figure. "Is this the grave of Reuben Ludlow?"

The figure nodded yes, then gradually faded away. As the spectrum melted slowly, lightning flashed and a heavy thunder rolled.

Brenda quickly glanced around, searching for an item to mark the spot with. A brown quart sized beer bottle tossed by an unknown visitor and laying haphazardly by the edge of the field, fit the bill perfectly. She stood this up on the exact spot where the figure pointed.

She couldn't believe what had happened to her when she gave the experience thought. Deep down she knew, beyond the shadow of a doubt, the dried skeleton of Reuben Ludlow lay beneath that bottle. She stuck a few sticks into the ground beside the bottle in case the wind or something moved it. She ambled at a quick pace back toward the cottage home, sensing she was being followed, yet beholding nobody when she glance all around her in every direction. She eased into the back door of the cottage house, going directly to bed.

When she awoke, the air inside the house was filled with the sweet aroma of fried bacon and freshly brewed coffee. Both of her sisters, Uncle Monk, and her parents were seated at the dining room table, patiently waiting. The freshly made cheese grits, the fried eggs, bacon, buttered toast with rounds of homemade pear and peach preserves, appeared very appetizing

"So ye finally made it in, eh?" asked Uncle Monk as she took her seat. "Ye're about to miss such a fine serving, let me tell ya!"

Brenda smiled, hanging her head and slightly chuckling. Her parents and sisters glanced over at one another, then over at Uncle Monk, seated on the end opposite her father.

"Let us say grace," announced her father, promptly bowing his head.

As they commenced serving their plates in organized rounds, Brenda cleared her throat.

"How long did the horse stable stand?"

Everybody glanced around at one another. Then Uncle Monk's face brightened, and he spoke up suddenly.

"Oh, until maybe the mid-1950s, I would suppose. That's when near 'bout everybody had cars, trucks, and tractors. Horses didn't have much use after that time, other than for recreation."

"That's only been forty years or so," Brenda said as she lowered her head slightly.

Everybody glanced around at one another.

"True, but why would you ask such a question, Brenda?" inquired her mother.

Brenda looked up, then swallowed hard before speaking.

"I had a paranormal experience last night."

"A para-what?," asked her entire family together.

"A paranormal experience, an experience I can't explain," she replied.

Everybody glanced around warily. Only Uncle Monk cracked a broad smile through his thick beard.

"Tell us all about it. I want to hear this."

"Alright. I awoke last night feeling very energetic, which in and of itself is unusual. I opened the back door and the shadowy figure of an elderly man with a long brown and gray beard wearing homemade boots, overalls, and a worn straw hat, stood there, and motioning for me to follow him."

"And you actually did so?" gasped and interrupted her mother. "Brenda, this was crazy! He could have been one of these drug crazed psychopaths around in these parts, this day and time, out to do you serious harm."

"Tell us what he showed you, child," inquisitively asked Uncle Monk, as his firm eyes narrowed, glancing back and forth from Brenda's parents into the Brenda's face.

"He showed me where the grave of Reuben Ludlow is. I marked the spot with a quart sized castaway beer bottle I found, and some dried sticks I picked up beside the site."

"Really?" gasped her mother, "Brenda!"

"Wait just a cotton tailed minute here!" affirmed Uncle Monk with a raised right hand. "This figure she described sounds like Reuben Ludlow. There is a family legend that his ghost would one day return to reveal the location of his murdered corpse. Soon as we finish eating, me and your Pap will walk with you to this site. We'll bring along our pick and some shovels, and all shall find out the truth in this dark tale of woe at long last."

"Brenda, are you being honest with us? Now speak the truth here, since if this is a lie, it's already gone way too far," her mother sighed, with a disturbed expression on her face.

"Everything I've just told you is the honest truth," affirmed Brenda. "It all happened, as I have explained. I never really believed in ghosts and all of this family lore about the estate here, but I do now. Surely these old tales must be gospel truth, as we have always been told."

"When we dig up Reuben Ludlow's bones, he shall finally be allowed to rest beside his adorable wife, Ruth," announced Uncle Monk with a comforting expression on his face. "We'll all pitch in to give him the proper burial ceremony he so rightfully deserved, yet never received."

When the morning breakfast was completed, the entire family walks outside to the barn. Father and Uncle Monk got two shovels and a pick, and the group makes its way toward the site of the old horse stable. When they arrive, a quart sized brown beer bottle surrounded by sticks stabbed into the earth still stood, as Brenda described earlier. Father broke the earth with the pick, while Uncle Monk scooped it up with his shovel. They had gone down four feet into the dark earth and white sand when Uncle Monk suddenly picked up a human skull in his shovel. This skull was split in the back and in the forehead. Astonished, they paused in their labor.

"I do believe this is the skull of Reuben Ludlow," said Uncle Monk. "He's been murdered, for sure, whoever it was."

"More bones should be buried down in the area with the skull. I can also see what appears to be metal holes for lacing, as if he'd been wrapped up in a canvas or some sort and buried in it," Father said.

Uncle Monk scooped a few more shovel fulls of dirt, then up comes three ribs. He scoops some more earth and five vertebrae come up with it. Now it seemed human bones were coming up with every scoop of earth. The long bones of the arms and legs came up, and two or three shovel fulls of unidentifiable small bones. After that, all that came up was white and dark earth.

"We'll need to have a police report made on this find," Father said.

"They'll send it in to a crime lab and investigate this matter. They can tell how old these bones are too. If there is any marrow remaining inside the bones, new technology could allow them to tell if he is related to one of us," said Uncle Monk. "I, on the other hand, don't need all of this fancy-smancy stuff. My gut tells me it's Reuben Ludlow after all of these long years."

"Look, all of you remain here with these bones. I am going to walk back down to the house and make the phone call to get this ball rolling," Father said.

Father walked away. In forty minutes, he returned.

"Well, they should be here in a few minutes," he said. "We will all simply wait here until they arrive."

An hour later, two squad cars and several expensive long black cars pulled up with it. The police officers exited out of the squad cars, and men donning black suits and ties exited out of the others. Several ladies donning business attire and holding media cameras made their way out with them.

One of the men walked up to Father and Uncle Monk.

"I am Branch Wilson, the murder investigator for Bath County. We will take possession of these bones at this time and secure the entire area. Sir, I would like to receive every name present, and then you are all free to go."

"O.K., thanks for coming out," Father replied. He gave an account of every person present to the police.

As the family began walking away, one of the media ladies approached them.

"Sir, I am Cathy Welsh with WBC News. Could any of you tell me anything about what is going on here?"

"Well, we were digging around and found some human bones, so we called the police," Father told her.

"What led you to begin digging here?," the lady asked Father. Father appeared nervous, standing and speaking before the camera as he was.

"My daughter there," he said, pointing toward Brenda, "informed us that a ghost appeared before her, leading her to the gravesite."

"Who do you feel is buried there?" asked the lady.

"A long-lost ancestor who we always felt was murdered," Father replied.

"What year did this supposed murder occur? Do you feel?" the lady asked.

"Seventeen Ninety Three," Father replied.

"Wow, that certainly wasn't yesterday," the lady replied. The lady walks toward Brenda, holding out her microphone. "Tell us about the ghost, mam."

"Maybe at a later time. Right now I only want to go back home and lay down," Brenda replied.

"This is interesting," the lady said in a loud voice. "What did this ghost appear as?"

Brenda turned and began walking with her family. She snapped back around.

"Not right now, maybe another time."

When the family gathered back inside and were seated in the Parlor Room, Uncle Monk turned and said;

"It's all over but the waiting now. After two or three weeks, we'll know every detail."

"What if the bones were recently dead and buried?" Sheila asked. "What then?"

"Well, I can assure you, gal, they are not recently dead and buried. I am shocked that we found any at all after so much time has passed, and due to the general acidic nature of soil around here," Uncle Monk replied.

The daily household chores commenced. One day moved into another, it seemed. Soon, there was a heavy knock on the front door. Father arose to open it.

"Ah, Mr. Wilson, it's good to see you again," he said with a welcoming smile.

"I wanted to drop by and tell you what we found."

Wilson followed Father toward the sofa, then seated himself.

"The bones tested back to the eighteenth century, so there is no need to worry about some recent crime spree. They were definitely the bones of a male, European descendant. The new DNA technology should allow me to take a sample from you, a direct descendant, and if we get a match, then you have located a long-lost male ancestor."

The man took a swab kit and swabbed out father's mouth to get a sample. He sealed the kit up with a smile saying;

"In a week we'll call you and tell you what we found," Wilson replied, as he arose and walked over to the door. Father opened it, saying goodbye to him.

The next Friday the phone called, and mother answered. It was Wilson who called to confirm that the bones were indeed those of a Ludlow ancestor. Mother turned to tell the others the good news.

"Looks like we've found the bones of Reuben Ludlow at long last," announced Uncle Monk. "Now we must all plan for a proper Christian burial. He was a good man, they say, and good people deserve proper burial arrangements."

"To this day there is a place for him right beside his dear wife," mother said.

"I think we should go all out," Emogene said after remaining silent for so long.

"You know it will be a media frenzy around here when we do," replied Sheila.

"I am sure the county historical society, the news and local newspapers, and many others will be swarming all around here," Brenda declared, "but then again, so let it be," she said with a sly smile, "so let it be."

Four days later, Drunken Run Estate was a swarm with people, media, and local government officials.

The chief elder, George Ebeneezer III, assumed a position by the newly dug grave site, and before the gathering crowd. He donned a colonial suit of dress and a fancy wig from the era.

"Greetings, ladies and gentlemen. I am chief elder and caretaker of the family chronicle. Truly, what we are witnessing before us is a moment of great historical significance."

The growing crowd clapped and cheered.

"What is most outstanding, however, is the process by which we came to stand where we are. Brenda, daughter of Kieth and Scarlet Ludlow, experienced an appearance of possibly Reuben Ludlow's ghostly spectrum. This apparition revealed the location of these bones, who we are almost certain are Reuben's. Reuben's whereabouts had been lost since the year seventeen ninety three, however. The family has long speculated that he was possibly murdered since that time. The suspect for this crime was dead within a month following the death of Reuben. No other possible suspects have ever come to light in this case.

With assistance of these kind local authorities, we know that more than likely he was murdered with an ax or possibly a hatchet. We know that these bones were a male of European descent, in his mid to late fifties, fitting the profile we have of Reuben Ludlow. With the assistance of recently developed DNA technology, the time period aligns with the scene and the person of Reuben Ludlow to a perfection. With confidence here and the authority vested in me, I humbly announce the discovery of Reuben Ludlow from the year seventeen ninety three."

The gathered crowd clapped.

"Friends, family, counselors, and caretakers of the estate, state officials, and persons interested, I humbly commit these bones into the earth beside Ruth, the beloved wife of Reuben Ludlow," the elder continued.

Beside the newly dug grave, a padded coffin of elegantly carved cypress wood stood. Two officials transported a glass box with the dark earth stained skeletal bones inside. They placed this inside the coffin, gently removing the top and sliding the bottom glass from underneath the stabilized bones. The lid on the coffin was closed as four men gathered, picking up the ends of two leather straps. Upon this leather, the coffin was held over the hole, then gingerly lowered inside. The opposite ends of the straps were tossed in beside the box as the pal bearers positioned themselves on either side of the hole.

"In the name of God Almighty, we commend the bones back to the earth in proper Christian form. Though none of us ever knew Reuben Ludlow, we do feel the connection through time in our own being. If this man's soul is not of peace, maybe now a perfect peace is forthcoming. With the power and responsibility vested in me, I allow all to pay their final respects before we commence the burial."

Nearly every person gathered held a white carnation. They formed a line passing by the grave with the coffin lowered inside, tossing the carnation, with some tapping on both shoulders and their foreheads as they did so. When the last person had spoken his final word and tossed his carnation, the pal-bearers commenced shoveling in the dirt. The crowd disassembled and began speaking among themselves. Seemingly in no time, the grave was filled in and the mound formed.

"Ladies, gentlemen, and media officials, the grounds and estate are opened for touring, and various forms of accommodation are provided at your convenience," the elder continued. "By the vineyard hall, there is wine in virtually every form and food is always being served. The souvenir shop is open today.

"Over the following months, there will be many forthcoming events scheduled. Be certain to book your place today, since these fill quickly. When you make your way down the gravel road there, pause at the recently constructed cinema and be sure to watch our new film outlining the estate's colorful history. There are also numerous areas where living history is reenacted, such as farming, plantation living skills, and techniques from the general era. There is no charge for walking around on the estate today, so go forward from here at your own leisure, and as always, may God bless."

CHAPTER TEN

THE DEAL

Brenda, her two sisters, their fiances and the sister's parents make their way from the graveyard back toward the cottage. It was nice having everybody around so they could speak. Uncle Monk was back at the grave speaking with the elders and some of the others.

"Ludlow's estate here certainly has a rich history," said Bennie as they walked along.

"I'll second that," replied Donald. "So tell us, Brenda, a bit more about this ghost. It seems you're the star of our show around here today."

"Well, in case you haven't noticed, I'm always the star of the show, honey," Brenda sarcastically replied.

"Oh, ho ho! Listen to her there," Bennie spoke as he laughed.

The two sisters glanced hard at one another. Sheila laughed underneath her breath suddenly.

"Yeah, we all hear her. She's the star of the show alright. Can't you see her there walking along in her tight emerald dress with the show girl sequins? Doesn't she appear in similarity to a movie star or something?"

"She looks like a beautiful picarona mistress, for sure!" spoke up Emogene.

Brenda only smiled, making no comment.

"Now that comment wasn't nice," Donald abruptly interjected, "she's your sister, for crying out loud here."

"Yeah, I know, and we both know her," snapped Emogene. "Why do you think she doesn't have any relationship going of her own? She's of responsible age for marriage."

"Oh my," gasped Sheila as she laid her open palm upon her breast, "she's in it for the money, right?"

Brenda made no reply. She only continued walking along in her natural, sophisticated manner.

"That's not nice," Donald replied again.

"We don't mean to pick on her, now, we're only being truthful here," spouted Emogene.

Donald couldn't help but glance over at the two young women he and his now companion Bennie were with as they walked. Both were donning blouse attractive dress, but they appeared rather proletarian department store when they moved around in them. Emogene held a decent form, but Sheila appeared nearly mid-sized in her dress for the occasion. Truth is, both were only proletarian professionals, he reminded himself as he fondly labeled the category, rather than energetic, successful enterprising entrepreneurs.

Brenda's dress was comfortably held in her polished form. Her coat kept the dress and her form in good taste. He had no question her presence alone would attract customers. Her intelligence, he fathomed, would certainly court sells.

"Tell me more about that ghost," Donald said with a warm smile, while silently hoping to break the ice forming around the group.

Brenda smiled, then began speaking.

"There is a family legend about one appearing. Ever since Reuben Ludlow, one of the originating elders, vanished, he was said to one day return to a descendant."

"So you feel you are her?" Donald asked, as he noticed the ultra-professional conditioned form with which Brenda walked along.

"I must be her," Brenda replied, the spectrum appearing to me fit the description handed down. He showed me where his body lay, and I am confident the funeral we attended was indeed Reuben Ludlow's."

"You know, you were a celebrity today," informed Bennie. "They evening news was all over this place filming you? The newspaper reporters were interviewing you, as was the state historical society."

Brenda smiled pleasantly, making no reply.

"You know, if Brenda wasn't so manipulated and conniving, she might actually be a nice person," Sheila spoke through a sudden snarl.

"I never could fathom how such a foul personality could garnish so much fruitful attention," Emogene chimed in. "She has these businesses simply handed over to her on a silver platter."

"Ladies!" Donald interrupted.

"Maybe it's her good looks, eh?" Emogene continued.

"It has to be her good looks," Sheila chimed in, "just look at her as she ambles along there, with that body and walk of a real porno queen!"

Brenda made no reply, only smiling, as if she held the situation under control as she walked along.

"Ladies, I must say both of you have assaulted Brenda for a while now, for several days in a row, when Donald or myself simply do not see any reason to give justification," Bennie said.

"The longer you stay in our family, the more the truth shall reveal itself," snapped Emogene. "You'll see with your own eyes in time."

Donald rolled his eyes, then turned toward Brenda, bearing an inviting appearance on his face.

"I understand what you do for a living, being an Urban Planner, but what are your business ambitions, Brenda?" Donald asked.

"My sisters are right. I have what I inherited. I do, however, have my own ambitions," Brenda announced with that same confident smile.

"I want to hear. Tell me all about it," said Donald.

"I am looking at investment, but not for the sole purpose of turning capital on my own behalf," Brenda said.

"That's interesting, but keep going," Donald replied.

"Well, it's like this," Brenda said as she paused, turning toward Donald. "If I can turn capitol for myself, to give myself validation, I can turn capitol for you."

"I like that. We both certainly want to turn capitol," Donald smiled back at Brenda. "What have you invested in thus far?"

"I have recently begun to invest in repossessed homes. These homes sell at foreclosed prices. I could do o.k. with only taking a loan out on the property."

"You certainly could in some instances," Donald said.

"But my inherited business shares my sisters speak of have given me an advantage. I can pay hard cash outright for the property, netting myself a massive discount."

"I like the sound of that," Donald said.

"I bought one outright a week or so ago. It was a one hundred fifty thousand dollar property for forty thousand cash. It is located in Wilmington, not far from the university there. I can half estimate needed repairs myself. I hired an inspector with a solid reputation who checked everything out for me. My contractor only charged twenty thousand dollars for the needed repairs. A nice loan from the bank covered that perfectly. I have only sixty-one thousand tied up in it for a complete redo," Brenda said.

"Who's the contractor?, Donald asked.

"Well, of course he's an independent," Brenda laughed.

"My family business associations reach into Wilmington, but we also have them in Charleston, and Savanna. We have them far away as Jacksonville, Florida."

"You heard of Lambert Incorporated?," Brenda announced with a slight laugh.

"Sure have. I know Harris, the owner, very well, and on a personal basis." Donald replied.

"His work is immaculate. Some claim his personal life isn't afoot," Brenda said, "but his work is beyond belief."

She turned to face Donald.

"And the quality of his work is all that concerns me."

"So, how did it go from there?" Donald asked.

"I've had three people interested already. It's only been sitting for two days! I honestly can't believe how sweet this deal has been, nor how smoothly it has gone down," Brenda announced.

"That's great, Brenda. The man's personal life is inconsequential, long as it doesn't affect the quality of his work."

"That was my logic in the matter," Brenda affirmed. "When things get to rolling, and I can turn three or four homes, netting me total take, I want to do my own financing."

"How much are you hoping to turn on this one project?" Donald asked.

"Before taxes, I'll turn ninety thousand dollars. After taxes, around sixty. That's why I've already located another home, this time by the beach in South Port. I'll pay eighty for it, but its worth will be two hundred fifty," Brenda said.

"I don't see where your profit margin is?" Donald said.

"This one is a much more elegant home in a pristine location," Brenda turned, smiling confidently as she spoke. "I'm only paying eighty for it, with fifty coming out of it from the other sale, and only thirty coming from my own personal savings. Once I turn this elegant home, I plan on seeking another at the price of my first one, and in so doing, substantially increase my own profit margin."

"Oh, I can see clearly now, and when your financing program is finally established, you'll have an income from at least two or three different directions," Donald said with sudden astonishment.

"Hmm, now it sounds like you're onto things, big boy," Brenda winked as they both giggled.

When the group made it back into the cottage, they sat in the parlor room. Mother, Father, and Uncle Monk remained on the side, not saying much, while Donald and Brenda somewhat separated from the others, who sat off to the far end of the couch, speaking among themselves.

"What you have informed me of today sounds really enticing," Donald said to Brenda.

"I'm glad you've enjoyed it. I saved it all, especially for you," she replied with a wink and a nod.

"I would like to ask you a personal question, if I may," Donald said.

"Fire away, I'm laying here wide open honey, and game for anything," Brenda replied curtly, as she rolled with a sudden burst of laughter.

"What is your personal profit margin from your enterprise gains?" he asked.

"Thus far this year alone, my personal in hand-profit margin from my real-estate, is eighty thousand dollars. I haven't been financing homes long enough to see a gain, but I've taken in ten thousand more besides. From my math, certainly next year should be a far more handsome year," she said as she slyly gazed hard at him.

"Would you say your profit margin was forty percent of the investment? Fifty percent?" he asked.

"At this point fifty percent, and no less," she affirmed.

"Could you turn some money for me?" he asked in a lower voice tone.

"Why not? Certainly! What is your desired percentage?" she wanted to know.

"A rock hard ten percent would be fine by me," he smiled as he spoke with a chuckle.

"How much are you investing?" she asked with a subtle, inquisitive smile.

"A hundred thousand, rock hard," he shrugged as he spoke.

"When do you plan on delivering?" she asked inquisitively.

"I keep no less than a hundred stashed in my briefcase at all times, in case opportunity finds me or I find it, whichever the case might be," he said with an air if authority.

As he spoke, Brenda smiled with her chin perched atop her fist.

"I really like of that, big boy!," she whispered, but sharply spoke. "There is only one teeny tiny problem here, however. We absolutely must make this deal all legal."

"What are you speaking of here?," he said.

"We need to document this on legal script. Cash is tough for anyone to trace back. Everything must be done out in the light, right?" she announced as he glanced up, without saying anything. She giggled suddenly, "well almost anything."

He cracked a smile, yet said not a word.

"Step outside to my truck with me," he asked as he arose.

"Ladies, family, please excuse us for about five minutes," Brenda spoke as she and Donald turned, walking toward the door. "We have business to discuss," she said as they both stepped outside, then closed the door.

Outside in front of the cottage, the automobiles sat. They slowly ambled toward a sky blue 1993 Ford F150.

"Oh, so this is your ride, eh?" she asked.

"This is her," he snapped as he opened the door.

"Wow, with an extended cab and all. That's neat," she said as she smiled, rubbing the interior along the doors and the dashboard.

"Yeah, that's right."

He took out a briefcase from behind his seat, opened it up, revealing ten stacks of ten one hundred-dollar bills. He counted it all out before her.

"Well, here it is, just like I told you," he said, turning his head to one side.

"Does my sister know about this?" she asked as she chuckled.

He sighed, "Look, I don't tell anybody my personal affairs, including your sister."

She smiled broadly with total confidence.

"I like that."

"Well, there is your money," he said, pointing toward the briefcase. "The legal papers are all inside."

She paused, gently licking her lips as she seized the briefcase handle.

"I'll take the papers now if you want, but spending cash on big-ticket items is tough to do. Why don't you meet me at the bank tomorrow, and you may slam that great big beautiful green wad you have hanging there, into my darling little bank account," she licked her lips as she seemingly purred.

"That's putting me to a ton of trouble, with work and all," he sighed as he reared backward, "but I can do it around high noon."

"Excellent, then I'll meet you over at Bridger's Old Waccovia, at twelve o'clock noontime," she affirmed.

They both exited the truck, ambling back into the cottage, separating from one another, and mingling with the others freely, doing so underneath the flickering eyes of the other two sisters. No questions were asked, and a rather pleasant conversation dominated the scene. Come eleven thirty the following day, both met at the bank foyer down town. Donned in suit and tie, Donald ambled inside while Brenda remained inside her car. Twenty minutes later, when Donald returned, he held a receipt out showing where he had deposited the cash into her bank account.

"Excellent," she affirmed with a thin, confident grin, "and you'll get your money back plus ten percent," she informed him with an emerging smile as she took the receipt from his hand.

Over a course of the next month, she invested the money into more foreclosed homes and creating financing options for potential buyers. When the loan ran its course, the price of the home was three times what its posted cost was. This meant that the payments received were three times what they would have been on the loan itself. It was a simple matter to hand Donald his ten percent increase, but she decided to make it really worth his time, booting him on a five percent tip, since now she could well afford to do so.

Donald was extremely contented and excited about his newly found success. Tax time when the new year rolled around made him wince, however. She casually met him down town one evening at the local train depot by the railroad tracts. The town council was discussing renovations and using the time worn structure as a meeting hall, and also renting it out to locals for holding community and family activities. Her own presence there was consequently justified.

"I tell you what. How much did you lose in taxes on our deal?" she asked him.

"I lost damn near thirty percent," he informed her. "I wish there was some sort of legal hedge out there allowing me to navigate around this heavy burden, or to somehow recoup my losses."

"What if I could create that hedge?" she asked him.

"That would be wonderful! What on earth do you have in mind?" he asked her.

"Preacher McAdoo Jolly has his own church. Do you know who I am speaking of?" she curtly asked him.

"Yeah, that early middle-aged man downtown," he promptly replied. "I think his church is over in Old Carver's Creek Village Square."

"That's the one," she smirked as she spoke.

"I hear he's loaded with dough," Donald chuckled underneath his breath.

"I don't know, but I am confident I can talk him into allowing us to use his church as a hedge. If you are game, that is. This man also operates a number of charity organizations throughout the county. We could send your money through these also, netting in at least half of savings, maybe more. I don't know as yet on exact specifics."

"How old is he now?" Donald asked.

"Maybe thirty-five," Brenda replied. "I've never had any problems speaking with him. To be frank, this preacher has geared an eye toward my curve ever since I was a young child. He thinks I don't know this, but I do. There have been unsavory rumors floating around among the young girls for years, since my own youthful time. It is known where he makes frequent flights to Thailand. We may only speculate as to what types of vacations exist where he enjoys a rather routine participation in. I'm certain I may pull this proposal of ours all off, smoothly as satin and silk," she cooed, as she sarcastically made an almost purring sound to her voice. "I honestly think this man is both a dog, and a real disgusting pig at heart, besides being a man of the cloth."

"Sounds like a real deal to me, and I am game as the best fighting cock to get this little endeavor of ours going!"

Donald spoke with true excitement in his voice, smiling at her while seated inside his brand spanking new Coupe DeVille.

Brenda returned his smile, glancing over her left shoulder, then slightly winking, before sauntering back over toward her parked car. Her emerald silken winter dress seemed to hug every contour of her finely toned hour glass body, he noticed as she stooped to enter. Her general mannerism and composure didn't have a single rough edge in it anywhere, unlike her two sisters, who seemed very unrefined now that he was getting to know Brenda much better on personal terms.

CHAPTER ELEVEN

THE TAX HEDGE

Three days later, Brenda motored on into the local pool room hamburger joint. In the back room, the sound of clicking billiard balls rang through the air. Boisterous speech seemed to accent a somewhat heavy atmosphere. Many came there to gamble, but the home-styled hamburgers were labeled by nationwide surveys and culture magazines as being among the best statewide. Famous political people often donned inside this particular well known stopping place located on the main thoroughfare, to include the governor himself. She knew this to be a popular haunt for the specific person she sought. Sure enough, around ten in the morning, he was there, sitting at the table by the window. She sauntered up, donning her best casual dress. Already a few male eyes in the diner glinted upward in her direction.

"Well, hello Miss Brenda Ludlow," the man said before he took another bite of his burger as she was walking up.

"You're paying more attention to that burger than me, but hello to you, Mr. Jolly," she replied back to him.

He chewed and swallowed.

"Let me order you a burger, some fries, and a cup of tea."

"Naw, I came here to talk," she said to him.

"It's on me," he said as he motioned to the waitress. "You eat and we'll talk, then we'll talk some more. How's that?"

A quasi-attractive middle-aged waitress sauntered up from their table. Her now obviously thickly painted face seemed worn, without any expression, as she snatched out her notepad.

"What may I fetch for you?" she asked in an overworked tone of voice as she glanced upward from the pad she held.

"A burger, lettuce, tomato, and cheese, fries and tea," he said with a smile, "for the lady, of course."

The waitress penned the order, turned, and walked away, back toward the kitchen.

"These are the best burgers anywhere around," the man said to Brenda, "and the price simply can't be beat. A full two dollars for all of that!"

"So how's life?," Brenda asked him.

"Things are going well, I suppose," he replied.

"You sill at the church?" Brenda asked.

"Yeah, I've been there now for fifteen years," he replied.

"Is that all you do?" Brenda inquired.

"Right now, yes. I have been teaching religious classes at the local tech school, Bath Community, but it's all hit or miss, I hate to say. I land a contract for this semester, then they may snag a more experienced person with a higher degree on the following one. I might not have a job next semester until he wants a pay raise. When they can't find any person willing to work for their bottom wage, then they call me back," he laughed. "The whole affair almost makes me angry."

"It almost makes a preacher cuss. Is that what you're trying to say here?," Brenda asked in dark sarcasm.

"Almost," McAdoo laughed.

"That's strange, cause I heard you were doing well," Brenda said with a puzzled glare on her face.

"Well, I mean, I'm not on the streets and I have plenty to eat, but small local church establishments are not what they were only five years ago, Brenda. I feel like all of it is fine sand running between my clenched fingers."

"Don't lie to me now. You're a preacher, for heaven's sake!" Brenda joked. "What about that house you live in? You absolutely must tell me all about it."

"What about it?" he snapped as they ate. "I mean, it was an old seventeen forty church building over on the Holly Hill Spring place. The new landowner was going to trash it, since it hadn't been used in more than eighty years. All I had to do was to pay to have it moved. I invested money to have it renovated up to standard, power and plumbing put in, then I simply redone it again to suit my own tastes."

"But nobody does these things for free, Mr. Jolly Mon," Brenda laughed, "and honey, it ain't exactly done on the cheap this day and time either."

"Well, I mean, it was cultivated over a course of time, you know. I didn't finish it all at one smack," McAdoo replied.

"Done it in stages, eh, over time?" Brenda asked as she sipped her tea through a straw, glancing across the small table at him as she did.

"Yeah, I mean, this is nineteen ninety-three," he sighed, "what kind of people can afford to take on such projects in a single whop?"

Brenda only smiled as she continued sipping her tea through

the straw. He took another bite of his burger.

"So who's the lucky misses?" she asked.

"Misses? Who? You tell me," he spoke before swallowing.

"Wow, really? I can't seem to recollect who the last one was, to tell the truth, but I know there was one," she laughed as she took another bite of her burger.

In reality, she knew there had never been a woman, at least in public. This man was still young, had money at least once upon a time, and still had a refined, well-toned, athletic type body. She never could deduce what his problem was with women, unless he truly was some type of in-the-closet pervert.

"You know, Miss Brenda, I preach the message, but even doing that takes money. I wish it didn't. Sadly for me, though, everything takes money, and I seem to have a critical shortage these days."

Brenda laughed as she drew the tea through the straw, then suddenly smiled rather seductively.

"What if I told you I had a proposal for you that might change your financial life?"

"I've been praying for such a thing," he said, as his eyes glinted into her cleavage when he thought she wouldn't notice.

"I tell you what, Mr. Jolly. Why don't we meet after the meal here? I don't know, maybe at your place, eh? We need complete privacy to talk this thing over, because I have an offer you'll never be able to refuse. This diner simply isn't right for facilitating the occasion."

A nervous composure fell upon McAdoo Jolly's form.

"Why don't we go watch the billiard game over there first? You have today free, don't you?"

"Sure, a bit of leisure is always appropriate before talking business. If it makes you more comfortable, Mr. Jolly Mon."

Both walked from the dining area to the back room. Male eyes glinted upward from the tables toward the perfect figure of Brenda. Male eyes did the same as the two stepped across the threshold where the games were being played. As she walked ahead of Jolly across the threshold, his eyes were drawn to the manner in which Brenda's business attire stuck to her perfect female figure. She immediately struck him as being a smooth mannered, educated entrepreneur, who could have and maybe should have been a centerfold angel. The coarse gamblers at the billiard table appeared uncomfortable by the two being present. The two took a seat when they became available. Jolly drew out his billfold, extracting fifty dollars in twenties and one ten, holding it in the air.

"I'm putting fifty on Buck Pruet there!" he announced, as a sleazy lady who dragged heavily on a Winston cigarette walked over from the table immediately before them to take it."

"Wow, you know these people?" Brenda asked.

"Almost all of them," he replied in a low tone.

"Are they church patrons?" Brenda asked as she smiled.

"No, but I pause in here to preach the message often," Jolly said.

"You don't look like you're preaching any message in here to me?," Brenda laughed.

He cut his eyes but made no reply.

"Besides that, I didn't think preachers ever gambled," Brenda chuckled as she spoke.

The sleazy billiard waitress stepped over to an ice cooler by the wall. She opened the top, retrieving two cold wet bottles of Coors Regular. She stepped back over to the two.

"Have it on the house," the waitress said. "Buck and all of table four appreciate the kind of wager. He won't leave you hanging, I assure you," she announced as she opened the bottles.

"Why not?," Jolly asked as he took the two bottles, handing one over to Brenda.

Brenda laughed, pretending to be astonished.

"Mr. Jolly mon, I never knew preachers gambled or drank. My, oh my, aren't you full of surprises?

She spoke as she caught his eyes glinting downward in her cleavage when he thought she wasn't noticing. He suddenly snatched them up into her smoothly smiling face. Jolly swallowed hard.

"We've talked enough about me. Now let's talk about you for a bit," he nervously spoke.

"O.K.," she smiled, "what do you want to know?"

"What have you been doing in the year or so since we saw one another last?" he asked.

"I work for the City Planning Department over in Mount Horeb Village," she replied, then she laughed.

He turned his beer bottle up, taking a long drag.

"So who's the man in your life?" he asked upon taking the bottle down from his lips.

"Honey, now I'm pure as the driven snow," she purred, "free and available to the right one." she winked.

"Woe now, listen to that!" he laughed as he turned the bottle back up.

Soon the billiard game wound down. Buck's opponent missed his shot. Buck walked around the table and was now lining up for the final shot on the eight ball.

"Looks like your man is about to make his mark," Brenda commented.

The cue-ball suddenly smacked into the eight ball, driving it hard into the left front pocket on Buck's call.

"The ante is all mine!," Buck announced as he held out his hand to the sleazy table waitress. The waitress handed him half the kitty, then dutifully carried the other half to Jolly, since he was the one who made the largest bet. The others all around winced.

"Today must be my day at long last," Jolly smiled toward Brenda, as he received more than a hundred dollars.

"It's refreshing when a man really knows how and where to place all his energy, as he stabs in the perfect direction to score a high ten, don't you think, Mr. Jolly Mon?" Brenda slurred with a chuckle.

"Only if you say so, my darling, only if you say so," replied Jolly while swallowing nervously.

"Look, Mr. Jolly, let me follow you to your place. We have figures to discuss," Brenda said.

"Sure, this game is over anyway, and these people were the best," Jolly replied.

Soon, the two made their way out the front door of Codger's Pool Room. It felt good to sit in the old booth type of seats again. Being away from home and tangled up in a professional career for so long caused Brenda to lose touch with the basic spirit of the area. The ride might have been fifteen minutes as she followed Jolly. She readily knew his home area and thought she knew where his house was. She pulled up in his yard, then exited out of her car to greet him underneath his porch.

The antique cast away church he refurbished was extraordinary, to say the least, she thought in silence. The steeple was long removed, creating a type of frame. A nice porch was placed on the front if the structure, underneath where she and Mr. Jolly stood before what appeared to be a very heavy door of solid oak. The hinges were antique H styled types painted a neat black.

"You've done very well, Mr. Jolly," she said with a pleasant smile.

"It's a product of great sweat equity, for certain," Jolly replied, as he unlocked his door.

When the front door opened, the foyer interior appeared to be somewhat down stairs inside a shallow basement. When the light flipped on, it was immaculately decorated with antique furniture, dark heavy wood, and elegant inlaid hand carvings. The couch was leather bound, and soft as cotton.

"Have a seat, please," Jolly said as he pointed toward the couch.

"Thank you, sir," she replied with a warm smile.

When she was seated, he sat maybe halfway between her and the opposite side. She glanced around in every direction, smiling as she did so.

"My, if anybody is hurting for money around here, I can't tell it," she told him.

"Never forget, my dear, looks can be deceiving. Honestly, my true intention is to head any potential calamity off. My crash hasn't arrived as yet, but if I don't do something, it most certainly will," he intimated.

"Hmm," she said no more than she glanced at him up and down, and the room surrounding her. She hoped he didn't notice her own glinting eyes, but then again, she didn't really care.

"Could I get you a drink, Miss? Ludlow?"

"Certainly, Scotch on the rocks, please, if you have any," she replied.

He arose, with his thin black cotton dress pants hugging his own toned form. She really liked his dark purple Izod shirt with its matching checkered tie. She also couldn't help but notice an outright bulge emerging from beneath his expensive black leather belt and running quite a ways down his left pant leg. It appeared to pulsate, she noticed. She was rather impressed in totality by what she saw, but didn't dare allow the fact of the charm from him be revealed. He handed her the drink over ice, while holding his own in his right hand, as he eased back down on the couch, maybe eight inches closer to her. She smiled and chuckled slightly as he did so.

"So Miss Ludlow, let's get down to business here. I am not a man to waste much time, as maybe you can tell. You said you had this proposal that would completely reverse my potentially negative financial scenario."

"Yes, Mr. Jolly, that I did," Brenda replied, as she sat facing him with her legs crossed.

"Well, I'm all ears. I want to hear every word," he said to her.

"Simply speaking, I need to use your church for a tax hedge, Mr. Jolly. Money amounts will arrive in chunks, rather than one massive amount."

"What is the first amount I would be handling?" asked Jolly.

"Thirty thousand dollars," she said. Her general expression was rather seductive after speaking.

"Wow, now that's quite a sum! I calculate maybe the Federal tax alone on six figs, eh? You must be very successful, Misses Ludlow."

She smiled humbly, gazing him directly into the eyes, yet never saying a single word. Her eyes were unconsciously glancing downward upon his more noticeable bulge. Somehow, in the conversation, he managed to slide closer toward her without her noticing. Maybe she was becoming distracted from the conversation, eh?

"I really need to make this drop, Mr. Jolly."

He slid closer until he sat immediately beside her. She only smiled warmly as he swallowed hard.

"What's in it for me?" he asked her as his eyes glanced up and down into her cleavage.

"Fifteen thousand, of course," she purred, with an inviting expression across her face. "That will be the first chunk, however. There will be much more, I promise."

"Hmm, I don't know, fifteen is good, but I need warm assurance," he said, as his right hand nervously eased upon her left thigh.

She continued smiling, seized his right hand, and then moved it back toward his seated form.

"So do I," she announced.

"Like what?" Jolly frustratingly huffed.

"Like paperwork?" she told him.

"Paperwork? What kind of paperwork?"

"I want a document detailing where I dropped thirty thousand dollars into your church fund," she informed him." An uncharted drop is never good."

"I understand! I understand," he huffed as he arose, stepping over toward his office. She heard some tapping on a keypad. In maybe fifteen minutes, he arrived back before her in a legalized form. She checked it over. All it needed was a signature from her, in every proper place.

"This all looks great!" she announced with a gratified smile.

She carefully folded it, replacing it in her own purse. She glanced upward toward Mr. Jolly, smiling as he eased over next to her on the sofa. She really liked his chiseled, mustachioed face and his cut form. She leaned over, kissing him deeply, as her own right hand slid upward upon his thigh, until it rested upon that massive throbbing bulge. She slowly rubbed it lengthwise, kissing him as he flicked his tongue against hers. She commenced gradually unbuckling his belt and unsnapping his pants.

She unbuttoned her blouse, reaching upward behind her neck, disconnecting her bra, allowing her rather voluptuous breasts to fall out. She slowly pulled down his pants, uncovering his arched organ, which stood up like a rather large snapping turtle's head. He messaged her breasts with both hands as she stooped to pleasure him orally, nearly absorbing his entire wand in graduated increments, as her delicate hands massaged his testicles. He gasped at the level of her artistry in doing so. Where did she learn such splendid moves? He wondered in silence. She was never married.

Though Brenda was a well-mannered, professional, educated,

highly successful businesswoman, her general demeanor bore such a heavy air of pervasive innocence. His poor mind simply couldn't make the connection with what he knew about her, and the intense pleasure he was experiencing, and her gracious honed skill level in delivering this pleasure. In no time, it seemed, they both were totally nude, making passionate love for what felt like the next two hours there on the couch. When they finally finished, after they replaced their clothing, she curtly informed him.

"I'll be over here tomorrow with the dough, at maybe high noon?" she announced with a satisfied expression on her face, as she turned and headed back out the door toward her parked car.

"That's fine by me," he gasped heavily, sagging backward upon the couch as he waved her on.

CHAPTER TWELVE

THE MAGIC

Brenda continued investing money for Donald all year long. When the end of the year finally rolled around, he was amazed at how effective her tax hedge was. He retained half of what he would have lost in tax had he not invested with her? Other tax hedges such as Roth IRA secured even more for him. When he leaked word to Bennie, he wanted to get in on the action, although all he knew was that Brenda could make and save a person's money. He didn't know the specifics as to how.

Donald dropped by the cottage where Brenda stayed on the family estate. His intent was to visit Emogene, but he couldn't help spending more time with Brenda. Her magnetic personality, her high-class standards, and the fact that she could magically make money grow, proved to be more than he could avoid.

Emogene began noticing. She arose from the end of the parlor couch in the cottage, walking over to where the two sat, engaging in deep conversation about business plans and actions to be taken. She was noticeably angry. The two glanced up.

"There you are Donald Grimesly, with your fancy suit, tie, and hat, not to mention your debonair ways. No doubt, you must be glamorizing Grimes enterprises, eh? And you sis, we all know you. You never dated a man, even back in high school, who couldn't prove his family fortune unquestionably. If he had no inheritance, then you had no place in your life for him. Like so many from the time claimed, he had to be swinging at least a rock hard twelve inches of solid gold! But all of us know who you are, sis. Who I personally have a problem with is Donald there."

"What? What is your problem with me, Emogene?" Donald gasped.

"You told me you loved me," Emogene began weeping as she spoke.

"I do, Emogene, I do love you, dearly and without question!" he arose from his seat, grasping her with both arms.

"But I've been noticing you for some time, Donald. I see a glint in your eye, but it's not for me," Emogene sobbed.

Donald lay her head against his breast.

"Look, times are tight for all business people right now, Emogene. I am trying to reel in a profit any way that I can. If what you are referring to is in regard to my association with Brenda here, then you are sorely wrong. She knows much about business going on. She is chief on the town planning committee. She sees maps the rest of us never will. She knows where development is scheduled to initiate ten years before it does. She's the only such contact I have, honestly." He informed her.

"My instincts are revealing possibilities here. I simply don't like," she fired as she suddenly firmed up. "It's not that I have anything per-say to be concerned about, at least that I can readily observe. It is just that I have this intuitive feeling, you see."

"Well, you are leaping into irrational conclusions here," Donald fired as if he were irritated.

"Oh yeah?, and what do you think about this situation dear sis," Emogene spouted in her direction.

She only sat decorating her face with a sly, confident smile.

Suddenly she shrugged, chuckling.

"I guess it's another lover's spat that all lovers have? That's my personal take on what I see," she smiled and laughed.

"You would say such a thing, wouldn't you, Brenda?" Emogene fired. "You're laissez-faire attitude makes me even more suspicious of your true intentions."

"Intentions? My, how we all leap into grand conclusions when the emotion leads us," she shrugged and chuckled, glancing over at her and out into the room.

"Ladies!, I know situations derived from misunderstanding can lead to tension, but my intentions were never to be caught up in the middle."

Donald firmly glanced over directly at Emogene.

"I may assure you my intentions are not what you're thinking right about now."

He turned, walking through the door toward his car parked out front. He started the engine, pulled back, then drove away, never even glancing in the direction of Emogene. As his car moved on down the gravel road out of sight, Emogene turned toward Brenda with an angry expression on her face.

"You are up to something around here, something wicked. You might be my sister, but you are an evil person, a true born succubus, if you will. You are cooking something up around here, and it's anything but righteous."

Brenda smirked with a chuckle and a gasp.

"Really, sis, me?" she said, placing both opened palms upon her breast.

Brenda stepped back into the house, going directly toward her bedroom. Her closet was filled with the best business attire money could afford. She chose a snug business formal attire with a coat to match. If she didn't have the perfect body to go with it, this dress wouldn't be appropriate. Once she was dressed, perfumed, and powdered, she headed out of her room toward the door.

"It would be interesting for me to know where you are headed right about now," Emogene fired as Brenda walked passed her seated on the couch.

"Of course, I have business affairs to attend uptown," she smiled confidently as she spoke.

As she drive down the gravel road, she instinctively knew when things bothered him. Donald would always be at Codger's Pool Room. It seemed as if all well-endowed business people, regardless of social class, always frequented this ageless local establishment. Old man Bow-limp Codger was a big time speculator and investor, however, and was highly successful at it. Associations with him, although he was seldom seen there, could be very beneficial indeed. Quite often, political operatives who worked for the establishment and found themselves canned away for sleight of hand on his behalf, could find their desperately needed thirty thousand dollar plus bail and expensive lawyer services through the financial generosity of old man, Codger.

Emogene parked in front of the pool hall out on main street, walking inside and going directly to the back room where the billiard tables were. Donald sat at table two with his back turned, placing bets on a husky diesel mechanic donning a cut off western shirt that he wore all seasons, named Pop Top Macgraw. He was called Pop Top because he was a prodigious beer drinker. No person knew his real name. He was a damn good billiard player, but he was also a renter evict-or, should one

179

need his services. Matter of fact, any job where violence was needed, Pop Top would gladly perform in the dark of night, and was good at getting the job done. He lived for violence, even traveling to places such as Burma and Thailand to engage in death matches for high dollar foreign spectators, so it was said. Brenda casually walked up, laying her right hand on Donald's shoulder.

"Somehow I knew I would find you here," she spoke as he seemed to jolt.

"Yeah, I thought I would have a burger, watch a little game, do a bit of my own wheeling and dealing, should the opportunity present itself," she said to her.

"How much you have riding on him?" she asked.

"Five hundred dollars," Donald spouted.

"Have you been met?" she asked.

"Yes, by five more you see gathered around.

"Three thousand dollars is a nice take for a day out," she said. "Are you sure your man there'll win?"

"Like clockwork every time," Donald replied with a smile.

Pop Top's opponent was up for the final eight ball shot, since Pop Top himself had missed every other shot but three. When the opponent glanced over at Brenda, she dropped down her cleavage, pretending it to be an accident. The man took his shot. He missed, as all of them did every time she ever did this. She learned over the years. Now it was Pop Top's turn.

Pop Top nonchalantly walked around the table like it was second nature until finally the eight ball shot was his. He pointed to the left front pocket, making the call. He slammed the ball in hard like it was shot from a gun barrel. The sleazy waitress, who also collected the player's betting kitty, shucked out fifteen hundred to Pop Top, then the same over to Donald. Pop Top walked over to Donald, shook his hand, tipped his grease stained cap to Brenda, saying;

"Thank you all kindly. It was a pleasure doing business with you."

Brenda glanced over at Donald, smiling confidently.

"So, what's next on the agenda?"

"Are you up for grabbing a bite?" he asked her.

"I'm not to game for hamburgers right now," she replied.

"No, I didn't mean hamburgers," he snapped. "We can come here and do that on any dark and dreary weekend. I'm talking about the Queen's Riverside Diner over by the old Tory Landing."

"Oh, wow-wow now! You did come into a little side stash there, didn't you, Donnie boy? Sure, why not?," she said as she smiled her thin, confident smile.

"Leave your car parked here and motor on out with me, if you will," he said, with a slight wink.

Both stepped out of the poolroom and into Donald's new Cadillac DeVille. Brenda never really paid his ride any attention until now. It backed out into the main street, then purred along smoothly.

"Doing business with you, for me, has already commenced paying off handsomely," he said to her.

"Well, I'm glad, because I work hard to be a success," she told him.

"That's why I am investing another hundred grand for you here soon, Brenda."

"You know, you're netting a thirty percent increase, eh?" she replied.

"I honestly can't find another better investment," he said.

"I've reaped a heavy profit, and I mean pure profit, at that. I am honestly thinking of running my entire enterprise through you, Brenda."

Brenda gasps.

"I don't know how to reply to that, except that I feel honored at the generous recognition."

"Then don't," he told her.

The car seemed to turn by itself into a narrow dirt road heading toward the river on the edge of town. It turned a corner to the right, and thereupon a flower covered hill sat an antique building. This building had been several things in its day. A hay barn, a specialty candle shop, an antique dealership, a gilded book store. Now it was an elegant diner by the riverside. Donald opened the car door on his side, walked around the car, and then opened the door on her side. The well-dressed two walked up toward the doorway, arm in arm.

"What will they think when they see us together like this?" she said to him.

"They can think what they want, but actually, this time of day it's mainly guest passing through town here from the beach on one end, or Cross Creek on the other," he said.

"My, aren't you smart? You had this all planned out, didn't you, Donnie boy?" she said, glancing over at him.

He opens the door, pausing by the cash register. The waitress appears, asking them to follow her. They were given a seat by the window facing the river at a bend.

"With early spring coming on, the flowers were beginning to bud. Something about pollen falling on the flowing water makes a pretty sight, don't you think?" she said.

"Doesn't this general picture suit us two?" he asked.

"Like how?," replied Brenda.

"It's becoming greener and so are we," he chuckled.

"That's funny Donnie boy. Is money all you think about?"

"No, Brenda, it's certainly not all I think about."

The waitress paused by, pouring empty glasses full of water, then moved on to the next table. Brenda tipped her glass, smiling as she glared at him across the top. She sighed deeply when she placed her glass back down.

"What surprises am I going to get out of you next, Donnie boy?"

"I wouldn't be precisely where I am without you, Brenda."

"But what about Emogene? Where precisely is her stake in all of this?"

"Emogene has a kind heart, I must say," he told her.

"Maybe true for you, but what I want to know is how much it weighs in pure gold?" she replied.

Donald gasped, then chuckles.

"I'm still waiting to find out myself, to tell you the truth. What I fear most is that Emogene nor Sheila are not business women. Two good heads motivated toward the same endeavor are better than one."

"Oh, yeah?" she smiled as she took another sip of water.

The waitress soon appeared with two more. Two fetched the platters, while one poured the rose wine and set a bouquet of red roses in the center of the table.

"If there is anything else you need, then let us know. We are here to serve you," they said. When the waitresses left their table, Brenda paused, gazing at Donald with that smile stretched across her face.

"Hmm, I must say, you are as sly as you are handsome, Donnie boy. How long have you and my sis been together?"

"Three years," he replied. "She's a good heart-ed woman."

"How did you two meet?" Brenda asked, as she raised her glass and sipped the blood-like rose wine.

"We met at one of the politicians' big barbecue dinners they have had at the tobacco warehouse. I think it was the one where Codger supported the governor of South Carolina."

"Which one?," asked Brenda.

"You know, that governor accused of inner-state investing, money laundering, and all of that corruption."

"Oh yeah," Brenda sighed, "That governor where a hundred women from way back when, came out of the woods and accused him of hanky-panky."

"That's the one," both of them laughed. "I'll never forget it."

"I bet you won't, because that governor won, and he made a hell of a lot o' people connected to him wealthy," she said.

"I didn't intend on speaking of that, but you know how things are. It's who you know," Donald affirmed.

"Yeah, and Clan Grimesly was right in the middle of that great take, eh?"

Donald chuckled, smiling, yet made no reply.

"You don't need any words, Donnie boy, I understand."

Soon, the lamb and horse overes were finished.

"Are you up for desert?" he asked.

"Another glass of this wine maybe, but I have my fill of food, to be honest, about everything."

A waitress appeared with a bottle of port wine, pouring them both a glass full. It felt really good to simply lean backward and enjoy the rich, thick liquid. Donald left payment in the leather folder. Sitting there with Brenda seemed almost surreal for reasons he couldn't explain. The very real fact of his newly found success couldn't be overlooked as being its own contributing factor in this sensation of natural intoxication.

Not much was said at the moment as they both eased backward, sipping the wine. When they finished, the waitress seized up the tab and the cash tip he laid I the center of the table, as they only sit smiling across the table at one another. Soon they both arose, heading out of the diner toward Donald's car. Donald opened Brenda's door, closing it as she was being seated. He walked around the car, opening the door and taking his own seat.

"For some reason, there's a sense of timelessness in the air today," she said as she slowly turned toward him, "and déjà vu, don't you think?"

"We live in an area thick with history and family tradition," he replied. "I mean, a block over stands an elegant church with bloodstains from the Revolutionary War.

"Wealthy people from the era, along with their descendants today, live along this main street here," Brenda said. She suddenly broke into a smile. "Who knows what kinds of personal battles they were fighting as these wars of the past were being fought?"

She cut her eyes over at him and slightly chuckled.

"Where are we going?," she asked.

"Riding, I guess. It feels good too, doesn't it?" he asked her.

"Yeah, that looks like Mount Horeb Church up ahead," she said. "It's kind of on the edge of town out in the middle of nowhere."

The car passed the colonial church, turning down a narrow two rut dirt road maybe a block passed. The majestic live oak stands with trees covered in hanging moss were absolutely beautiful. They might have driven four hundred yards when they over passed a creek on a cypress wood bridge. To the side of the road immediately passed the creek was a hill, with a massive ancient live oak standing on it. The car tucked itself away in the shade of a tree in a space, seeming as if it were made for it.

"This sure is a nice after lunch spot," she told him. "It's almost as if it were made for this car."

"It's something different," he replied to her.

He opened his door and hers, and they both stood beside the car. They slowly walked over toward the tinkling creek.

"What kind of history does the place have?" she asked.

"Well, the church was once part of a grand estate."

"Was it Mount Horeb Plantation I used to hear about?" she asked.

"That's it, way back when families owned the enterprise, and prospered from it, rather than everything being owned by banks, corporations, and strange people we know nothing about, as it all is now," he sighed.

"But Grimesly and Ludlow are changing that back around, sir Donald," she smiled.

"Maybe," he sighed, "we can certainly try."

"I don't recall ever seeing any sort of plantation house any-where around here," she said.

"It's been a ruin for the past forty years," he told her. "The big house sits covered in vines just around the bend up the road there, to the left two or three hundred feet. I deer hunted with the Mount Horeb Hunting Club for years. We once held unof-ficial meetings inside that ruin."

"What kind of unofficial meetings?" she asked hesitatingly.

"If you know anything about that hunting club, all of us were Masons, you know."

"So what?," Brenda fired.

"We formed our own break away branch of Masons. Our branch was steeped in ritualistic symbolism. We often held se-cret rites inside that dilapidated mansion house at midnight, so we wouldn't be discovered."

"Sounds freaky," Brenda laughed as she glanced over at him.

"We even held seances a few times, gazing into crystal balls and mirrors with candles flickering beside them," he informed her.

"Were there any strange occurrences?" she asked.

"During the summer and fall electrical storms, we often caught glints of shadow people late in the evening and at night," he told her.

"Really?," she gasped.

"The owner was said to have been a particularly vicious Revolutionary War veteran. He hated any person who was not part of his own family."

"What was inside the old house?" she asked.

"Not much of value. I found part of a flint-lock gun and some china. There was an antique iron for clothing.

"Let's ease over there!" she gasped. "The car is tucked away here. One must be right up on it to see it. Let's go!"

"Alright, but there is not much to see," he reminded her.

Slowly, the two ambled up the narrow dirt road to the first bend. She looked to the left and could see a large building structure covered in vines.

"These vines conceal the beauty once present in this magnificent structure," she announced as they turned away from the road and began waking.

They both stood before the staircase, wide at the bottom, narrowing off at a moss stained foyer.

"It is a place of its day, that's for sure," Donald said.

"How did these people get so rich way back then, Don?" she asked.

"Providing money lending services, and financing services back down to the populations surrounding them," he said.

"Like buggy repair and taking orders for clothing?" she asked.

"Exactly," he replied as they walked up the stairs. The door going into the house was ajar.

"And building their own family banks?" she asked.

"This family certainly had one," he said as the slightly opened door swallowed him up. Brenda followed after him.

Even in the dirt and decay of time, this old house proudly maintained its appeal. She counted six empty rooms on either side of the hallway. The hallway dead ended at a large central room with an out of place ripped leather couch on the edge. A table sat near the couch.

"Here's where we held our séances and ceremonies," he said.

"I wonder if we could provide money lending services now?" she asked.

"Perish the thought, I tried, and it's illegal in virtually every state, unless one accepts depreciating collateral," he replied. "Some states feign allowing individual people to lend money, but the legal red tape is onerous, to say the least."

"Who in their right mind would do such a thing as accept depreciating collateral?" she laughed as they took a seat on the couch.

They both fell in, since the couch was so soft. She particularly noticed how he sat supporting her body against his. She could feel what she felt was a slight bulge shoved into her lower back.

"So families way back then had a right to own their own banks, but we don't?" she laughed.

"And haven't had it since the Great War here," he smiled, as he leaned over to kiss her.

She submitted, and the two were laying across the top of the couch, with him kissing her heavily in the mouth and down her neck. He flipped her buttons skillfully and soon the dress, the bra, and her panties glided off gently. A rumble of thunder ensured as the two continued on in their actions. As a patter-patter of light evening rain fell, the sensation of them being in the house seemed like hours.

When the act completed with him riding her viciously from behind, he somehow felt as if a hook had been set. As this sensation astonished his realization, a peal of rolling thunder crossed the skies above the house. He gazed deeply into her eyes, and he saw not the eyes of a satisfied lover, but those of a confident engineer. She only smiled broader as he seemed terrified at what was now revealing itself. He breathed heavily as he suddenly scrambled to replace his clothing.

"Why so quick to redress when we could just lie here, holding one another, listening to the rain, savoring the blue flashes, and what I perceive as being a wonderful Gothic feeling in general?"

"I have an uncomfortable feeling," he announced. "We must go from here soon," he glanced over and told her.

She seized his neck tie, an obviously expensive one with its Italian design. She tossed it over his head, dragging him toward her.

"Oh no, Donnie boy, I don't want to go. I want to play some more."

"Well, please pity me, Brenda, because I don't have the time."

He grabbed the neck tie, tossing it over his head.

"Donnie, Donnie, Donnie," she sighed, "we have so much we absolutely must discuss, especially now."

"Like what?" he fired as he struggled to replace his clothing.

"You've been doing well, Donnie boy, thanks to me. You must admit it, eh? Well, now it's my turn to prosper a bit. It's only fair, right?"

He froze in his tracks, glaring at Brenda directly in the face.

"Like what?" he fired through clenched teeth.

"Sign over Emogene's share of your family enterprise she'll gain upon your marriage with her, to me. You own a share already, I already know. She is no manager, she can't do you any long term good." A smile leaped across Brenda's face. "I mean, is she even good in bed? Will she do tricks for you as thoroughly as I do? You must give me all the credit where it's due. I know what you like, big boy. One is money and the other is a woman with no inhibitions."

"I don't know," he fired, shrugging his shoulders.

"Go fetch the paperwork and let's make it official now."

"I don't know about all of this. Brenda!" he whined.

"You always carry your paperwork inside that briefcase you keep locked up in your car, Donald. Go fetch it for me, boy! Then if I feel like it, I might ease backward on this couch and let you lap a little more, like the pathetic puppy dog you are."

"I don't know, Brenda!" he screamed, nearly coming to tears.

"You either do it, or you'll and all of Clan Grimesly shall be cut out of any future business dealings with Clan Ludlow, because Emogene is going to find out just how naughty you've been today. You go fetch those papers for me, now!, big boy, then jump down here and do like a puppy dog does when I ease back. You were all into it a minute ago. I may only wonder just what Emogene will think?"

Donald huffs out of the old house into the rain, then returns in fifteen minutes. He opens his briefcase, thumbing through some papers. He pulls a handful, then throws them before Brenda. She picks them up, scans them well, then returns them.

"Sign up, Donnie boy!"

Donny breathes heavily as he reluctantly signs the papers. When he finishes signing, the deed has been done. She holds the papers, scanning them carefully to ensure their authenticity. When she is confident all loose ends have been tied, she speaks to him again.

"I'll leave you copies on the mantle tomorrow in a sealed envelope with your name on it, when you visit Emogene. The envelope will have a sticker of an old thirteen star colonial flag on it."

"Get your damn clothes on, woman!" he snarled at her as she gradually leaned backward instead, gently spreading her legs.

"Oh no, Donnie boy, you have another job to do for me first. So why don't you just hop down to it now, like a good little boy? Else I might make a sly report back to Emogene, the IRS, and a few others, on just how bad you've been these days."

Five minutes or so transpired.

"I own you now," she purred through tightly clenched teeth, as she patted and rubbed the back of his head. " Now, let's get something straight right now. You're going to do everything I tell you, just as I command. Don't you just love being my pathetic little hump puppy, Donnie boy?, but don't you dare stop to answer. You savor your new candy there until I tell you that you are free to come up for air."

CHAPTER THIRTEEN

THE PURSUIT CONTINUES

Carvers Creek Village sat outside of Mount Horeb-town, fifteen miles or so. It was an old cross road village at a creek fork, a quaint kind of place with an appealing timeless beauty to it. The fork was actually outside of town, maybe a mile and a half. It was called Swift Ford, since the water moved so quickly and was difficult to cross back during the colonial era. At the fork stood a colonial era church. The structure was traditional A framed, with a step shelter or small porch. A nice steeple sat atop this A frame, in which hung a large bell. This bell rang incessantly down through the ages to announce church every Sunday morning at 1000 hrs.

On the inside was a rather large sanctuary capable of containing a thousand people, in what appeared on the outside as a small building. Above the sanctuary was the loft where parents didn't like for their children to sit, since the community dissidents and misfits often sat there to play, hide or sleep, when well-meaning family members forced them to attend. At the front stood a wooden podium, behind which sat a fully dutiful, devoted twelve member quire. Preacher McAdoo Jolly proudly assumed his place behind that podium every Sunday morning as he had for the past ten years, and a very dedicated following always attended. This particular Sunday morning, a heavy sensation of difference hung in the air, however.

"I want to address the subject of people living duel lifestyles. I'm talking about people having a public life in the church and living private lifestyles. The bible, however, says we are either hot or cold, never in between!"

Among the late arrivals, dazzling attired, Brenda casually walked inside, sauntering down the aisle like a gilded carnal goddess, sitting on the front seat immediately before the podium. While the church didn't appear as much, still it held an atrociously large expense account. She couldn't help but ponder on this matter as the preacher now nervously stumbled through the morning sermon.

"We can't focus our eyes and minds on heaven, with our feet and hearts among men. With our mouths we can't praise God and the scriptures, while we sin in our own choice of actions," he announced in a shaking voice.

Brenda sat there smiling while the preacher spoke. When the service ended and the people exited, Brenda stepped back inside the church building, making her way toward the rear rooms where she heard stirring. When she walked silently into the room immediately behind the choir loft, Preacher Jolly was organizing his books and meticulously counting his incoming tithes for the morning. The preacher had his back turned toward her as she approached on panther's feet.

"Tis good to see a man hard at work, being dedicated to the word so on a Sunday morning. Wouldn't you agree, Mr. Jolly mon?" she purred in a manner that somehow rubbed the preacher's nerves raw, as her words startled him. He signed deeply.

"What could I help you with?" he said without turning around immediately. He then suddenly spun around in his leather swivel chair.

"We need to discuss some more business," she firmly informed him.

"Business? Not now, I'm too busy at the moment. Come back around 1600 this afternoon maybe, and we'll talk then."

Brenda pushed the door firmly shut, then calmly and very confidently approached him, pausing before his very face.

"No, Jolly Mon, we're going to talk business right now," she affirmed upon an inflexible face. A sudden smiled cracked, bearing great confidence behind it.

"Be out with it. I don't have much spare time in my hands," he curtly informed her.

"O.K. then, since you don't have much time for socializing and monkeying around, frankly I need to make another drop," she told him.

McAdoo sighed deeply.

"How much this time, for Christ's sake?" he spouted, as if he hated to hear the news.

"Three hundred thousand dollars, American."

"What!" Jolly exclaimed while suddenly attempting to muffle the speech. "How can I justify this money? I mean, if IRS auditors should come in here tomorrow, how might I justify such a stupendous write off?"

"Add some shrubbery, build onto the sanctuary, and paint this antique decrepit building, for heaven's sake." She bore the witches a smirk as she hesitated. "Put in some crystal on those colonial candle chandeliers, for crying out loud around here. Otherwise, appears like you've a big problem here, oh thou preacher man."

"Well, I'll inform you politely, Brenda Ludlow, you're deeply stuck inside this kimchi pool with me, darling," he said, as his own confident smirk cracked his hardened face.

"Oh no, you had better check carefully over those papers again. There is another name on that signature besides yours, alright, but it isn't mine."

Quickly, the preacher fumbled through his briefcase, finally discovering the papers. Sure enough, the other name listed was Donald Grimesly, in what bore an astonishing appearance of a male signature. He simply couldn't fathom the mechanics of all the mounting negativity he was bearing witness to.

"Well, I'll be damned," he muttered beneath his breath through his clenched teeth. He glanced upward, directly into Brenda's face. "What kind of game are you playing with me, you friend? You filthy rotten hussy."

"That's right, and you, honey, are my little dumb-ass, butt-licking fool."

Brenda leaned directly over into the preacher's face.

"You listen to me, Jolly Mon, and you listen well," she said as she pointed her right index finger directly into the preacher's trembling face. "Now you are going to take that money, write another legal form and accept what I hand back to you, or I'll dime everything out about you to the IRS; and the whole world will know of your secret sick perversion for little children and your illicit affairs with prostitutes, not to mention the adult males and females you have forced your way with. That's right, the kind proprietress, Aunt Sadie Benton, down at Sister Sadie's Bake Oven in Bennettsville, told me all about you not long ago. I even know the names of the grossly young women underneath her employment that you were with!

"I'll claim you have been eyeing me since I was nine years old, which is the truth, you disgusting lying buzzard! I'll say you forced yourself on me. You have that, right? You and all of your business shall be eternally ruined while you rot away in some dank dungeon somewhere, if you don't wind up with a noose around your neck or a bullet through your dark heart! I mean, damn you to everlasting hell for hiding behind the word and using it to gratify your pathetic greed and to veil your disgustingly sinful lifestyle!"

His eyes widened in utter astonishment, and he breathed heavily as she spoke.

"When are you going to make the drop?" he struggled to ask her, dropping his head as he asked the question.

"Tomorrow at one thousand hours. In here would be best, where we are behind closed doors. You draw up the paperwork in the meantime. Make the tax write off for Donald Grimesly, as they have been thus far. I want to inspect this paperwork for myself tomorrow and receive a certified copy before I drop the money. You and your church here get a whole one hundred fifty thousand dollars! Isn't that nice? How many other preachers, or anybody else in these parts, can honestly boast of such? You can net such a fine living from allowing us good people to take much needed tax write offs, eh?"

McAdoo Jolly gazed deeply into space through widened, horrified eyes.

"And to just think that I so willingly allowed such a thing," he gasped, as he barely managed to speak.

Brenda suddenly fires her opened right palm out, slapping the preacher solidly across his face.

"You allowed it, you hypocritical filthy pig. You; and you are going to do something else for me before I leave here, to consummate our new deal," she paused as she smiled seductively. "You have that, Jolly Mon? You may call me the avenging angel sent in to provide retribution for the sins of men."

"What must I do now, on top of what I have already done?" he gasped as he nearly came to tears.

Brenda fired her right palm out three consecutive times, slapping him solidly across his astonished face. He grasped his astonished face as if he didn't realize what had just occurred.

"You are going to fall down on your knees right now, you dirty, filthy, rotten dog, and worship me, your divine master and your goddess," she spoke through tightly clenched teeth. "That's what you are going to do!," she raged. "I am dying right now to make your grossly filthy face glisten."

"No! No!," he gasped. "I mustn't after I just preached the word."

He plead as he melted before her as she stood before his desk. She seized the top of his head, forcing him farther downward upon his knees. She turned with the desk to her back and he lifted her skirt, slowly easing down her silken panties.

"I own you, you're my dog to train as I please, to do my bidding, and nobody else!," she growled through tightly clenched teeth as her viscous slaps on the back of Jolly's head gradually transformed into easy petting strokes. She arched her back deeply, then released, groaning as she did so.

"That's right, you lick me like candy everywhere down there, you good-for-nothing dog, and stab me hard with your tongue like you're mad at me. That's what you may do to exercise your pent up frustration and anger!"

The following day, Brenda met again with Jolly, finalizing the deal and making the drop underneath her own specified conditions. After pausing at the poolroom for an outstanding noon day burger and a cup of tea, she finally made her way back to the cottage. When she arrived, only Bennie and Sheila were around. Bennie stood from the couch as she walked up upon entering.

"I am so glad to see you, Brenda. We hardly ever see you. You parents are always asking about you. Where have you been?" he spoke as he smiled.

"I'm a businesswoman, and it's a never ending labor of love," she curtly informed him. "I feel as if I am married to the enterprise, rather than to a man."

She chuckled underneath her breath as she spoke.

"We understand, and can see, your dedication. We can also see your pride for Clan Ludlow, its history, and its business endeavor."

She moved around as she hung her light coat in the closet by the entryway door.

"We have been talking about much of late between us. Sheila and I have, Brenda," Bennie said.

"You're so successful at what you do. Donald has nothing but kind words about how excellent you are as a woman and business associate."

Brenda suddenly paused before him as he spoke.

"Eh?," she said as she leveled with him, "how kind of him to speak that way?

"Yeah, I mean, he speaks as if you've really done well by him. I haven't heard any comments in the past, say two months, but I have heard much in prior times, and all of it was positive."

She suddenly continued walking back toward her bedroom, desiring more casual indoor wear, not to mention a hot shower. The hot shower felt great after a hard night and day's work. She must have stayed inside for an hour. She eased out the door, donning her genuine ostrich feather house coat. Prior to putting on her clothing, she often took a drink. The bar was located at the far side of the den, away from the couch. She eased out to the door, grabbing a bottle of seven year bourbon, pouring herself a nice shot. She glanced over at the couch. Only Bennie was there.

"Where is sissy?" she asked.

"She stepped out for some cheese and milk. She won't be out but a minute."

Brenda poured herself another shot.

"You want one?" she politely asked.

"We need to talk," he said to her, as if he felt uncomfortable doing so.

"Am I that tough to speak to?" she asked. "Do you see me in my house coat, make you nervous or something?"

"No, nothing of the sort. I know Sheila and yourself haven't ever been on the best of terms," he said to her.

"Look," she exclaimed, "I see your sheepish little eyes glinting, Benjamin, just come on out with it!"

"It's nothing of the sort, I assure you, Brenda Ludlow. Your sister and I have been talking."

"And?" Brenda fired.

"We want you to manage my portion of my own family enterprise estate, and your sister's portion of Ludlow enterprises. We both think you, and us, would make a marvelous team. All you must do is agree and endorse the documents, right here and now, today."

"Let us wait until sissy returns. I don't believe what I am hearing. I must be hallucinating or something, if I am not flat out mad and insane."

She walked on back toward her bedroom, putting on her evening slacks for hanging around the house. As she was finishing, she heard the front door of the cottage open up.

"You're back just in time," she heard Bennie announce.

"In time for what?" Sheila replied.

"I broke the news to Brenda about our partnership."

"How did she reply?" asked Sheila.

"She preferred to wait for you before commenting," Bennie replied.

"How considerate of her. Matter of fact, it's too darn considerate, to a point that I don't feel comfortable, Bennie," she heard the voice of her sister announce through the walls.

"You heard Donald a few weeks ago, darling, and we are not getting along too well handling the family enterprise ourselves. Why not allow her to handle the headaches, and us draw a percentage, so that we might go on and enjoy our lives?"

"You're the man of the house. You do what you feel is wisest, although my feminine intuition is warning me, Bennie."

Brenda arose, walking out of the bedroom, into the parlor where her sister and Bennie were. She took a seat opposite of them on the couch.

"What's on? I know what I have been told, but please tell me again so that I know I am not losing my mind," she spoke with a long sigh as she ran the fingers of her right hand through her hair.

Bennie laughed.

"Well, it's all pure and simple, as I have said already, Brenda. We've already discussed this matter between us. There was much dissension and disagreement, but we finally reached a consensus," Bennie said.

"Which was?," fired Brenda.

"We're failing," Bennie firmly intimated. "We're on the verge of losing outright. That's why we are signing all of it over to you. All that we are asking is a mere after tax thirty percent. The other seventy is all yours, Brenda. Should something ever happen to both of us, then all of it is automatically transfers over to you. Sound like a winner to you, Brenda?"

"If you know you are sure, then let's do it! I can make the business end of things prosper. You just be sure you are sure, because once that signature is down, there is no backing out. Signed, sealed, and delivered means exactly what it says. You both have me on this?"

Bennie produced a new black leather briefcase. Carefully, he retrieved a handful of documents. He gently handed them all over to Brenda. Brenda began flipping through them. She soon realized reading and signing them would take time, maybe three or four hours.

"This is outstanding. It may be tomorrow before I deliver them back, signed and everything," she said as she flipped through the papers, pausing to read now and then.

"No problem," Bennie replied.

"And sis, you're sure this is what you wanted?"

"We never saw anything eye to eye. Our entire lives were one great big squabble. We were never close, like family should be," Sheila said.

"So what made you decide on me, pray tell?" Brenda asked.

"You are the one who can make it happen. Donald confirmed all of this for us. We need a huge turnover, Brenda. All we are asking is thirty percent in royalties. The other seventy is all yours."

Two days passed and Brenda lay the folder down before her sister, Sheila.

"The papers are all in there, signed, sealed, and delivered," announced Brenda.

It was a load of trouble organizing all of this business enterprise the first month. There were lawyer's fees, permits, taxes and back taxes that needed paying. When Sheila's take arrived in her hands, she was sorely disappointed.

"Is ten grand the best you can produce for us, Brenda?"

"What about all the unpaid taxes and mismanaged balance sheets? I am the one who has to organize this, since you lacked the ability!" Brenda raged. "Ten grand is exactly thirty percent of what I turned for the month on yours and Bennie's business enterprises."

"I don't believe it! You're holding back on us," Sheila exclaimed.

"You both are out of your cotton picking minds! Am I gonna have to show you every little detail, month after month, so that you'll eventually believe me? I mean, come on with this!" Brenda said.

The following month generated a much better take, but the situation for Brenda was the same. Whines, cries, and accusations of holding out were callously and very rudely thrown into Brenda's face. The less the couple could have done was have been thankful someone somewhere was willing to organize their disorganized heap. Sometimes Brenda regretted taking on the responsibility, considering the overwhelming lack of gratitude.

Late at night, she would often walk out the front door to the swinging chair on the live oak tree by the dirt driveway, swinging back and forth in the comfortable half-moon glow and nighttime air. The mental escape from business concerns felt very relaxing. In the far distance, she would hear the hoot of an owl and the wail of coyote, along with the shrill call of a Whip-Poor-Will somewhere among the largest live oaks. Now and then, she would notice the distant flicker of a shadow spectrum in the soft moonlight.

CHAPTER FOURTEEN

THE BIG MOMENT ARRIVES

It had been almost a year now since Donald signed over his own portion of his family estate to Brenda, and she had been placed in charge of Emogene's inheritance by the Ludlow family elders. In the end, such was honestly the best move that could have ever occurred. Her sisters simply could not uphold the strong Ludlow family tradition of business and enterprise. They lacked the intellectual capacity for excellence, preferring only to embrace rude frivolities that failed to even make her laugh.

There were a number of reasons why her sisters failed so miserably at virtually everything. One of the greatest strikes against them was their own idealistic level of moral expectation and sense of social duty. In business, as everybody knows, the only true moral is increasing one's bottom line. Every other consideration is secondary, no matter how much entrepreneurs may attempt to feign otherwise. Let it be said here, where the only religion is whatever it takes to win, and undeniable proof of the supreme divinity in charge of enterprise and negotiation is the magnitude level of one's own success.

While swinging underneath the live oak in the moonlight, Brenda had given the Ludlow family history and traditions great thought over the past year. This new DNA technology is a fabulous achievement, she reasoned with herself. All areas of what makes a person human are linked to genes, including personality, health, intelligence, and one's likelihood of success in general. No doubt, she had reasoned in silence as she swung, there was a gene for raw creativity, and those most likely to be successful in business.

A family will soon be able to literally isolate both the physical and intellectually superlative elements inside its own patrimonial diadem, then extract any element running counter. Thus, every child born would be outstanding, rather than only a rude base average sum total determined by an inescapable fact of history or chance of nature. Such dawning technology had to stand among the most spectacular achievements of mankind, no matter what any idealist and moralist attempt to claim otherwise. Clan Ludlow deserved to stand among both physical and intellectual god-men, where all sub-plateau humanoids only bow in service to them. This silent inner thought, when it flashed through her mind, often made her smile in public when there was otherwise no reason to.

There had been a great stir for a while all across Ludlow Estate. The antique plantation chapel nearby was now fully decorated with spring time flowers. The azaleas, roses, lavish tulip beds, and chrysanthemum were blooming. The marvelous wisteria hung the sweet odor of lavender honey all throughout the air anywhere on the grounds. The song birds were singing sweetly. Sensations aroused on the inside were those of complete exhilaration at what the forthcoming year holds in store. The talk of anticipated adventure saturated virtually every conversation, from one perspective of consideration or another.

Brenda found it exciting, to her own astonishment, going down to the local bridal shop for the purpose of selecting the most elegant bridal dress. The elder females traveled with them, since no event occurred inside Clan Ludlow outside of elder approval. Money was never a factor for consideration, since the entire clan contributed.

Weddings were very important to the family. Such was the reason elders chose partners for young family members. Certain factors must be present in families selected, such as physical features, intelligence quotas, and an ever prevailing factor of family achievement.

A family must possess physical appearances of British Royalty. Spanish Royalty might work at times, but the general preference was Scandinavian to British. The family absolutely must be filled with surgeons, successful prosperous business owners, property owners, successful creative people, statesmen, and high end government employees on some admirable level.

Average rank and file was simply not acceptable, and often viewed as being an outright insult to the Clan in general. The future of Clan Ludlow rested in a youngster's personal choices and associations made. Associations with lower species of humanity, was simply not allowed, and family members were willing to take drastic measures in discouraging it. A prevailing fear among elders always was one of imposing government policy, compelling an opposite approach. The very thought insulted every conviction the elders in charge held. Who among the Clan was going to carry the astonishing torch of Ludlow superiority into its dazzling new apex?

There were others among Clan Ludlow held into an identical cast, but her sisters were not admirable family members, according to her own comprehension of family standards and expectations. Their associations, their fruitless pondering, their entertainment, their humor, their choices in careers, if they had any, were far too purulent and base for membership in this blood clan. This was the reason she seldom, if ever, laughed at any of their so called jokes. Thankfully her sisters submitted to the will of Clan Elders who dutifully selected their mates, but they didn't truly deserve them, from a blood right perspective as it relates to superior accomplishment.

The day selected was the fifteenth of April. This was the date the estate was signed over to the state's historical society. This was also the day Drunken Run was acquired by the first Ludlow, the day the first timber was laid in the manor house. There had been many firsts on this day in Ludlow's history over the years.

The plantation chapel was actually rather large, as far as chapels go. The building alone covered maybe half an acre, if not slightly more. It was actually an old wood framed baptist church building still used for services. The title of chapel was more of a nickname the elders assigned. The fifteen feet tall solid oak double doors seemed massive, yet simple to open with a minimum of effort. Once one was inside, the place felt heavy with the Holy Spirit.

Brenda was actually recruited to participate in the ceremony, but chose only to play the part of the spectator. She enjoyed the idea of watching, and feeling that somehow she played a part in the culmination of this event. On the day of the event, she took her seat among the family members. She stood proudly with the others as the bride and groom entered. She was a witness when the parson asked the sacred questions.

"Dearly beloved, do you take this man as your lawfully wedded husband?" he said.

"I do," was the reply.

"And do you sir, take this beloved lady, to have and to hold, and to cherish, until death do thus part?," asked the parson.

"I do," was the reply.

When the golden band symbolizing eternal union was placed

upon her sister Emogene's left hand, Brenda couldn't help but wonder if it would really go unbroken. What was he thinking as he placed this upon her hand? Did he secretly desire another somewhere out there? How much did he pay for the ring? Where did it originate? Was it the one of his great grandmother, as heirloom tradition dictated?

After the couple made their exit, every person made their way back to the manor house on Drunken Run Estate. It was in here where the wedding reception transpired. No expense was spared. The entire affair was catered, lasting well after sun down. Men were allowed to dance with the bride, and women were allowed to have a final dance with the groom. Brenda assumed her proper place, taking her own turn at dancing with the groom. She sensed an air of nervousness within him as she did so.

"Well, the finalization in our negotiations has at long last been made, Donald," she whispered into his ear.

"Emogene senses something is up," he replied.

"How do you know?" Brenda asked as a smirk jerked across her face.

"I can tell it in her general mannerism," he replied.

"Have you informed her yet?" Brenda curtly asked.

"No, not yet," was his reply.

"I'll leave the choice do so and the job itself, up to you Donald," she smiled.

"Thank you," he replied as they continued to dance.

"How do you think she shall react when she does find out?" Brenda asked.

"She'll make my life miserable. I may be rested assured," he replied.

Brenda only smiled in complete satisfaction to herself as they danced.

The day after the wedding, Brenda motored back out to McAdoo Jolly's church. He always left the front door to the church wide open when he was in the back rooms working. It was a dumb move, but he always did so. Honestly, there was much that McAdoo Jolly did that was dumb, for lack of a better descriptive word. She gingerly pulled the front door closed as she eased inside on the cat's paws, making her way toward the back room behind the choir loft. He kept his back toward the door, and sneaking up on him granted her a special effect on approaching him. Tension seemed to hang thickly in the air.

"So I see you're hard at work again, oh Jolly Mon, eh?" she said.

He appeared to leap out of his skin, forcing himself to turn around. It was immediately obvious he didn't want to speak with her.

"What might I do for you, I shudder to ask?" he strained to say.

"I have another task assignment for you," she announced as she slowly approached him, "and you're going to accept it," she firmly stated.

His eyes were firmly fixed upon the lower curvature of her well-proportioned body. She chuckled slightly as she noticed.

"So what is it this time?," he hesitatingly asked.

"Here is twenty thousand hard cash," she said as she tossed it out on his desk. Jolly thumbed through it, licking his lips as he counted the amount.

"So what must I do now?" he squeaked as he gazed upward

from his desk.

"You're going to visit Pop Top MacGraw over at the garage where he works first light tomorrow. Tell him Bennie McNeil got a new wine colored Ford F150 maybe six months ago. He's already talking about getting an oil change, and he always goes in that garage. You drop ten thousand down in front of Pop Top and tell him to break the nut on the front wheel carriage pinion bar. Tell him to wear gloves and never touch anything. If he refuses your offer of ten, offer twelve grand, but no more. Anything left over after ten, you may keep as your own for doing this job," Brenda said to him.

"What! What kind of coo-coo bird has been nesting in that head of yours now? There is no way in hell I am going to do this, Brenda!"

"You're gonna do it, or else I'll destroy you with all I have on you already. You're gonna do it just like you're gonna take care of all my most perverted fetishes when I want you to, bitch! Do you hear me? You are gonna do it!" she screams as she slaps him four consecutive times across his face with her opened right palm. "You're a bitch, but you're my otherwise worthless bitch, and I own you, Jolly Mon! At least you are good for something when you are my pathetic bitch. Do you have that? I own you Jolly!"

The preacher hung his head, running his fingers through his own hair.

"My God, oh my God, what have I gotten myself into?" he whined. He began to weep.

Brenda suddenly fires out her right palm, slapping the preacher viciously across the side of his hanging head.

"Shut up your pathetic blubbering, you filthy piece of trash! I know you love it when I speak this way to you," she growled through tightly clenched teeth.

"By the way, before I leave, I have another oral task for you that I have been desperately craving for a while now. Let's just say it's a secret addiction I have that absolutely must be satisfied from time to time."

She began snatching her panties down.

"No! No! Oh no," he whined as she seemingly ripped her panties off, "not this! I simply don't feel right about doing this, Miss Ludlow."

"That's right, you call me Misses cause mine is made of candy. It's been awhile now, but you are so damn good at it," she told him as she tossed her panties to the floor.

"You sit down in that chair, and I am going to throw my left leg up onto that desk, and you are going to lick the flavor off my lifesaver until I command for you to stop. Do you hear me, you dog?" she growled as she tossed her leg up, turned around, and bent over. "Now you are employed by me for life! Do you have that? I constructed you from raw dung, and crafted you into an astonishing success, Jolly, and now you must do for me part of what you are good for. The other part is to simply follow my orders, or I'll surely lay you to waste!"

CHAPTER FIFTEEN

THE REALIZATION

Four months passed, and Brenda was taking in profit hand over fist. She was tempted to purchase herself a brand new Alexis, but she withheld on the urge. Too many questioning eyes might take notice, she reasoned with herself.

The wreck was devastating. Bennie and Sheila were driving along interstate 95 and suddenly crossed headlong into oncoming traffic. Both were laid up at the hospital in Wilmington, she had been informed, and were in comatose. Both were scheduled to be transported to Chapel Hill very soon. Three days later, they were moved by air transport. Brenda decided to motor out and pay them both a visit.

The receptionist informed her that they were located in room 302 and 303 on the third floor. The entire facility held a heavy, dismal sensation in the air. Other family members were gathered inside, paying visits to both. She entered her sister's room first. Her sister appeared to be slumbering in her bed, although she had numerous scars and bruises upon her body that were all too obvious. Her mother wept as she gazed upon her.

"Why do you cry, mother?" Brenda asked. "She's in one of the top medical facilities on earth. They'll save her."

"They're only human, child," her mother told her. "The head surgeon has already informed us to prepare for the worst. The elders are preparing her grave as we speak. She shall soon lay with the others in the family plot, my intuition informs me."

"What about Bennie?" Brenda asked her mother.

"Since they were not yet married, Bennie's family will be responsible for him," she said.

"But I like to think positive. They'll both make it, mother."

"And I do likewise, but I am also a realist, child. When a chief medical specialist at Chapel Hill or Duke informs one his time is nigh, the odds are definitely not with him being otherwise," spoke her mother.

"I have asked many questions about everything over the years," said Brenda, glaring off into space. "Is life even worth living, anyway? I have often found myself saying it isn't."

"Child, one's destiny is in their own hands," replied her mother. "What we make it is what it is."

"I have been told that all my life," said Brenda, "but is it really? What could Bennie and Sheila have done to prevent this great misfortune?"

"Child, in spite of all the questions, we are supposed to keep our eyes focused on the light at the end of the tunnel," her mother said. "Your greatest fortune in life was to be born into Clan Ludlow. Your financial future is secure, which is far more than most ever have, I can assure you. You shall only marry into the best of bloods. We have your back on that. You may witness the burger flipper at one of the fast-food places, or the street sweeper, and have confidence in knowing that you'll never have to take such a position only for mere sustenance. Others have no such choices in life, and would love to exchange places with you. I can solemnly promise you that much, dear daughter."

Her sister continued to lay in compete comatose as Brenda and her mother spoke. Brenda couldn't help but feel she somehow heard their words as she lay. A sudden twitch in her lip was almost as if she wanted to speak, Brenda imagined. She decided to step into the other room to visit Bennie and pay respects to his family.

When she entered Bennie's room, he also lay in comatose there in the bed. His mother held her head in her hands. She walked over, laying a hand on the elder lady's shoulder.

"What's his status?" Brenda gently asked.

"His surgeon is the same one your sister has," his mother informed her. "The prognosis is grim, same as your sisters."

"Which surgeon is that?" asked Brenda.

"Dr. Jim Dyson," his mother replied, "and a very fine doc he is," she sobbed.

"What does he look like?" asked Brenda.

"His body is cut, somewhat muscular," spoke Bennie's mother. "He stands maybe six feet two and wears a thick black mustachio. He combs his hair straight back, parted slightly on the left side. He's tough to miss and far too handsome for one to simply ignore."

"I don't have the right words to speak," exclaimed Brenda. "I sincerely hope the doc is wrong."

The door opened suddenly. In walked three nurses and the master surgeon himself. Brenda instantly recognizes him.

"Hello," he said, " my name is Dr. James Dyson. I am the surgeon in charge of the case with this man and the lady next door. Who are you?" the doctor asked Brenda.

"I am Brenda Ludlow, sister to the lady next door. You know, this man was her fiance."

"I heard she had one, and we'll do the best we can for both of them, but right now, the general prognosis is not good."

"What credentials do you possess?" Brenda thought to ask.

"I come from a long line of medical professionals reaching more than four seventy year generations backward," the surgeon informed her. "My people have been medical experts dealing with beast and man. I haven't time to speak right now, Mrs. Brenda. There is much work to do."

The doctor spoke a few incomprehensible words to his assistants, and soon they were wheeling the bed of Benny away.

"Where are they taking him?" Brenda asked his mother.

"Into the intensive care unit for operations," his mother replied. "Your sister is already there now."

"Did it happen while I was in here?" Brenda asked.

"Oh doll, they got your sister right before they picked up Bennie here," his mother exclaimed.

"Have they said what the prognosis is?" Brenda asked in a near sudden gasp.

"Not good," his mother said. "There is brain, liver, and heart damage from this crash, not to mention damage to the spinal column, the doc told us, Brenda. The elders in both families are right to proceed with funeral preparations."

"I don't want to hear that!" Brenda exclaimed in tears, with both hands over her ears.

"You are one of the household adults now. You must hear it. Such possibilities are always a reality,"

Bennie's mother stated.

The statement of Bennie's mother echoed as if it were made on the threshold of a virtual nightmare. Somehow, it seemed, she was mysteriously transported away from the dismal scene. She awoke in her awoke in her own cottage bedroom. She arose, nobody else was home, it appeared. She walked through a vacated home, although in the far distance on the outside, she thought she heard voices. Suddenly, the front door opened and Emogene strode through.

"Get your clothes on now," she thundered.

"Why, what on earth's going on?" Brenda gasped.

"Your sister's funeral, that's what!" Emogene told her.

"When did it happen?" Brenda struggled to ask.

"Evening before last," Emogene told her.

"Where was I?" Brenda struggled to ask.

"Unconscious. You passed out when the announcement was made, and we feared a mental breakdown of some sort," Emogene told her.

Brenda rushed back to her room, putting on her long coal colored silken dress and sable head veil. Her sister wore antique black. There was no note of joy in any of this. When her clothes were donned, both loaded up into her sister's car, slowly motoring out toward a crowd gathered by the old family cemetery. The elders were taking their positions. Her sister's opened coffin stood upon a pedestal near to the open grave site covered on every side by flowers.

The general sensation for Brenda was beyond reality. For her, she couldn't believe what was occurring. Had she been possessed by some demon? Cursed? When she pondered a possibility of being cursed, an inexplicable sensation of solving the puzzle fell upon her, but why? The elder, George Ebeneezer III, positioned himself to speak.

"Dear family, friends, and associates, we have gathered here today for the purpose of bearing witness to the finalizing conclusion of a terrible story. Things in life happen, with no explanation, I might say. We are all aware of these realities, are we not? This scene is so tough to fathom, much less accept, but in the end, all of us have no alternative choice. May we all now align single file and walk past for the final observation?"

The crowd formed a single file line. Each person walked past, laying a white carnation into the coffin. Her father wept bitterly while her mother attempted to climb into the coffin with her sister. Several elders rushed to restrain her, taking her to a parked vehicle where it was said they would give her a calming injection. Her sister almost appeared at her best laying in an eternal slumber. Brenda said "goodbye forever, sister," as she did the holy catholic cross sign by tapping both shoulders and her forehead. Brenda couldn't help but wonder if her sister knew anything, or everything, or simply lay there enveloped in an absolute oblivion of endless comatose.

The graveyard assistants soon closed the coffin, lifting it for transportation over toward the nearby open grave site. As they did so, the elder commenced speaking.

"Ladies and gentlemen 'tis always such a pity when life expires, but so much more during the person's best years of youth. What might have Sheila Ludlow ever become? Who might she have wound up being? None of us shall ever know now. She was a hard worker who loved family and friends. She was a lady dedicated to a love of family, community, and dedicated to preserving its history. She was soon to be wed. Her fiance' also is being laid to rest at this very moment. Such a tragic story with

218

broad effects this is."

The coffin was being lowered as the elder concluded his address. The grave was being filled while the final address resumed.

"In the name of eternal God in heaven, we commend this humble corpse. The body is merely a vessel for containing the soul. This vessel of dust is returning to the earth while the soul ascends into a new life beyond. If she is guilty of sin, oh Lord, please purge her, per our humble request, and allow her entrance into your divine realm. For we ask this in the name of the Holy Father, The Son, and the Holy Ghost, Amen and Amen."

CHAPTER SIXTEEN

ANGEL OF DEATH ON THE MOVE

The past six months were too much for anybody to ever forget. The family, what remained of it, sat before the large table in the cottage home where Brenda was raised up. Uncle Monk, her parents, Emogene and Donald, sat around for morning breakfast. Uncle Monk cleared his throat as he sipped his coal colored coffee. The others quietened.

"I've consulted with the other family patriarchs, such as George Ebeneezer, and the conclusions are all the same.

"What conclusions?" asked Emogene, as her eyes rather nervously flicked over toward Donald.

"The most gifted family member should run Sheila's piece of the show here, and that's Brenda. We are compelled to proceed forward due to the realities of accomplishment. Few others in the family her age can even come close, I am sorry to say."

"Something doesn't appear right in this somehow," reiterated Emogene with an uncomfortable glint in her eyes.

"Appearances and opinions are inconsequential," replied Uncle Monk. "What we proceed forward upon are facts, and the finalizing note has already been signed, sealed, and delivered as I speak."

Emogene glanced around the table, hesitatingly, announcing somewhat nervously.

"I have more news along those same lines. Bennie signed his total inherited share in his family stake over to Brenda, so she nets this in the bag to boot."

"Yes child, the family is already aware," pleasantly informed Uncle Monk.

Uncle Monk turned toward Brenda, bowing gracefully as he spoke.

"Unto the most gifted and accomplished go the spoils. No person your own age in Clan Ludlow is qualified more than you. The elders have all spoken."

Brenda only smiled, making no reply.

Emogene glared at Brenda hard, then glowered around the table into every blank face present, snapping back in the direction of Uncle Monk.

"When does morality ever become an issue in this family, Uncle?"

"Morality? On whose watch?" replied Uncle Monk.

Emogene gave no reply.

"Where lies the charge of immorality? What specifics are being defined as immoral?" Uncle Monk asked.

Emogene commenced to sob as she spoke.

"Brenda has always been a gold digger. The whole family should know better," Emogene gasped.

"When does ambition become immoral?," asked Uncle Monk. " Give me a better specific, please, and I shall make an appeal for reconsideration of the choice already made. However, I may assure each and every person, right here and now, where such considerations in anticipation of negative possibilities have already been made. Any suggestion of a possibility for immorality has been overshadowed by raw gilded accomplishment, hence the deliberated conclusion stands firm upon its own legs."

Emogene slowly turned toward Brenda, gritting her teeth.

"I hope you are happy, sister!" spouted Emogene, glowering hard at Brenda.

Emogene arose from the table wearing an angry expression, walking into the rearmost area of the house. Donald soon glanced around nervously, arising from his seat and politely excusing himself, then followed.

"Convictions without justification have no place in the logic of this family," spoke Uncle Monk in unerring confidence.

"We're kind of amazed ourselves," spoke Brenda's mother. "Family conflict has always been present, however."

"I am analyzing the encompassing situation carefully," replied Uncle Monk. "I wonder who Brenda shall marry. Are there any indications of possibility?"

"None that we know of, and no interest in doing so, indicated," spoke her father.

Brenda arose from the table, going into her bedchamber. She donned her best business attire, being a calcimine mid-thigh level lace skirt. The immediate appearance on her delicately shaped, proportioned body form was very elegant, to say the least.

"Going out dressed so well already this morning, child?" her mother asked inquisitively as Brenda walked past the couch.

"I'll not be gone long. I have a few matters to address and close out this morning," she spoke as she walked out the door of the house.

Brenda allowed her car to warm before moving on out. She motored down the hard surfaced road for twenty minutes, then turned left down what appeared as a narrow two rut dirt road bordered on either side by tall standing oak trees, eventually curbing leftward directly into McAdoo Jolly's drive way. She exited her car, walking up to stand on the steps underneath an extended antique shelter. She knocked three times. There was no answer. She glanced around, noticing his primary vehicle parked underneath a live oak shade tree. He was definitely home; she muttered to herself. She knocked three more times. The door creaked open slightly, and a trembling, rather pale, gaunt figure of McAdoo Jolly appeared. He donned a mysterious black cloak and hood.

"Ah, 'tis only you," he gasped. "Come on inside," he said.

"Who else were you expecting?" Brenda spouted with a chuckle.

"We've both got trouble, Brenda, real trouble," he replied with a cold shudder as he shut the front door of his house.

"Who's got trouble? Why?" she inquired with a hard look.

"They're asking questions, Brenda," he whispered, glancing all around.

"Who's asking questions?" Brenda spouted.

"Four IRS agents have already stopped by here, looking all around. They dropped by the church, asking if this building and grounds were all there was. I warned you in regard to all of this business about using the church as a tax haven to an excessive extent, Brenda," Jolly whimpered. "You've abused the honorable privilege. Now all of this activity must be justified. There are cracks in our system, Brenda, and these investigators are gradually seeing through them."

Brenda smiled with confidence at the preacher. She walked into the house as if in absolute control, taking a seat in a leather swivel chair by a desk. She spun around playfully, laughing with a sick child-like glowing glee as she did, pausing suddenly to face him with an angry glare in her eyes.

"Sounds like you've got problems to me, big boy," she said as she glanced upward into his face from the seated chair.

"There's more, Brenda," he nervously sighed as he spoke.

"Like what?," she asked, as she began glowering at his crotch area. Her angry expression suddenly transformed into a harlot's smile. Every now and then, his coal black cloak would part as he spoke, revealing tight purple bikini underwear, and a massively large bulge snaking nearly all the way across his midsection. In his fear of the emerging developments, he forgot all about it. Brenda released a demonic chuckle as she began licking her blood-red lips.

"An investigator dropped by here. He claimed he had spoken with Pop Top regarding a few matters of serious concern. Brenda, he asked me if I knew Pop Top."

"So, what did you tell him?, oh Jolly Mon," she asked as she gently tugged upon the string belt of his cloak. The cloak slid open.

"Yum, I hope this gracious lollipop you are blessed with is as good today as it was the last time I tried it," she gasped, licking her lips and smiling a harlot's smile. "I'm kind of hungry, Jolly Mon. I have a real fondness for a nice, big, juicy snake, Jolly."

"He said Pop Top mentioned my name," Jolly shuddered, "and told him to speak with me, Brenda."

She commenced kissing the bulge in his thin purple bikini underwear. She paused, glancing upward as she began gently messaging his bulge. "Did you ever have any other business with him, other than what I put you onto?" She lowered again to kiss the bulge in his bikini underwear.

"I was double crossed in a real estate deal a year or so ago," Jolly gasped as if he hesitated to tell her. "I paid Pop Top handsomely to even the score. So he set fire to the man's house and barn on my behalf, reducing it to ashes."

Brenda eased down his underwear, commencing to kiss and lick his huge testicles, and his ever growing organ as he continued speaking.

"Hmm, yum, so what's the problem?" she smacked when she drew backward, while glanced upward and speaking, then continuing on with her deed.

"The man and his family perished in the flames," he struggled to say and breathe as Brenda swallowed his huge erect shaft all the way down to his stomach.

"So what are you going to do about your growing problem, there?" she gasped when she finally backed off.

"I milled around and found a biker with a beef against Pop Top," he struggled to inform her. "Something about a dope deal MacGraw flinched on once upon a time. I paid him to take care of Pop Top next Saturday over in old man, Codger's Pool Room," he struggled, flinched, and gasped to say as Brenda hungrily flicked and licked her unnaturally long tongue all over his erect pulsating organ and upon the front and back sides of his retracting billiard ball sized testicles. She loved hissing like a poisonous viper when she did this, for reasons she could never explain.

"Well, you've been a good little boy, Jolly Mon, now haven't you?" she said in a whinny child-like voice when she finally backed away.

The two made their way into Jolly's home. Brenda ripped off her clothes, falling backward across the couch. Jolly, in spite of being an impractical, idealistic nerd with all of his faults, was a red hot lover, never holding back on anything. She liked that, a man with solid nerve, and game for anything when it was her heart's desire. She loved it when she could command him to do something, anything, and he would jump down and simply do it, without hesitation. When the action finally climaxed, reaching its grand conclusion as he assaulted her from behind with his mighty sword of flesh, she glanced around to inform him of another money drop arriving where she needed the write off. He fell off onto the bed upon reaching climax, gasping for breath.

"Brenda, I simply can't! The IRS agents have already been showing up on these premises, asking dozens of questions. We'll be audited come tax time, if not in court before," he pleads.

"You know the penalty for noncompliance with my commands! Now do it, or else, Jolly Mon."

He began weeping.

"I'll be ruined!," he sniveled.

"Jump down here and gratify me orally, like you already know I like, and do it now! I want you to savor my life saver, now!" she growled through tightly clenched teeth.

When he did as she asked, as he was drawing backward, she slapped him violently seven consecutive times on the rear of his head and ears.

"That'll teach you to be bad and even think of disobeying my orders!"

When it all finally ended, Brenda arose, replacing her clothing, and heading slowly toward the front door. She paused before stepping out, turning toward Jolly, slumping backward upon the bed, weeping.

"You shut up your pathetic crying. You have too much work to do for any of that. I'll be back to check up on you in a few days. You hear me, Jolly Mon?"

Jolly glanced up toward Brenda.

"How can you continue doing this to me? A bigger question is why? I am going into permanent ruination. You know that by now, don't you?" he whimpered as he wept.

Brenda never made a word in reply as she turned and headed back out toward the door. She pushed the door snugly, too. The preacher sat idle, glaring hard at the door she exited from for a period, feeling like hours. He had nowhere to go, and not much more to say.

The next weekend finally came around, after an enduring, involved week at the Urban Planning office. Friday afternoon, she decided on a whim to drop by Jolly's place for another visit. She paused at the door, knocking.

"Jolly, you home?"

She glanced around, spying his automobile parked in the yard. He was home alright, but something didn't feel kosher about the general scene. She glanced around furthermore, spotting his wood shed and barn up against the tree line across the yard from the house. She casually walked over. The wood shed was a three-sided barn, underneath which stood a stack of freshly cut and split hard wood of various sorts. His barn stood nearby.

She noticed a trail in the dried leaves going around the barn behind it. She followed this trail, and as she rounded the corner there she saw the stiffened body of McAdoo Jolly hanging from a nine inch diameter limb of an ancient live oak tree.

At first the sight astonished her, but the stiffened hanging corpse of the preacher gently turned in the light morning breeze, causing an eerie, inexplicable calming sensation to fall upon her. She gazed upon this corpse for a few moments, then slowly turned, heading back across the yard toward her car. She entered it, driving away slowly, deciding it was time to return home. A mysterious sensation of unquestionable satisfaction coursed through her veins as her car moved forward along the highway.

Tonight was a special time for her, she reflected as she parked. A certain guest promised in sincere earnest to pay her a visit. She had been seeing him in secret for some time, often traveling way up into Durham to meet with him. Going to such great lengths for anybody was totally out of her character, to be honest about it. It wasn't that her family wouldn't approve, oh they were going to adore him high above all others; it was only that the time of her relationship would not be appropriate, all other considerations being made.

When she arrived back home, she spent the remainder of the evening lounging around with the family. Old rivalries even appeared to calm somewhat, she told herself. Eighteen hundred finally rolled around. A heavy knock was heard on the front door. Uncle Monk carefully opened it. Before them stood a somewhat tall, slightly muscled man, wearing a thick black mustachio. He wore his coal black hair slicked back and parted to the left side.

"What may I do for you, sir?" asked Uncle Monk.

"Is Brenda home?" he asked rather humbly.

"She sure is, right over there on the couch," Uncle Monk replied as he pointed. "Who are you now? I feel as if we've somehow met before."

"I'm Dr. Dyson, James Dyson, to be precise. Most refer to me as Jim."

He casually strode over toward Brenda with a macho aspect of the natural limp in the way he moved. She liked that about this man. She calculatingly allowed them to near being intimate on three occasions already, but then tactfully withheld submission at the finalizing moment. Her intent was to set the hook solidly, then reel this man in. Not only was he a master surgeon, he was also an accomplished business man all in his own right. He was self-made. He originated from a long line of medical professionals, but he labored intensely for his own success.

Besides that, she was already being sexually satisfied in every way imaginable, but not for nothing, mind you. No son of a pig was ever going to touch her, even in the slightest, unless he paid her demanded price down to the very last dime, in full. There was something in it for her other than mere gratification alone, or the act in question simply wasn't going to happen at all. If she found he wasn't hung enough or wasn't any good at using it, she would still go through the motion if he handed her enough in her personal requests to go with it, yet she never refrained from finding another wealth laden stud to carry her on through.

This man, however, she was going to pursue differently, and she always got what she wanted. Way back in high school, her entire eleventh grade English class was asked to describe itself individually, in a single word, and only the word bitch sufficed to intimate her story the way it needed telling; and she was proud of the fact, even way back then. Frequently, she wore tactfully revealing clothing standing in good taste, only allowing him to have a hint at what lay in store. If only he continued being a good little boy. He took his seat immediately beside her on the couch.

"My, how you seem mighty cheer-filled today, Miss Brenda," the doc said with a happy clip in his speech..

"Well, I have so much to be cheerful about, Dr. Dyson," she replied with a smiling glee.

"Don't we all, if we only search for it a bit?" the doctor replied in an agreeing tone of voice.

"You know, some of us sit on top of the entire world, and don't even realize it. Wouldn't you agree, Dr. Dyson?," Brenda said.

"There may certainly be times when one could find him or herself in an advantageous position, and not know how to take advantage of it, that's for sure," the doctor replied in a courteous voice tone.

"Life is funny like that, I think," Brenda said with a slight chuckle.

"You certainly have a glittering smile stretched all the way across your face, that's for sure," the doc said. "What grand adventures have you held the winning hand in, Miss Brenda?"

Brenda continued to smile away from him, then sighed on a cheerful note, turning to face the doctor.

"So let's talk about your adventures, doc, enough about mine."

"My adventures? I work night and day in the surgical room. I tried hard to save your sister and her fiance, as I have so many others. I have high moments when I succeed, and low times when I fail. It breaks my heart to see people and families hurt, so, as I know, yours certainly has," the doc said.

Brenda sighed deeply.

"Indeed, the going has been very tough for all of us. All we may do is look forward to the coming day, and try to make the most of it, Dr. Dyson," she said.

"Does it ever improve, Miss Brenda?" asked the Doctor.

"Each passing dark day seems to somehow hold a spec of light in it more than the one before. That's all that I can say right now," said Brenda. "I force myself to smile while I search diligently for some type of good in it."

"Have you found any as yet?," politely asked the Doctor.

"Only that sissy and Bennie are in a better place. No more ruthless competition. No more strife. No more envy. No more pain." She turned to face the Doctor. "No more disagreement, only a never ending state of dreamlike slumber for them both now. Such is the only good in it I can find."

The doctor continued speaking about business, about friends, and his family. He wore white casual sports pants, a white sports coat, with a shiny purple satin formal night time events shirt.. His shirt had the top two buttons loosened. A solid gold chain hung across a tanned, somewhat hairy chest. Her eyes scanned downward when he wasn't noticing, down his stomach, down to his belt.., and his lower area. She could see much explicit detail in outline, and was greatly impressed, but fought with herself not to notice.

She was going to reduce this man into a groveling, wasted heap of quivering flesh, laying helplessly at her feet first, feasting from the palm of her hand and granting her every request in property and gold, before he could even dream of any carnal pleasures happening. She feigned complete innocence when she merely pecked him, after even an expensive date. She knew what she was doing and was the world's best at it. Nobody anywhere couldn't tell Brenda Ludlow anything.

In time, the entire story was out all over Mount Horeb Village. Pop Top was met at old man Codger's Pool Room by three patched in bikers. Some claimed the group called themselves The Rowdy Buccaneers, other claimed something else. The three bikers challenged Pop Top to a thousand dollar billiard game. Pop Top took the challenge. When he lost, he didn't have the pay out on him, so the three took him down, and when his pockets were riffled, he didn't have but a hundred dollars on him. They pressed him to ride with them, telling him to take a ride or a bullet, his choice.

They carried him deep down in a place known as Bingo Swamp by the locals. It was near another area known on a map as Colen Williams Bay. So the local legend claims, both of his hands were tied behind his back, then a nine millimeter was placed directly upon the back of his neck where the skull meets, and the trigger pulled. His twitching body sank down into the dark bourbon tinted, slow moving water, where the alligators and the man-sized catfish had him reduced down into morsels inside two hours' time. Soon even the bones were gone.

Some fisherman discovered his weathered and worn castaway boots by the shore, his hat and his shredded cutoff denim shirt were found floating in the water. The police dredged the place, turning up nothing, as was expected by the locals. The three mysterious bikers claimed by local legend were never found.

Soon an investigation into McAdoo Jolly's obvious suicide produced suggested connections, but nothing definitive could never be ascertained. It did vaguely appear where Jolly paid the three twenty thousand dollars for the job, but no details could be pieced together as to why, or in regard to details leading to the payment, if such a payment ever occurred at all, law enforcement intimated.

The secret in regard to Jolly's tax hedge was out, however. While Jolly and Bennie were out of reach, Donald was beginning to feel the heat when investigators thundered on his front door at 0300 in the morning. The tension was mounting, but Donald knew nothing, and the investigators had not yet proven where any misdeed was done, even on Jolly's part. Everything at this point was only suspicion, but at the same time it was all enough to arouse deep curiosity on the part of Emogene, so she commenced her own investigation into matters at hand.

CHAPTER SEVENTEEN

NEW SITUATIONS AND TRYING CIRCUMSTANCES

Donald Grimesly was pretty darn successful financially. He was married to Clan Ludlow now for a couple of months over a year. His business endeavors were excelling beyond anything he could have ever imagined. Deep down, however, he gradually hated the fact that credit for this excellence went to Brenda Ludlow. How was she accomplishing such feats of turning everything she touched into gold? Accomplishing such levels of excellence could never be done in today's America by legal means, as most thinking people know who have attempted achieving financial excellence. Maybe these investigators continuously dropping by asking questions was a hint of possibility. His wife, Emogene Ludlow, certainly thought so.

"It's all falling into place with me now, Donald," she said. "I knew I smelled a rat in all of this business, since it simply sounded way too good to be true!"

"What in heaven's name are you speaking in regard to, Emogene?" he asked.

"It's all going back to the same source. My gut is telling me, and that source is my sister, Donald."

"Oh yeah, well, what does she have to do with anything?" Donald asked.

"She has plenty, Donald. She was often seen in Codger's Pool Room speaking with McAddo Jolly. The filthy pig called himself a preacher, but he was in really only an aging shiest-er, outright thief, and a horrendous pervert besides everything else."

"So what are you saying, Emogene?" Donald asked.

"I'm saying I sense a possibility where Jolly was using his church as a tax hedge," spoke Emogene with firmness in her voice. "That was how he could afford those fancy cars and the heavy fixing up on that old house he lived in, not to mention the nine thousand dollar large screen TV I have always heard about, with the most advanced satellite viewing system. I bet we both can guess what that filthy, perverted son-of-a bitch spends his time watching. That hypocritical bastard keeps American Ecstasy in business! Personally, I wouldn't let my dog go to his church."

"So, what's with it, Emogene?" Donald asked as he held both palms up and out by his side. "I mean, damn all of this ridiculous talk here. So what about it? Frankly, I don't give a happy damn what Jolly does myself."

"Those investigators came here, Donald. Your name must have been tied onto the write off claim somehow. That means you've been allowing my sister to invest our wealth, I'll bet!"

"So what if I have? She's good at turning profit, Emogene," Donald said. "You can't deny reality, like Uncle Monk said, no matter how much you may want to."

"So that's it, eh? My sister has been behind the scenes all along in this glittering new success of yours, huh?"

Donald made no immediate reply. He only struggled with

himself to remain straight faced through the verbal assault.

"Well, you just wait," spouted Emogene. "I am going to confront her over at the old cottage home when she finally arrives today."

"So what are you making of it, Emogene?" Donald asked.

"What am I making of it? Well, Mr. Glittering Success., let's just say I know my own sister, and I don't like the smell of things around here. All of this around here smells more like shit right now than ever before!"

Emogene huffed out of their new apartment in town, motoring on down to the cottage back at Drunken Run. It was near three in the evening, and Brenda would be home soon, if she wasn't already. When Emogene walked through the door, Brenda was seated on the couch calmly speaking with her parents and Uncle Monk. Emogene huffed over to where she sat.

"Could you step outside with me, for a moment?" she gasped in near rage. "We have a bone to pick between us," Emogene said.

"Sure, but what's bugging you, sis?" Brenda half chuckled in surprise.

"Just step outside for a moment, please," Emogene spouted.

Brenda calmly arose from her comfortable seat, politely excusing herself, heading toward the front door. Emogene opened it and the two ladies stepped outside, carefully closing it behind them.

"An investigator arrived in our place the other day, asking what we knew about the death of McAdoo Jolly," Emogene asked. "You know that, don't you?"

"I don't know anything about this, sis. What's it all to me, anyway?" Brenda gasped as she lay her opened right palm upon her chest. "What on earth did I have to do with anything, sis?"

"This thing doesn't take a genius for me to figure out," Emogene spouted. "I know you. You may fool most of the people some of the time, but you never have fooled me."

"Be out with it, sis," Brenda shrugged. "Please, I'm visiting with family today, myself."

"Donald's name was on that write off docket. You have been seen on several occasions in Codger's Pool Hall with Jolly in the past, Brenda. We are doing very well financially, to be honest. I can connect the dots here."

"Oh yeah, so what about it, eh? What's the problem, then? You should be thanking me, if such is the case here, sis."

"I highly suspect you many have intimidated Donald into handing over a share of his family enterprise because I know how you work, Brenda. You do nothing for the gift of giving. You always demand a beneficial exchange, receiving loads more than you ever pay out. God only knows what else might be going on!" Emogene gasped as tears welled up in her eyes.

"Oh yeah? Well, if that's the case, then you had just better get home so that you may keep an eye on your poor little hubby then, eh?"

Brenda smiled confidently, as she poised herself like she firmly controlled the scene she was abruptly caught up in.

Emogene turned, stomping off toward her parked car.

"This is not the end, and you haven't heard the last. I can promise that, Brenda," she roared as she opened the driver's door and stooped into her car. She virtually leaped into her car, then backed down the drive, and rode away.

Inside thirty minutes, Emogene was back at her and Donald's apartment. Donald sat on the outside deck gazing outward into the trees overlooking the old Tory Landing Park, bearing a disturbed expression upon his face of anticipating the worst. Emogene snatched open the door, huffed across the living room floor, ripping open the back door to the deck.

"We must talk, Donald!" she nearly screamed.

"Talk? About what?" he asked in earnest.

"Come on inside here, about much, to say the very least."

"What did your vixen sister have to say this time, Emogene?"

"She didn't say much about anything, but I smell a great big nasty rat in all of this."

"I don't understand," he said with a gasping sigh.

"It's the fact of what she didn't say, and isn't saying, that matters most here, Donald."

"Be out with it, woman! What in hell's name are you driving at here?" Donald demanded. "I demand to know what specifically is going on with all of this."

"Don't you dare stand there and tell me a bald faced lie, Donald Grimesly!"

He shrugged his shoulders.

"Did you sign over your share of your family estate and your own enterprise to her?"

He made no comment, only glanced down.

"I thought so, and I know she consummated the deal with you, didn't she, because I well know how my bitch sister operates?"

He glanced down, saying nothing.

"I thought so, you filthy rotten, dim-witted dog!"

Still, he held his head down, saying nothing in return.

"She always consummates these deals to give you a solid damning stake in the association, so that she might flip a switch in the future and invite your total emotional, financial, and social destruction. She would send you into prison or the graveyard, if she could do so with no lines reaching backward to her. What astonishes me most is that you and all the others are too damn foolish to see through this Satanic scheme of hers. Look what men get by allowing their greed laden minds to be soaked, and their God-forsaken cods to do their thinking for them! Look at all of this family disgrace and destruction that has been invited into the Ludlow household at large. Some have even claimed over the years that June Ludlow, from way back during the days of our family patriarchs, was cut from the same slice; and the reason her father, Reuben Ludlow, was murdered was due to her own gold digging and secret carnal shenanigans."

"You stand there making all of these claims and suggestions, but how can you verify them, Emogene? Any mind and mouth can make a claim, proving it is a very different story altogether," Donald told her.

"Well, just for your information, I've put an investigator, who is also a lawyer, onto all of this. This one will fetch me all the proof I need for you. I didn't commence anticipating the worst-case scenario yesterday, you dumb-ass bastard!"

"And should you receive it? What then?" Donald asked, with a wide-eyed expression on his face.

"I'm going to snatch the rug out from under your very feet, upon which you now stand, and allow you to burn for eternity in the same purgatory she will, right beside her, with her! You both deserve each other, Donald Grimesly."

Donald chuckled.

"Don't go over the edge so quickly here with this, honey. Calm down, you have nothing to fear here but fear itself."

"Don't you dare try to coddle me, you vain glorious bastard! I'm going to leave here for a while, Donald Grimesly, and speak with my attorney. He's been researching on my behalf for more than a month now. Since you are my husband, he can delve into your records and complete information. When I return, we'll have a few tidbits to hash out, right here and now."

"How can you stand there saying all of that? How do you know?" Donald sighed. "I know you are only excited. I forgive your harsh words, darling."

"My intuition is telling me so, Donald, and it never leads me down a dead-end path."

She turned, stepping out the door, slamming it solidly behind her.

Donald crashed down upon the soft leather bound living room couch with his face in his hands, as the sound of her car starting and tearing out filled the air. Deep down he knew the entire facade would be uncovered, where he signed his entire enterprise holdings over to Brenda. His tax hedge with preacher Jolly would eventually be uncovered, he thought out loud to himself. He would spend many years in prison for tax evasion, not to mention spending hundreds of thousands in back payments plus interest. After being released from prison, he was destined to have what remained of his enterprise holdings, savings, and retirement accounts confiscated, and to live life as an outright slave to the US Federal and North Carolina State governments. He was ruined for life.

From every angle considered, however, the only person deeply involved in this tangled web of deceit with absolutely no lines reaching backward was Brenda, the demon succubus, who devised all of this negativity for everybody surrounding her. There was no method of ensnaring her in this situation. He gazed into space blankly for what felt like hours. He signed deeply as he angrily seized up a sheet of notebook paper from a desk in the corner of his living room den and commenced writing.

To Whomever discovers this note.

May 9, 1995

Dear kind reader,

If you are holding this note in your hand, more than likely I will only be a name carved onto a tomb stone somewhere, and an unsatisfied ghost in your living room. Somebody somewhere must set the record straight. Brenda Ludlow arranged for the tax hedge with preacher McAdoo Jolly. She laid with me in an effort to set a hook on me, where I couldn't shake away from her control. She compelled me under threat of blackmail, to sign over all of my inherited family enterprise and those of my own.

Brenda Ludlow created the tax hedge with McAddoo Jolly, more than likely utilizing the same tactics of seduction and blackmail, especially with him being a preacher and owning a respected church establishment. She was the one making those horrendous money drops on my behalf. I know the only names on the docket were mine and Jolly's, but she was the primary motivator in this, I tell you. She was a master mind at covering her own tracks. I also bear a suspicion where she is behind all of this death around here, such as Pop Top MacGraw, and even Jolly himself. Maybe she was even behind the recent deaths of her own sister- and brother-in-law! I simply can't believe how nonchalant everybody is around here, in regard to all of this manifesting negativity. Her own clan, Ludlow, even appears to disregard any possibility of her involve-

ment. I have no choice but to act very soon on my own behalf. I do
sincerely apologize to all the surrounding innocents.

Sincerely

Donald Grimesly

When he completed his writing of the note, he folded it carefully. He glanced around the den, noticing an antique mahog-
any china cabinet up snugly against the wall in the kitchen
area. He knew there was a secret, difficult to notice a drawer
in it, behind one of the main drawers. He dropped the folded
note into a zip up leather change purse, then stashed it inside the hidden drawer on the backside behind some jewelry
boxes filled with expensive, time honored, heirloom gold and
diamond necklaces. It would be awhile before any of this was
discovered, which his plan out of courtesy was for the other
family members on both sides. Nobody else knew about this
drawer, and few visitors even noticed the china cabinet at all.
He wanted at least two years, or even more, to pass before anybody discovered the note. About the time Brenda felt this dark
cloud had passed, all hell would come crashing down upon her,
he secretly hoped as he wrote and stashed the note. The truth in
this entire tangle must be told, however, sometime.

After carefully tucking away the note, he stepped back into his
bedroom. Inside the oaken nightstand drawer lay a black thirty
eight Smith And Wesson snubbed nose revolver. He removed
it from the drawer, taking a seat on the bedside, slumping into
deep despair, gazing at the pistol he was holding in his lap
for what felt like long, enduring hours as he sat spinning the
ammunition cylinder with his right thumb. The bullets were
meticulously downloaded with less powder and heavier lead,
generating a semi-silencing effect by eliminating the sub-sonic
crack when the bullet exited the barrel. He wanted the bullet to

mushroom and stick inside his target, not merely pass through.

Outside the apartment, the only sound heard would be a more heavy thud, known from experience of shooting invading rats and possum in other people's homes, barns and warehouses, to seldom arouse attention. Few neighboring residents or pass-ers-by would ever notice, if indeed there were any. He heard a car pulling up outside his front door suddenly. Instantly he recognized it as being Emogene's.

CHAPTER EIGHTEEN

THE FINALIZING PHASE

Again, the entire Ludlow clan was gathered at the old family cemetery on Drunken Run Estate. Two elaborately decorated caskets with silver inlaid handles sat beside two freshly dug holes. Flowers covered the ground surrounding them. They were to be buried beside Bennie and Sheila. The families formed a single file line moving past the two coffins. Both corpses lay face up in their best dress, as if caught up in enduring slumber. Sobs filled the air, which exploded into sudden wails of grief. The parents attempted to climb into the coffins, and had to be escorted away, where they were given tranquilizing injections of drugs. Elders from Clans Grimesly and Ludlow assumed the fore there inside the iron fence, while the families gathered outside by the graves.

"On this day, tragedy has indeed struck our families again," spoke George Ebeneezer, with a solemn Uncle Monk standing by his side. "As the children of Israel were struck, so the Angel Of Death has now struck us, again. What are we, clans of Ludlow and Grimesly, to make of this? Is it divine retribution? Might it have originated from the hand of Satan? Where have we all gone so sorely wrong? Or is it that we are only human, and simply destined for such experiences? We have now cast our chrysanthemums and our holly among the dead, to fend away evil spirits. We stand here in earnest, saying our desperate prayers. What else now may we do? What may we all do now except wait until it is our turn one day, and go where all of us shall meet again on the other side?

"Why did such a horrible event have to happen?" spoke Uncle Monk. "Furthermore, who is responsible? Some lone villain appears to have entered into that apartment, according to investigators. Whose out-of-place tracks were there? Whose pistol did the shooting? The one discovered at the scene was not registered underneath any known name. May God Almighty render judgment! The walls know who did this. The spirits in the room know who is responsible. May the heavy boom of judgment and eternal damnation fall upon the guilty?"

After the address from the elders and various family members, the two coffins were finally lowered. Workers shoveled loose dirt piled close by into the holes, as grieving family members wailed aloud. Soon the people scattered, most entering their vehicles and slowly driving away. Some few walked the estate grounds at Drunken Run. The manor house was open, tours were free. Only one was running today, however. A few people on the grounds were tourists, speaking in their strange accents, as they behaved, believed, and thought in ways causing many locals to view them as bizarre foreigners.

"My, oh my, this Ludlow family sure has a far out history," one of them would stop and say. "How come you people around here are so weird?" another would ask. "Look at this. It's all over the front page of the morning news."

An overweight middle aged woman struggled to open up the front page of the Mount Horeb Village Tribune and show it to several family members as they somberly trudged passed.

"Mysterious intruder murders locally famous Ludlow daughter, Emogene, and her husband, Donald Grimesly," she reads.

"Is that who is being buried out there as we turned in?" another standing beside the one holding the paper would ask, wearing an unfamiliar expression on her face and speaking in a voice that could barely be understood. Nobody today felt like pausing to answer their less than kosher questions and simply kept on plodding past.

Brenda sulked as she walked down toward the manor house. Another outsider paused to ask more rude questions and make chastising, opinionated remarks.

"Just how wealthy is this family? I say, I hear their levels of wealth are astonishing, according to what the tour guides all tell us. People in New Jersey, or Connecticut, or even in California, could never amass such grandiose levels of land, money turning real-estate, and wealth. You know, far as I am concerned, all of their wealth should be confiscated by the government. That's right, confiscated I tell you! its old money made from the sweat soaked backs of belaboring innocents. Poor people taken advantage of, I say. All of this good-ole-boy politics and subtle prejudice is horrible, and utterly unbelievable in our own day and time. You simply are not going to find it where my family is from, I tell you. I find it very strange how the past still lives on down here."

Brenda slightly raised her head to lightly chuckle as she continued walking passed,.

"What past? America doesn't even have one," she would reply without smiling, finally pausing and turning in the direction of this crass man and his entourage of tourists. "I was in Italy and Spain recently, and looked at buildings commissioned by Julius Caesar still in use. I saw people living in farm houses first constructed during the Roman era, and you, ignorant out-lander, speak about America's three hundred-year-old past as if it even has a history yet. Your shallow mindedness is pathetic,"

246

She shook her head from side to side and chuckled again as she glared. She bit her tongue to keep from telling this particular middle aged man to go back wherever the hell he was from, but decided her saying it wouldn't do any good. With these people oozing their way into local politics, she never saw benefits they generated going to any of the local people at large. They only increased repressive regulations enforcing their own idealistic social convictions, making it needlessly tough for enterprising individuals to conduct business; yet she, the urban planners, and other local business people were forced to endure this crass, self-righteous talk from them on occasion. It was almost as if they imagined themselves being on some sort of social crusade.

If she felt like doing it, she would tell these cock eyed sons-of-bitches something, but today was not the right time. Besides that, they were paying tour fees into the estate, purchasing from the gift shop, and making food and wine purchases from the estate vendors, where the whole family and the local government received a nice kick. She, the estate, the local government or the family, didn't need some anti-Drunken Run Estate backlash from idealistic tourists far and wide, considering how given to emotional sensibilities and assumptive conclusions these people were. After she made her peace, these people would only glare hard upon her as she slowly walked on by.

As she walked along, she thought it felt lonely being a sole survivor in her branch of the family. Her mother and father were all to pieces, and would be so for a long time coming. She struggled at the thought, her, the only one remaining from three. She was required by the situation before her to make the very best of what she was thrust into. Doing this was all part of Ludlow's survival, she silently whispered to herself. She was destined by inherited genes in her veins to make it, however.

It always seemed like death came around Christmas time. She often found herself spending an unnatural amount of time wondering why during the passing weeks. When spring finally arrived, she and many others were relieved. With the sun shining so brightly, there seemed to be a promise of new life. Clan Ludlow held a need for this realization when the time came for it. On May twentieth, the family reunion was here again, and the manor house and Drunken Run Estate buzzed with a flurry of activity. Outsiders were even allowed to witness these events. The intellectual elders, Uncle Monk and George Ebeneezer III, assumed their appointed positions as the house filled up with people.

"Family, associates, and friends of the estate, 'tis so good to see you all here once again," George spoke donning his expensive suit and tie, yet appearing more than a philosopher than a businessman. "Much has occurred in Clan Ludlow during recent times, but we are not going to dwell on that today. None of us may change past events. Humanity simply doesn't yet possess such abilities, eh? With the sun glowing outside to such a degree, we all must direct our focus on new promise for success.

"Today I bear a declaration standing all on its own. Television and newspaper reporters ready thyself for the spoken words and dazzling manifestations."

A wave of chuckle and ovation moved through a swelling crowd.

"Clan Ludlow has a new angel among us, who, in the glitter of her own transfiguration, shall transport the scepter of success on behalf of the patrimonial inheritance and family brood. Based upon careful, studious examination by the gilded seven elders, she shall be the one among us and our youth, who shall escort the clan into new intellectual, social, and economic heights."

A gasp and another ovation wave moved through the gathering crowds.

"She was voted most likely to succeed in the local high school, crowned valedictorian was the Dixie Tobacco festival beauty queen, and hailed by statewide newspapers and national magazines as being the most gifted among local entrepreneurs. She has held chairs in various urban planner associations, local and statewide. She was even selected by a national committee to facilitate instruction in the skill of urban planning at the University Of Hawaii!"

The crowd excitedly clapped and cheered.

"Allow me to introduce, if you will, the honorable, successful, and very talented, Brenda Ludlow."

Brenda arose from her seat. Her affluent business dress seemed to hug her endowed, elegant female figure. When she walked toward the microphone, a brisk recollection flashed through her mind regarding all the many dozens of erotic films she had secretly performed in over the past years, as the swelling crowed cheered on for what felt like an hour. In truth, she had tremendous fun jetting out to exotic Caribbean and Mediterranean sites, and to various places throughout California, Spain and Europe at large, with magnificent accommodation on a studio dime, where she was paid more than six figures for a mere seven shoots a year, revealing and performing all unhesitatingly before the camera. Her special character had won dozens of film awards, such as Best Starlet, Best Film Award, Best Visual Effects, Best Anal Scene, Best Threesome Scene; surely the extenuating list is exhaustive.

Not only did she profit from the venture, she was wholly gratified, according to her every fantasized situation and relished act. Yet, she bore no regrets on account of it. All of this action was occurring in conjunction with her other enterprise efforts over time. Every consideration was second nature to her by now.

Such extreme avenues were only part of what being truly financially successful in today's America demanded. It wasn't how one played the game to her. All that mattered was winning; since in the end reasons why one lost were totally irrelevant to the judgmental masses, even if these reasons for one's failures were absolute truth. She covered her tracts brilliantly in all past endeavors. She utilized a false name and a clever disguise while being filmed, so she held great confidence she would remain totally anonymous for life, while relishing in recollections of titillating deeds performed and the many lavish cash blessings they generated. She even had her own personalized lines of lingerie, night time party dress clothing, and personal products. Still, to this day, she held private dance routines for customers willing to pay her price. There were stores all across America selling her videos and the products, not to mention newly developing websites. Did any of them know?

Nobody knew, she told herself, not even Dr. Dyson, who she had been seeing for some time now. She shook the percolating thoughts from her mind, now compelling herself to smile as she assumed an authoritative position before the gathered crowd.

"Thank you, thank you. I am utterly at a loss for words with this announcement."

The crowd gasped as the ovation continued.

"That's quite unusual for me, is it not?"

A light wave of laughter ensued.

"Surely today must rank as one of the happiest of my entire life. Even so, as I relish the accomplishment of a childhood dream, allow us to bow our heads in remembrance and respect for my sisters Emogene, Sheila, and all the others who have gone on prior to this day."

There was dead silence as every head slowly dropped. When they lifted, she continued.

"I stand before you today not as one above you, but as one among you. Do we not have a duty to ourselves, our patrimonial heritage, our success, and the continuing grandeur of the clan? I encourage all of you to raise your offspring as I was, thanks to both of my parents. Raise your kids to value excellence, heritage, piety, chastity, and a continuing success of the family at large. I say, continue on in our long held tradition of arranging marriage, since all youth are prone to irrational passions of emotion, rather than solid convictions of reason."

The crowd cheered enthusiastically at her words.

"In the end, it all comes down to our own personal convictions. Do we want state owned and operated schools indoctrinating our kids with ideologies alien to our own patrimonial belief systems? Do we want our youth, the flower of the entire Bath County population, to mingle with sub-intellectuals, who do not value our own patrimonial heritage and convictions, nor share in our genetic destiny for success? Worst, good Lord forbid, would we want our sons and daughters to marry one of these gross-blood inferiors?"

The crowd gasped.

"I sincerely think not. I am telling you this because I perceive a real threat in time to Clan Ludlow, and all the gilded clans who dwell in such grandiose comfort behind our walls of accomplishment, if we allow an emerging imposing government to have its way. The crusading amoral out-lander among us simply does not share in our own visions of elegance for ourselves. We cannot allow him to prevail in our legal and local political system. I know well what I speak of, since I am head of the local urban planning association. Our future destiny commences at this very moment, with the choices we make and the paths we, as individuals, take."

The crowd clapped.

"On a sunny note, still yet there is much to cheer. While I realize we have long been receiving donations from political connections in conjunction with the estate management here, the legalized kick from tours on Drunken Run Estate was finally approved. Now each and every direct member of Clan Ludlow shall receive a decent check in the mail every month."

The crowd clapped and cheered.

"A portion of the estate on the backside has been leased for apartment complexes. This lease is equivalent to twenty percent of the rents harvested by the complex. This complex is scheduled to take in more than five hundred thousand dollars a month. This calculates down to Clan Ludlow, receiving more than one hundred thousand dollars a month. Isn't this news wonderful?"

There was a long clap and cheer.

"Now divide that amount between the family members to see what each shall receive. This amount shall arrive in on a monthly basis. Imagine that!

There was an extended clap and cheer.

"My personal advice is to receive this money and use it to start up new family enterprises, maybe in another county or state, since our traditional home place here is being organized to take care of itself, while you still receive your income from enterprises it accommodates. The beach area is beginning to prosper. South Carolina is a more accommodating business environment. Charleston has a very rich history and is surely a place I highly recommend investigating for entrepreneurial endeavors. Think farther out than Drunken Run Estate and Bath County here, my gilded sisters and brethren. Many Southwestern states are extraordinarily welcoming to those with business ambitions."

There were many cheers and claps from the gathered family crowd.

"The city with golden streets, Las Vegas, shouldn't even need mentioning here."

The crowd was almost ecstatic.

"There is Saint Augustine, Florida, for our consideration!"

The clapping commenced again.

"When the spirit of adventure moves, never forbear on seeking these exciting places out for fun and profit."

Cheers and claps extended.

"In the end, our personal destiny lies inside our own hearts and hands. What we choose to act upon, the choices we all shall make as individuals, will dictate how we end up. There is no magic involved here, but if we continue to work together as a single unit, all of us may achieve that much more, and faster."

As the crowd continued cheering and clapping, George Ebeneezer III stepped up to the microphone. He turned toward Brenda.

"Brenda, I just want to say as an honored patriarch, that Clan Ludlow is very proud of you."

The crowd whistled as George Ebeneezer removed a golden diadem from a large leather purse.

"I present you here with a cherished family heirloom, hailing all the way from Aberdeen-shire, Scotland."

The gathered crowd was ecstatic.

"This award had been granted only to the most accomplished in the Ludlow clan," George announced as he carefully and gently placed the diadem upon Brenda's head, while she gasped in utter astonishment, near to a point of fainting.

"I, George Ebeneezer III, as clan patriarch and elder, hereby crown you Gilded Queen Superior. Your name has been assigned to the Timeless Chronicle Of The Blood, see here?," he said, as he opened an antiquated large leather-bound book, pointing to her feather signed name, in company with a multitude of others dating back to the year 1500. "Only individuals with those glorious physical and intellectual attributes common to an ancient temple priesthood are assigned inside these pages, Brenda. As always, my lovely queen, there adamantly must exist a heavy aura of accomplishment to accompany these."

He turned, facing the crowd, glancing over occasionally at Brenda as he spoke.

"Henceforth, Brenda, I proclaim here where it shall be you who transports the golden scepter of dazzling Ludlow success into a new dawning future. You shall be the guiding light, the astonishing brilliance, importing a divine wisdom, illuminating our own future brood through an ever emerging bleakness of authoritarian transgression and banking dynasty financed corporate tyranny. Because of you, Brenda, upon the ashes of all others surrounding us, Clan Ludlow shall ascend into a spectacular staggering oasis of eternal brotherhood, and the glory of Clan Ludlow shall surely endure for a dazzling infinity!"

The crowd clapped and cheered ecstatically as a silken purple robe was surprisingly placed over Brenda's shoulders when she stood, and an elegant symbolic silver and gold scepter was placed in her cradling arms. She and the family elders humbly bowed. Now, at long last, a true childhood fantasy was achieved.

CHAPTER NINETEEN

COMMENCEMENT OF A NEW ERA

More than six months had passed since Brenda was crowned Gilded Queen Superior. Jim was somewhat different, going to great lengths in accommodating her, catering to her every heart's desire with cost being absolutely no barrier, taking her virtually anywhere. He was like a bass on a hook willingly submitting to the reel, at long last. He was now a tail wagging, the docile silhouette of a man. In his own way reminding her somehow and for some unfathomable reason, of a cheerful puppy elated only to be in her company.

One night she sat on the couch in her parent's living room, dressed in a casual mini-skirt, but not the short kind. In their talk and their play, he had come to sit on the floor between her legs, with his back to the couch. She caught him glancing up her skirt at her crotch as he turned to position his back up against the couch, so she gently ran her fingers through his hair as they joked, laughed, and talked about foolish pondering.

Nothing intimate had yet occurred. She barely even kissed him in any depth, even after dating him for so long. She felt that her astonishing successes in life and her fact of holding him back were sources for the reason she was so successful in manipulating her relationship with him. She often pondered kicking his tires a bit, but she wanted so much more from him first.

One night he was down before her while she sat on the couch, and the unthinkable occurred. He faced her while he positioned himself between her legs as she sat. He reached down, producing a small red box tied with a wide green ribbon, since green was her favorite color.

"This is my Christmas gift to you," he lovingly said to her.

She received it, carefully opening the small box while she smiled. It was a golden ring with a genuine fifteen carat diamond cluster in the center.

"Wow, I can't believe it!" she gasped. "Thank you, dearly."

"Will you marry me, my love?" he asked her.

She didn't know how to reply at first. Her breathing stumbled a bit. She had never really seriously pondered the question, but since it was he who asked her, she would grant a sufficient answer.

"Yes, I will!" she replied to him after some time, with smiles and tears. Saying so and tactfully agreeing, especially since she knew her family already approved, would be another golden feather of accomplishment in her already loaded hat.

"What about us doing it on June first? That gives us a good six months to prepare. We can do it right here on Drunken Run Estate. Us having this wedding in spring time like that will surely be a cheerful note on all of this past negativity, don't you think, dear Brenda?"

"Sure, why not?" Brenda gasped and chuckled slightly. "The family shouldn't have any problem with us doing it here."

The wedding was going to be an all-out affair, they finally decided, with the news media being present and it being opened to the public. When within Clan Ludlow, weddings were generally private affairs. Having their wedding in such a fashion would complement as it ushered in the coming opening of their new family vineyard on the backside of the estate, opposite the apartment complex, Brenda cunningly decided when she pondered creating a venturing debut to market newly developing enterprises. Big plans for this new vineyard were already in the making, with rental cabins, a restaurant serving traditional menus, an antique museum and shop near the vineyard wine store. All of this new endeavor was to be leased out to an agency known as Dynasty Associates, consisting of seasoned professionals specializing in running magnanimous business enterprises.

Dr. Dyson suggested that the family act as father Abraham did, allowing the proxy and the government to have their commander shares of the profit, while he simply opened more shops in the city of Ur. Brenda and Clan Ludlow at large, had other more important business affairs to attend anyway, so the general concept fit perfectly to the present situation. With the internet slowly moving into vogue, a nice Ludow Family Estate website was already being developed by professional designers.

After much later debate, rather than having the actual marriage ceremony at the family manor house, they would do it at a near cathedral sized First Baptist Church in Mount Horeb Village. The elegantly crafted stone church building was more than two hundred years old, so it fit the scene of tradition perfectly. Having the actual wedding inside this sanctimonious time-honored structure would be a compliment to her innocence, so her new fiancé, Dr. Dyson, intimated to her later on during the planning stage of the wedding.

She was very happy he felt that way. She smiled broadly at the silent fact of her playing the cards dealt out by opportunity and fate into such an astonishing winning hand. Only the Grand Reception, it was finally decided after much more debate, would occur inside the old manor house back on Drunken Run Estate, as many others already had been over the generations.

Finally, that long awaited day arrived, and the church congregation was filled to overflowing, while the cameras flashed and the news media moved all about. Several hymns were played, then the elders spoke in succession, telling of Clan Ludlow's past grandeur, and the dawning of its newly coming glory inside this ceremonious event. When the great pipe organ finally commenced playing "Here Comes The Bride," the massive front doors opened to the huge congregational room, and Brenda stood with her long white gown trailing and the bridesmaids giving assistance in carrying it.

When the tuxedo donning groom appeared at the podium of the church, Brenda commenced walking toward him, being ushered in by her father. She assumed her position beside him as he stood. When the music ceased, the parson took his position at the podium between the groom and the bride. When the music ceased, the parson made his famous address.

"Dearly beloved, do you, Brenda Ludlow, take this man, James Dyson, to be your wedded husband, to have and to hold, until death do thus part?"

"I do," she responded.

"And do you, James Dyson, take this woman, Brenda Ludlow, to be your loving wife, to have and to hold, until death do thus part?"

"I do," he responded.

"And do both of you forsake all others in this bond of matrimony, in sickness and in health, for richer or poorer, for the remainder of your natural lives, until death does thus part?

"I do," replied Brenda.

"I do," replied James.

"By the authority invested in me courtesy of North Carolina State, on this day of June sixth, nineteen and ninety-six, I pronounce you man and wife. You may face one another and kiss the bride."

Brenda and James turned, facing one another, and he kissed her right on that day. Brenda's slightly lifted leg tactfully highlighted the occasion of the many cameras present.

"I present to you Mr. and Mrs. James Dyson!," spoke the parson as Jim ceased kissing, and the couple turned toward the congregation.

The gathered crowd clapped and cheered.

They both proceeded forward underneath showers of rice and flowers, making their way outside toward James' new automobile. Slowly they would ride back over to Drunken Run Estate. Already cars and pickup trucks were gathering around the big house for the magnificent party event. When the couple entered into the banquet hall of the plantation manor house, the first toast made the introduction.

"Ladies and gentlemen, here we are at long last. The king of the Duke and Chapel Hill medical staff marries the Gilded Ludlow Queen Superior, eh?" spoke the Grand Master Of Ceremonies.

The gathered witnessing crowd gasped, then laughed and cheered.

"The world shall never be the same again, let me tell you," he continued.

There were play skits, games, drinks, loads of food with many varieties, song and dance until late into the night. Around 0100, the people began melting away. As they exited out, many would ask;

"Where are you going away on your honeymoon?"

"To Hawaii, maybe, or the Greek Islands. We don't know yet. The island of Crete really rings a bell with me," she told them.

"Are you going to live around here in Mount Horeb Village, or relocate away?" many guests asked.

"We are going to live in my apartment for now, but maybe after Christmas time we are going to move," she replied.

"Oh yeah? Move? Where to?" they would all ask.

"We're thinking Fort Worth, Texas, since Texas is so good for business right now. North Carolina seems to be moving into a backdrop for enterprising entrepreneurs, but somehow alright for retired people, I guess," she would say. "Ludlow Enterprises is set regardless, however. Let the state and managing agencies tend the place, while we, among the family, harvest in a cash crop."

Finally, the reception ended, and the couple made their way out. This night would be the big event when her "chastity" at long last would melt away, as far as he knew anything about. Then again, since this bond was sanctioned, she would still retain her chastity. He curtly informed her late one evening. Brenda smiled warmly as she allowed him to proceed forward in lieu of that motivating thought on this one magnificent first night. She had lived her life to the fullest. She was ready to remain in one place now, relishing in the self-perpetuating rise of her own profit margin, and living to only enjoy the time she had yet remaining on earth. After Christmas, the two commenced packing up. "Texas bound or bust," they would say as they rolled out.

When they arrived in Fort Worth, Brenda already had an

investment program up and rolling, purchasing foreclosed homes, hiring a crew to recondition them, then renting them out or putting them up for sale. Gradually, she shifted over to commercial properties. Most of this money was invested into IRA and stock accounts in various well-established money lending institutions. She soon arrived at a point where a few quick phone calls from her own living room literally turned tens of thousands in dollars. Her husband continued on in his surgical practice at one of the local hospitals. Now and then, the new couple would vacate to Spain, Italy, Dubai, Germany, or France. They were considering a four month worldwide tour. All was well, and the two got along perfectly from that time forward.

CHAPTER TWENTY

DRUNKEN RUN ESTATE 2020

Time has passed and all the Ludlow elders have faded into the grave, including Brenda's parents. Most of the Ludlow youth have moved far away from Mount Horeb Village. The cottage home Brenda was raised up in is being rented out and maintained by a national property management firm. The old plantation manor home and grounds are now a thriving corporate enterprise and park largely owned and operated by the State Of North Carolina, minus a few enterprising developments.

This estate provides employment for the local community and is an iconic meeting area for government and business leaders. The population at large in the entire developed area of Bath County, has changed from being one of heritage Scotch-Irish families, into an amalgamated congregation from afar, who strangely appear in likeness to invading twenty-fifth dynasty Egyptians speaking in bizarre accents the elders, or even Brenda and her sisters, would have barely understood. The few remaining heritage locals rarely venture outside, preferring to remain behind tightly locked doors, dwelling merrily inside the world they once knew, now relegated to the imagination by an intimidating ocean of imposing difference insulting every ideology and conviction of personal and national destiny, history, and constitutional tradition ever held.

The unique atmosphere of individuality has also faded with its heritage people and the elders. The local history is barely mentioned anymore, except at Drunken Run Estate, but only then, in a manner appearing to indirectly elevate, suggested negatives found in Ludlow's family history; such as the legend of June Ludlow's life, the fact of the family once possessing bond-servants, and the ghost viewed by a largely atheistic alien population as being myth. Taxes are atrocious. Working for cash payment now is nearly a capital offense. Owning firearms is such an onerous red-tape deal that few do, which is astonishing in a place where everybody, young and old, once did, not so long ago. People are now sent to prison for writing or speaking personal opinions criticizing the new society or government, and living unsanctioned, off the grid non-mainstream lifestyles. Conversation all around heavily questions the general national direction. Is it truly one of new technical advancement, as leaders claim, or of dawning tyranny?

Brenda Ludlow Dyson and her husband, Jim, are up in age now, nearing sixty, and living happily together in the State of Texas, which stands as a grand exception to many other states. Jim was playing around on the internet late one night and accidentally discovered innumerable clips from Brenda's old video productions. He struggled to recognize her character, but finally matched the faces of Brenda and this well-endowed mask wearing, Cat-Woman like person sporting short bunny ears, up with a Google search. Her innocent face, as he knew it, was right there beside that identical face in Cat-Woman's mask, heavily soaked in all of its syrupy undiluted glory, even to a point of dripping profusely from her broad toothy smile and chin. The breath virtually exited his body as this unsettling realization gradually manifested on the screen before him.

He mentioned these erotic clips he discovered to Brenda. After some silent time, she finally admitted herself as being guilty, informing him of the entire story in regard to the hundreds of movies her infamous character once starred in. He bitterly struggled with the issue for a while, eventually relenting and forgiving her, as she secretly anticipated he would before admitting to anything. After all, such was her life before his time.

"The bullet already fired can't be replaced back into the gun chamber," he sighed, saying to her with his face buried in his hands. "You are still reaping royalties from these clips when people download, I presume, so in the end maybe I can find a way to live with it."

Brenda only held his head close to her breast, reassuring him in an easy, innocent voice that her loyalty was eternally bound to him, and to him alone.

Once in a while they'll visit Mount Horeb Village, attend the First Baptist Church where they both were married, while stopping by the homes of a few cousins and some old friends. Occasionally they will pause by Drunken Run Estate and the old family graveyard, speaking cheerfully to their own late teenaged daughter and two young adult sons about family history. The daughter often says she wants to work for a year as a government employed tour guide on the estate, when her senior year of high school completes. Brenda is highly encouraging.

Codger some time ago sold his famous pool room to an out-lander from way up in New Hampshire, or somewhere like that. Rumor is that old man Bow-limp Codger's son, Alfonzo, held back on a secret ingredient used in his cherished burger recipe, because something about them simply doesn't taste the same anymore, so days every long-time customer who visits. It is an ageless local custom to do such things when one sells a restaurant or another enterprise, in case a member of the business founder's family ever wishes to open up his own shop in another place. He could once again recapture the long time loyal customer base, so the general belief goes. Often these family visits would wind up here as the sun was sinking downward.

Most people walk on passed with nary a single glance, as the couple dines by the large window in the poolroom or ambles down the sidewalk on main street, since now there are so many living inside town limits who have no blood heritage or history in the area, and wouldn't know who the real Brenda Ludlow ever was. The warm family atmosphere once present seems now to have melted away, like frost on the morning grass does with the arrival of spring. All of this bothered Brenda once upon a time, but her business ventures are still pulling in an ever-growing profit margin to a staggering degree, and in the end she finds her complete happiness in that sole acknowledgment alone.

Not very long ago in the past, Brenda was compelled to return with great reluctance, since a damning note was discovered in an old china cabinet left in Donald's place, sometime after he and her sister perished. She got herself the best local lawyer, an honorable Captain Worthington, hailing all the way from New Orleans, who had been a long-time resident in Mount Horeb Village, answered a few direct questions, paid him fifteen thousand dollars, and such was the end of it. The trying ordeal was finally over with for good, since absolutely no evidence could be found to substantiate any claims made in the note, or otherwise.

A seemingly implicating note was also found inside the wall of McAdoo Jolly's home, when the state assumed possession of the structure following his death and was renovating it for sale. This note was also presented in court, but when Jolly wrote the note, he had handled freshly cooked bacon from all indications, and the grease from it attracted mice, which ripped and smudged the note into indiscernible shreds. This somewhat smudged and faded fragment of evidence was consequently dismissed as being insufficient.

Now Brenda is totally free for a duration of the ages. Her reputation and soul are now perfectly cleansed, purged pure as the snow white gown she wore walking down the aisle, and her own body was on that special night when she finally submitted to her overly anxious husband; who once salivated heavily at the jowls every time she wore an elegant, but snug, expensive dress, she had long noticed. Sometimes she chuckled to herself when she recalled wearing a thin bikini bathing suit. If they ventured up the road in springtime to Crystal Lake or farther out to Myrtle beach, that virtually sucked her lower extremities; only to witness the astonishment in her then boyfriend's eyes, and amazingly hold him into a continuing pursuit in likeness to a cave sorceress's enchanting charm, but such is a story better left untold so far from the time. Truth is, if we have lived life to its fullest potential, all of us should have at least a few similar intriguing tales to spin.

The couple's daughter, Elenor, finally graduated from Fort Worth High, then filled out the North Carolina State application for a twelve month employment stint as a tour guide on Drunken Run Estate. A quick telephone call by Brenda to a local North Carolina State congressman firmly secured the position for her. Young Elenor enjoys escorting these hoards of strange visitors coming from the beach back inland, then stopping in town to shop, and finally visit the unique historical site and park of Drunken Run manor house and farms.

Agra-tourism really is a huge deal in this day and time. Vineyards have now replaced tobacco farms, and the old wood and kerosene fired log barns Brenda was once familiar with are now museum relics tourists and their children love walking through.

This sight often emits an eerie feeling to those from the era of Brenda's age.

As Elenor casually ambles along throughout the estate, leading the visiting entourage, she commences her tale with accounts of the founding patriarchs, the legend of June Ludlow, and the passionate murder of her father, Reuben. Like her mother, she doesn't hold back on anything, entertaining gasping guests with every luscious detail of her own unique version of the story she has to offer; such as the curse being leveled on her family due to the carnal escapades of June, and the Ludlow family finally discovering the truth when the mysterious ghost of Reuben Ludlow appeared to her dear mother two hundred years later. Accounts of other bizarre, almost daily paranormal occurrences on the estate add spice to the tale already told, and an air of enchantment to the family estate. Since her own surname name is Dyson, she may freely spin this nearly true tale of intense passion without any tourist ever perceiving her own direct blood connection.

The final pause on her tour was at the old family graveyard. Out of courtesy on the last note, she asks visitors if they have any statements they wished to make in regard to anything they heard discussed. One day, two immaculately dressed, rather unusually affectionate, obviously well educated, over-sized late middle-aged ladies gazed off rather blankly toward the grave stones, then quickly glanced over toward Elenor, sighing deeply.

"You know," said one in a barely discernible accent, but a manner of speech Elenor was growing increasingly familiar with, "we are from California, but are of rather recent Polish extraction, when compared with this family, Ludlow," she informed in a direct, serious tone. "We have also lived all over Illinois, throughout Connecticut, Delaware, and Maryland, for a period of years. We finally retired from the university system back in Hartford, Connecticut. I must say after hearing this account of yours in regard to this incredible family, Ludlow, and likewise visiting these sacred grounds, an unsettling thought just struck me hard, like a bolt thrown down from the heavens beyond."

"Freely speak your mind," replied Elenor, with a healthy young smile, shrugging playfully with a light, inviting chuckle.

"I have more than fifty years of time observing a developing new American femininity," continued the lady, "in various locations found throughout the general national interstate panorama."

The woman suddenly chuckled before speaking again, while almost holding back on her forth coming statement.

"Eh? Be out with it now," smiled Elenor politely, but with a slightly puzzled appearance upon her face. "We don't believe in keeping good secrets to ourselves in this neck of the woods, honey."

The woman struggled as she attempted to somewhat pull herself together before continuing on. She sighed deeply again prior to commencing.

"The very thought almost knocks me off my feet, that strangely somehow, at least a rather juicy piece of Ludlow's daughter I might say, still yet dwells inside us all."

Reverend Crown Publications

reverendcrown.com

Blaze Goldburst brings to you a lot more from the book world:

Merchandize, videos, gifts, giveaways and a lot more.

Get yours now.

visit:

blazegoldburst.com

For more information, SUBSCRIBE to Blaze Goldburst

on YouTube, follow us on all social media sites using

@blazegoldburst

ABOUT THE PUBLISHER: REVEREND CROWN PUBLICATIONS

Reverend Crown Publications is the No.1 Traditional Publisher for aspiring and rising authors. We believe that traditional publishing should be accessible to all and not just be limited to a few. Your prosperity is our priority.

Visit reverendcrown.com for more information.

Book Cover by Blaze Goldburst & Saurav Dash